# STRANGLEHOLD

## A JACK DRUMMOND THRILLER

### RENA GEORGE

ROSMORNA

# INTRODUCTION

*A killer on the loose. The body count is mounting. Time is running out for him to be the good guy.*

A strangler is stalking Glasgow's red light district targeting prostitutes. The body count continues to rise as pressure mounts on Detective Inspector Jack Drummond to catch the killer.
But the murderer is playing them...luring them into the shadows where they will find no clue - only another body.

No woman is safe as the tense game of cat and mouse escalates. Drummond can't protect them all, but maybe he can keep young Evie off the streets before the killer strikes again.

As the murder hunt switches to the Highlands and Drummond links up with DS Nick Rougvie, the truth begins to emerge.

Will they be in time to prevent another killing? Or is it already too late?

Stranglehold is the first book in Rena George's exciting new crime thriller series featuring surprising plot twists, compelling characters and a flawed cop who likes to dish out justice with his fists.

# ONE

THEY FOUND her the Saturday before Christmas. She had been strangled and her body dumped amongst the chip papers, plastic burger boxes and used condoms discarded by those who frequented Glasgow's Barras.

At 6 a.m. it was still dark, but market traders were already arriving to organize their stalls for what was building to be the busiest day of the year.

Detective Inspector Jack Drummond looked around him, avoiding staring back down at the body. Murder was worse when you knew the victim. Maggie Burns had been a sex worker whose soliciting activities Drummond had long since turned a blind eye to. Arresting these women was pointless. He'd tried that. Maggie and her mates would be right back on the streets as soon as they were released.

'Poor soul.' Detective Constable Gail Swann was heaving a sigh beside him. 'The killer couldn't have chosen a worse place,' she said, shaking her head. 'We're going to be so unpopular with these market people.'

Drummond's attention was now on the uniformed officers he'd instructed to cordon off the lane. 'Tough,' he said, narrowing his eyes, but he knew she was right. The place would soon be teeming with Christmas shoppers hoping for that last-minute bargain. And the traders definitely wouldn't be happy about all the police activity affecting their business. Well it wasn't his problem. Discovering who squeezed the life from poor Maggie Burns and left her in this miserable back lane was his only priority.

'D'you think she'd been to the gig over at Barrowland, boss?' Gail asked.

Drummond thought of the posters he'd seen advertising the appearance of the rousing Scottish rock band and shook his head. 'I doubt it,' he said. 'Not Maggie's style.'

Gail's head snapped up. 'You recognize her?'

Drummond nodded. 'Maggie Burns. She's a hooker.' He forced himself to glance back to the body. 'Who found her?'

Gail gestured to the end of the lane. 'He's back there.' She consulted the notes she'd hurriedly punched into her phone. 'His name's Alec Millburn. He's got a music stall in the barras.'

'What was he doing down here so early?'

Gail sent him a look that suggested he needed to get out more. 'It's Christmas, boss. It'll be a busy day in the barras. He wanted to get organized for it. Should I get him over here?'

Drummond was watching a police photographer, his camera clicking as he moved carefully about the crime scene recording every angle. 'Yes,' he said. 'And find out who operates that surveillance system.' He nodded to a CCTV camera. 'I want to see what's on that.'

Gail headed off up the lane, tugging up the collar of her jacket as a sudden breeze sprung up, sending the dropped chip papers and fag ends into a macabre dance.

Drummond frowned, switching his attention back to

the crime scene. Dr Nell Forrester, forensic pathologist for the procurator fiscal's office, had arrived and was on her knees by the body. 'Anything for us yet, Nell?' he called over to her.

She straightened up and stretched, pulling a face. 'Patience was never your strong point, Jack. When I have anything definite, you'll be the first to know.'

He grinned at her. 'Late night?'

'None of your business,' she snapped, but he could see she was smiling. 'There's one thing I can tell you. Our lady wasn't killed here.' She indicated the area around her. 'No sign of a struggle. I'd say she was dragged here from the end of the lane.'

Drummond had already reached that conclusion after inspecting the scene. His brow wrinkled. 'I thought that, but it makes no sense.'

Nell shrugged. 'When did murder ever make sense?'

Drummond frowned. 'I still don't understand what she's doing here. The killer couldn't have chosen a busier area. They must have known she'd be found.'

Nell turned back to the body. 'You're the detective, Jack, but I'd say the killer wanted you to find her.'

He pulled a face, turning as Gail approached with their witness. The man was tall, lanky, scruffy – and definitely not looking happy.

'How long is this pantomime going on for?' he growled at Drummond. 'You do know I'm trying to run a business here and your lot won't even let me into the building.'

Drummond resisted the urge to point out that his murder investigation was way higher up on his list of priorities than this man's naff record stall. He took a breath and smiled. 'We do understand how inconvenient this must be. If you could just bear with us a little longer–'

'Inconvenient?' the man exploded, not giving Drummond the chance to finish his sentence. 'It's not about being inconvenient. It's about getting shafted. We'll all be bloody shafted if you stop the punters getting into the barras.'

Drummond was having trouble hanging on to his patience. 'We'll do our best to minimize the disturbance, sir. Now if you could just tell me how you found the body.'

Alec Millburn's face contorted into a grimace. 'I've already told her.'

Drummond gave him a hard stare. 'Well now I'm asking you to tell me.'

The man let out an impatient sigh. 'OK, it's like I told her. I get here early. There are always new batches of records to sort out. I run an orderly stall.' He glared at Drummond. 'You do know it's only three days to Christmas? If we don't make money today, then we're screwed.'

'The body.' Drummond sighed. 'Just tell me about finding the body.'

Alec Millburn opened his arms. 'Nothing to tell. I was coming down the lane and there she was.' He ran a hand over his greasy hair. 'It wasn't pleasant. I bloody nearly threw up.'

'But you didn't?'

'No. I phoned you lot.'

'Did you touch the body?' Drummond asked.

The man looked horrified. 'Touch it? I couldn't even look at it again. Of course, I didn't bloody touch it.'

'Was there anyone else about when you found the body?' Gail Swann asked.

'Just me.' He threw Drummond another irritated scowl. 'Look, how much longer will this take? I need to get in at my stall.'

'It will take as long as it needs to, sir,' Drummond said. 'We'll let you know when you can get into the building.'

'Well it better be soon, or you'll have a riot on your hands.' The man was still mumbling to himself as Gail escorted him back to the top of the lane.

'Did you hear that, Dr Forrester?' He raised his voice. 'Our witness is predicting a riot if we don't get things moving.'

Nell got slowly to her feet and shook her head. 'Like I said...so impatient.' She glanced down at the body. 'I'm done here. They can take her away.'

Out of the corner of his eye Drummond saw a young PC hurrying towards Gail. From Gail's shocked expression it wasn't good news. She was moving quickly to join him, drawing him aside and lowering her voice to a whisper. 'We have another body, boss.'

Drummond's heart sank. 'Where?'

'Round the corner.'

'You'd better come too, Nell,' he called over his shoulder, strutting off at such speed that Gail had to quicken her pace to keep up with him.

They followed the PC out of the lane and fifty yards along the road before turning into another dimly lit alley. The body could have been mistaken for a pile of rags strewn across the broken, narrow footpath. A uniformed officer was beside it shining a torch on the scene.

'We need to get another forensic team down here,' Drummond said, holding up an arm to stop anyone else from advancing on the body. 'And some decent lights.'

He instructed Gail to rustle up more backup as he grabbed his own phone and tapped in the number of his senior officer, DCI Joey Buchan. She didn't appear to appreciate being disturbed on her day off. He held the phone from his ear as she let out a string of expletives.

'I'll come down,' she ended sharply, before cutting the call.

'Great,' Drummond muttered. 'We'll leave it all to you then.'

He had no problem with female senior officers, especially ones he'd had a relationship with, but Joey was bitter. She left him in no doubt that he wasn't her favourite person, but what had he expected. Nobody appreciated being dumped, even if their relationship had been going nowhere.

Joey Buchan had her sights set on fast-tracking her way to the top. Even if his team had a speedy result and arrested their killer, or killers, he knew the woman would find a way to take the credit.

He sighed, turning back to the scene. The smell of cheap wine in the alley was nauseating. His eyes were moving around the area. In a far corner he could see the discarded wine bottles, cans and other detritus left by the rough sleepers. Was this killing the result of a fight between vagrants? Was it a coincidence that it happened on the same night and in the same area as their first body? Drummond frowned. He didn't believe in coincidences.

'Looks like this one's been stabbed, boss,' Gail Swann said, coming to stand beside him.

Drummond was watching Nell Forrester slip an object she'd just picked up into an evidence bag. She held it up for him to examine.

'It's a coin purse,' Gail said, squinting at it. 'Not the kind of thing a rough sleeper like him would have.'

'No,' Drummond said thoughtfully. 'But the dead woman round the corner might have had something like this in her handbag.'

'So, the murders could be linked?' Gail was staring at him.

The poor devil lying in front of them covered in blood didn't look like he had the strength to strangle anyone, let alone a robust woman like Maggie Burns. And why would he? Drummond doubted if she'd had anything much worth stealing.

One possibility might work though. This wino could have stumbled on the body and saw it as an opportunity to grab what he could. It might explain the empty coin purse. If it belonged to Maggie, Drummond didn't think it would be too difficult to prove.

The downside of this theory was that if it was right then the murder scene would have been seriously contaminated. The swish of activity to his left half an hour later brought more bad news. DCI Joey Buchan had arrived. And she was looking rough. Her mousey brown hair had been scraped back in a bun and she wore no make-up. 'OK, update me,' she snapped when she'd reached Drummond's side. Her top lip was curving in distaste as she glanced at the old man's body. No 'Good morning,' or 'How are you, Jack?' But then he could hardly expect that when he'd called her out so early and on her rest day.

He chose his words carefully. 'We don't know for sure if the bodies are connected but we've recovered a purse next to this one that could have belonged to the other one.'

'And what does that tell us?'

'Maybe that this old boy found body one and robbed her and then came back to his nest here.' He nodded to the litter of empty bottles, cardboard and newspapers. 'If that part's right then it looks like he was killed and robbed himself, possibly by one of his mates.'

Buchan was already spinning on her heel and marching

off. 'Round them up and bring them in. All of them.' She ordered over her shoulder at him. 'And show me this other crime scene.'

Drummond didn't miss Nell's amusement at his muttered curse. He pointed a warning finger at her as she giggled. 'Run along now, dear,' she grinned. 'Mummy's calling you.'

He frowned back at her. 'That remark will cost you.'

'Can't wait,' she called after him as he followed Joey Buchan out of the lane.

Joey had already reached the first crime scene when Drummond caught up with her. Maggie Burns' body had been removed to the city mortuary. One of the forensic officers was heading towards them. The plastic evidence bag he was holding contained a card showing a black silhouette of a cat and mouse. 'This was under the body,' he said.

Drummond pulled a face. Was their killer trying to tell them something? He hoped not.

'That's all we need...a joker as well as a killer.' She swung round with an impatient sigh. 'OK, tell me what we know about this one.'

Drummond repeated everything he knew about the victim. 'Nell Forrester doesn't think she was killed here, but the post-mortem will tell us more.'

Buchan gave him a sideways look that said did he think she was an idiot. Her eye was already on the CCTV camera. He pre-empted her.

'We're getting the tapes,' he said.

She gave him an irritated look. 'Witnesses?' she asked.

'Only the one who found her.' He nodded to Alec Millburn who was still remonstrating with a uniformed constable.

'The traders are getting restless,' he said. 'They want to

get to their stalls and sort themselves out before we open the place to the Christmas shoppers.'

Joey Buchan blew out her cheeks. 'Christ, Christmas! I haven't even thought about it.' She turned to him. 'What about you, Jack? Bought all your pressies yet?'

Drummond blinked. He was used to his DCI's mood swings, but this change of tack took even him by surprise. 'Err...no, not yet.'

'We should all go out for a drink,' she said. 'I mean the whole department.'

'Err, right! That would be good.'

She spun back round on her heel, firing out a catalogue of instructions. 'Check the CCTV tapes. Talk to her hooker pals. Talk to her family. Why this site? Why dump her here? Find out what's so special about it. Is there a Barrowland connection? Did the old boy rob her of anything else, if so, where is it?'

The staccato list of orders was fired at him in her usual annoying way.

Drummond tried not to groan as he rolled his eyes.

'Right! I'll leave you to it.' Joey said. 'Let's not mess about with this, Jack. The top brass won't appreciate getting a strangler for Christmas.' She moved her face in closer. 'Just catch this bastard!'

Gail came forward as Buchan retreated up the lane. They both stared after her. 'Makes you feel we should be clicking our heels and saluting her,' she said.

Drummond sighed as he watched Joey Buchan reach the corner and disappear. 'Yeah,' he said. 'She'd like that.'

# TWO

'Doesn't help us much,' Gail said, back in the incident room, as they watched the shadowy CCTV images of a figure in a track suit dragging the limp body of Maggie Burns into the lane. 'It could be anybody. He knows the camera's there. Look how he keeps his head down.'

Drummond agreed. The killer knew what he was doing. He'd worn dark, non-descript clothes that could have been bought anywhere. The stalls inside The Barras were laden with the stuff. And what about the card he'd left with the body? Was he really audacious enough to think he could play a game of cat and mouse with them? Drummond had no intention of entering into that. He watched the killer move away, head high and shoulders back. The man was too confident, too arrogant.

They continued watching as other officers joined them. 'Fast-forward it,' Drummond ordered, and then pointed. 'There! Go back.' They could see movement by the body and a figure emerge from the dark.

'It's him!' Gail Swann turned to the others. 'It's the old man.'

The figure was shuffling up the lane and almost stumbled over the body. He stopped, staring down at it before squinting around him. Apparently satisfied no one was watching, he stooped down and made a grab for Maggie's bag. The detectives watched him rifle through it and snatch out the purse before tossing the bag aside. Drummond grimaced as the tramp yanked the dead woman's pendant from her throat and pulled a bracelet from her wrist.

'Did we find the jewellery?' DCI Joey Buchan had come up behind Drummond and was watching the screen over his shoulder.

'Not so far,' Drummond said, nodding to the young detective operating the CCTV equipment to fast-forward the video again. 'Wait! Go back! What's that?' He jabbed a finger at the screen.

The officer replayed it. They were staring at a shot of the old man staggering back up the lane. A shadowy figure appeared from a doorway. The old man stopped, cringing away, protecting himself as the short stocky figure pushed him roughly up the lane.

'Do we have any footage that tracks this pair?' Drummond's tone was urgent.

'There's this,' the officer said. He'd switched to another camera that had been trained on the dark area where the man's body was found.

There were shocked gasps as the detectives watched the two figures on the screen grapple with each other. One of them produced a knife and plunged it into the other. The figure slid to the ground as the attacker bent over him, pulling out the knife and wiping it on the victim's coat before stashing it back into an inside pocket of their long, ragged coat. Drummond watched in disbelief as the attacker ransacked the victim's pockets and found what looked like the pendant and bracelet the tramp had ripped from Maggie's body. They found her purse and emptied the contents into their hand before tossing the empty purse away.

Drummond tilted his head at the screen. 'Is it a woman?' He screwed up his eyes. 'Anybody recognize them?'

There was a unanimous shaking of heads.

A uniformed PC came into the room carrying a tray of coffees and paused, focusing on the indistinct images.

'Wait a minute, I know who that is,' he said. 'That's Annie Bishop. She all but haunts The Barras with that old pram of hers stacked up with rags.'

'I know who you mean,' DC Murray Anderson chipped in. 'And if it is her, she'll be out now cashing in on what she's just killed the old man for to buy drugs.'

Gail shook her head. 'I doubt if that lot will buy many drugs.' Her brow furrowed. 'Poor old devil. Why did she have to kill him?'

As the officers watched the woman hurrying away, three more people emerged from the shadows and approached the old man's body. They stared at it for a few seconds and then one of them raised his hands to his head and rocked it, another let out a loud wail. The third person hurried away and the others quickly followed.

'Looks like we have some eyes witnesses, boss,' Gail Swann said.

Drummond sighed. 'Bring them all in...and arrest that Annie woman.'


Drummond stood in front of Maggie Burns' door. It wasn't the most impressive of Glasgow tenements, but he'd seen worse. There was no response to his police knock. None of the residents here would be early risers. He used his fist to batter on the door. Eventually, it opened slowly and a tousled-haired, bleary-eyed black woman squinted out at him. 'This better be world shattering,' she said.

Drummond produced his warrant card. 'Can I come in?'

'Could I stop you?' She moved aside as he passed her.

'If you're after business, you're too early.' She yawned, pushing her fingers through her mass of crimped red hair.

'It's about your flatmate,' Drummond said curtly.

'Maggie? What's she done? If she wants me to bail her out again, she's got no chance.'

She slouched across the room, pulling on a tatty red silky dressing gown before turning to give him an irritated scowl.

'Let's start with your name, shall we?' Drummond said.

'Leisha McTaggart.' The woman scratched at her stomach.

'We're investigating a serious incident,' Drummond said. 'Were you with Maggie last night?'

She was more alert now. 'Yes. What's happened? Where is she?'

'Did you see who she went off with last night?'

Leisha frowned, confused. 'I don't know. I wasn't watching her every move. I was more interested in who was stopping for me.' She pushed her messy hair out of her face and screwed up her eyes as though trying to clear the fuzz from her head. 'She got into a car...a black car, I think. Has something bad happened to her?'

'I need to contact her family.'

'Maggie doesn't have any family, at least none worth bothering about.'

'But there's somebody?' Drummond said.

The woman nodded and then shook her head. 'I think

so...I don't know. You haven't told me what's happened to her.' But she didn't need to ask more. His look said it all.

'She's dead, isn't she?'

'I'm sorry, Leisha.'

'How...how did she die?'

'That's what we need to find out. I'll have to go through her things. We didn't find a mobile phone on her. Did she have one?'

'We all do. Benny likes to keep in touch with his properties.'

*Benny Saul.* Drummond frowned. They all knew Benny back at the nick. He was a well-known Glasgow pimp. But it was the man he worked for that interested Drummond. Big Mal McKirdy – hard man, gangster, and 'godfather' of the city's drugs' scene. If anything dodgy was being moved around the city you could bet Big Mal had a finger in the pie. He'd never been caught. He was too clever for that, but his luck wouldn't last forever, and Drummond would make sure he was there to play his part in bringing the man down.

'Properties?' he said, turning back to Leisha. 'What does that mean?'

'Saul calls all us women his properties. When he has special clients, he phones us, tells us what to wear, sends a car for us.'

Drummond's brow wrinkled. 'How often does that happen?'

'Not that much for the likes of me and Maggie. It's the younger lassies who get most of the calls.' She paused, her top lip curling. 'Saul's special clients like 'em young.'

'But you and Maggie still had phones?'

She nodded.

'Could Maggie have left her phone here?'

Leisha gave a little laugh. 'Are you kidding? There's a black eye and a cracked rib waiting for them that doesn't take their phone everywhere.'

Drummond felt a rise of anger. 'Saul would beat you up?'

She nodded. 'Him or one of his gorillas. Same if any of us try to get out. Saul doesn't like it when women go against him. He knows exactly how much I earn on the streets and if I don't hand it all over when he calls...' She put a hand to her scrawny neck. There was no need to finish the sentence.

Drummond had a thought. 'I don't suppose you or any of the other girls ever take pictures of your punters?' She gave him a look that suggested she thought he was mad.

'No. Why would we do that? We're out there looking for business. Punters would run a mile if we started snapping them.'

Drummond could understand that, but it still didn't mean it never happened. He frowned. Could that have been why Maggie got herself killed? Had the killer taken her phone because he knew there was a picture of himself on it? It was something to think about. 'Can I see Maggie's room?'

Leisha nodded to the wall. 'It's through there.'

'Show me,' he said, standing back as she led the way. He'd been expecting it to mirror the chaos in the rest of the flat, but the place was orderly. The bed was made up with a patchwork quilt, and pink bows adorned the bed head. Some clothes hung on hangers from the wardrobe doors. His glance passed over the cheap clock radio and pink-frilled table lamp on the bedside table. There was a drawer and he slid it open, checking through the contents. Hand cream, hairbrush, paracetamol. Nothing that helped him.

He turned back to Leisha. 'Did Maggie keep files of important documents, letters?'

She shrugged. 'I've no idea. Maggie keeps...' She corrected herself. 'Maggie kept all that kind of stuff to herself.'

Drummond went to the wardrobe and flicked through the clothes on hangers. There were pitifully few items. His attention went to a shoebox on the top shelf and he lifted it down. It was full of papers. He began to flick through them. Maggie was certainly organized. Paid bills were paper-clipped together, unpaid items were in a see-through plastic sleeve. At the bottom of the box there were articles, clipped from celebrity magazines. None of it looked significant. He was hoping there might be an address book. There wasn't. Maybe a detailed search of her room might throw up more clues. 'I'll take this stuff with me,' he said.

The woman's thin shoulders rose in a shrug.

Drummond hesitated. 'One more thing.' She looked at him, eyes full of dread. She knew what was coming. 'We need somebody to identify the body,' he said.

Her brow knotted. 'Do I have to?'

'Think of it as doing one last thing for your mate.'

Leisha McTaggart reached for a cigarette from the packet on the table. Drummond struck a match and lighted it for her. She took a deep drag and squinted through the smoke. 'Doesn't look like I've got a choice.'

# THREE

GONE WERE the days when Glasgow hoodlums lived in city centre slum tenements. Drummond ran his eyes along the smart frontage of the Cowcaddens flats and wondered how many tricks Saul's girls had to turn to keep him living in this style.

'I've been here before,' Gail said. 'Saul's flat is on the top floor, the penthouse suite.'

'Why does that not surprise me?' Drummond said sourly, as they made their way to the impressive entrance hall.

'D'you think he already knows about Maggie?' Gail asked, her attention on the row of buttons lighting up as the elevator moved silently up the floors.

'Of course he does,' Drummond said. 'The city's jungle drums wouldn't be doing their job otherwise. That's if he didn't kill her himself.'

'He's in the frame then?'

Drummond gave her a sideways frown. Everybody was in the frame until they caught this murdering bastard. He pasted a smile on his face as the door opened and a slickly dressed Asian man fixed them with an irritated expression. 'Mr Saul?' Drummond forced a smile as he produced his warrant card and Gail did the same.

Saul's eyes rose heavenwards. 'What d'you want? I'm busy.'

Drummond nodded to the flat's interior. 'Perhaps we could step inside?'

'Perhaps you bloody couldn't,' Saul said. 'What d'you want?'

'It's about one of your girls, Benny...Maggie Burns.'

'Never heard of her,' Saul said. 'Is that it?'

'No, it isn't.' Drummond's foot was already in the door. 'It would be in your interest to co-operate. Pimping is still illegal.'

Saul's frosty look went from one to the other, but he stood back allowing them to pass into the flat, pointing to the large, expensively furnished sitting room. A young blonde in a tight-fitting red top and black leather miniskirt moved away from the window and stood nervously in a corner. 'Make yourself scarce, Marie,' Saul said, and the girl slipped out of the room. He turned to face Drummond. 'So, what's this all about?'

'You live very well, Benny,' Drummond said, looking around him. 'For a pimp, that is.'

'I'm an accountant.'

'Are you now?' Drummond locked eyes with him. He knew it was true. The man *was* an accountant. He also worked for Big Mal McKirdy and ran a stable of prostitutes on the side.

'Will this take long?' Saul said.

'Depends how well you co-operate. Shall we start again?' He paused. 'Maggie Burns. When was the last time you saw her? And before you waste our time denying you know her; we will be checking her place for fingerprints. If we find any of yours there, then it won't look good for you.'

Saul looked away. 'OK. I've met her. What about it?'

'Maggie's dead, Benny,' Drummond said, watching him. The man tried to feign shock, but his acting wasn't great. The woman's demise clearly wasn't a surprise, but was that because the city's jungle drums had reached him, or was it because he'd killed her?

'We'll need a statement about your relationship with Maggie Burns,' Drummond said as Gail slipped a notebook and pen from her bag. He didn't want to give Saul time to concoct a story by offering him the option of coming to the police station, but the man knew his rights. He glanced at his watch. 'Look, I really am pushed for time right now, but I can come down to the nick later, although I don't know what kind of statement you expect. I hardly knew the woman.'

'Just make sure you're there before 4 p.m.,' Drummond said, not bothering to hide his distaste as he glanced around the plush room. He could feel Saul's eyes on them as they walked away and knew the villain would be reaching for his phone as soon as they were out of the door.

Outside the building they sat in Drummond's car looking up at Saul's flat. 'What now, boss?' Gail said. 'Big Mal McKirdy's place?'

He pulled a face. 'Naw. Let's get back to the nick and see what Nell Forrester has for us.

'You do appreciate I've had next to no time to examine these bodies let alone carry out the post-mortems yet,' Nell Forrester said, dismissing Drummond's attempt to give her his most endearing smile.

'You shouldn't put yourself down, Nell.' The teasing grin was still there. 'Come on, tell me. What've you got?'

She sighed. 'It's the scarf the killer used.' She indicated it on the bench by her microscope. 'It's got DNA on it.'

Drummond's brow wrinkled. He was processing what this might mean. 'Do we know if it's the killer's DNA?'

Her look was scathing. 'I'm a pathologist, Jack, not a magician. If you find me something I can match it with, then I might be able to help you. At the moment all I can say is that it could be the killer's DNA, but it would not prove he – or she – was the killer, only that they had touched the scarf. Actually, not even that. The DNA could also belong to a close member of the killer's family.'

Drummond cursed under his breath, but he knew she was right. They would need to round up a few suspects before they could pursue this line of investigation any further and so far, their only suspect was Saul. Drummond wasn't confident he was a real contender for their strangler.

'Do we know if the killer was a man or a woman?'

'Not for sure,' Nell said. 'But if it's a woman, well, put it this way, she must be a very strong six-footer.'

It confirmed what they saw on the CCTV. 'So, a man then?'

'I didn't say that.'

Drummond blew out his cheeks. 'What about the other body? Anything on that?'

Nell shook her head. 'A few bits of string in his trouser pockets and a filthy hankie.'

'Could the killings be linked?' Drummond asked.

'In what way?'

Drummond shrugged. He was pitching about in the dark.

'Anything's possible, I suppose,' Nell said, her violet

eyes glancing up at him in a way that made his insides quiver. 'The killer of our first victim could still have been at the scene when the old man turned up and began to rob the victim. He, or she, could have been so incensed that he killed the old boy.'

'That would mean the killer had the knife on him,' Drummond said, knowing it was all hypothetical because they had the old boy's killer on CCTV, but he enjoyed hearing her theories.

'Maybe he, or she, was in belt and braces mode. If the strangling failed then he had the knife to fall back on,' Nell said.

Drummond slid her a look. 'You're joking. Right?'

She laughed. 'Sorry, Inspector. I was only playing devil's advocate.'

'Your input is always appreciated, Dr Forrester,' Drummond said. He was wondering how she would react if he suggested they should go out for a drink one night. He was still wondering about that as he left the mortuary and headed back to the station.

'Any ID on the old man yet?' Drummond asked as he strode into the incident room.

Gail looked up from her screen. 'According to the police computer he's William George McDade from Skye – a petty thief who steals mainly to fund his alcohol problem.'

Drummond pulled a face. 'What about his killer?'

'Well that's where it gets better. Annie Bishop has admitted everything. She stabbed the old boy when he wouldn't hand over the stuff he took from Maggie Burns' body. She said she hadn't meant to kill him, only to frighten him. But he made a grab for her and the knife went into him.'

Gail looked up at him. 'Not bad getting at least one of the murders solved within hours.'

'You did well, Gail.' But his eyes were already on the whiteboard. Someone had put up a still from the barras CCTV. He moved in for a closer look at the killer. Even if this guy had been his best mate Drummond doubted if he could have recognized him.

# FOUR

'Sabre! Sabre, come!' Liam Stiller shouted into the dark as he paced the edge of the waste ground. He called again, impatient for his German shepherd to come bounding back. Where was the dog? He checked his watch again. Almost 7 a.m. He didn't have time for this, he was already on a final warning for his timekeeping. And to make matters worse it had started to rain. With an irritated sigh Liam headed out across the site, his head torch picking up only shadows. And then he heard Sabre bark. He called again, cursing. What was the dog doing? It was then that he spotted Sabre in the distance, pawing at what looked like a mess of rubbish somebody had dumped. Liam hated fly-tippers. They had respect for no one, not even themselves.

'Here, boy!' he commanded, but Sabre was more interested in his find than obeying his master. Liam stomped forward, grabbing the dog and snapping the lead on his collar. 'What the devil are you playing at?' he muttered. 'I don't have time for...' But he didn't finish the sentence. His head torch had caught the bundle that had attracted his dog's attention and he drew back in horror.

The woman's eyes stared up at him from the dark. She was splayed out like a rag doll amongst the rubble – and she looked very, very dead! A wave of nausea swept over him. He'd never seen a dead body before.

Liam stumbled back, clutching his stomach. Sabre, sensing something was wrong with his master, began to yank excitedly on his lead. Liam's only thought was to get out of there. The steady drizzle had turned into a downpour. He splashed over the rough ground, the beam from his head torch bouncing off the dark shapes of grass mounds and bushes, each one more sinister looking than the one before. Any of these shapes could be concealing another body. Liam ran faster, Sabre at his heels, as he made a frantic dash for the safety of the road.

They only stopped when they reached the pool of light from the street lamp. Liam fumbled for his phone, gasping for breath, not daring to look back. He punched in 999.


Drummond was swilling down a couple of paracetamols with a mug of strong coffee when he got the call. 'It's another body,' DCI Joey Buchan said, firing out the words like bullets from a gun. 'Over at Pollokshaws. Looks like she's been strangled.'

Drummond cursed, his fragile insides churning over as he grabbed his coat. It was the last news he'd wanted to hear that day. Six weeks had passed since Maggie Burns' murder and the team had been daring to believe her killing had been a one-off. It still might be. But another strangling didn't sound good.

It was half an hour before he got through the early morning traffic to the south side of the city. It was still raining heavily and the forensic team had already erected a tent and set up their powerful lights when he arrived at the scene.

Nell Forrester turned up in her white coveralls as Drummond squinted down at the body. 'You look terrible, Inspector. Heavy night, was it?' Her expression suggested she had no compassion for his hangover.

He cleared his throat. 'I recognize her,' he said flatly. 'She's another hooker.'

'Really?' Nell's eyebrow arched as she turned and knelt by the body and opened her bag.

'It's the same as before, isn't it?' Drummond said.

'Too early to say.'

'But she's been strangled, and it's another scarf, albeit a red one this time, but another scarf.'

Nell sighed. 'You're not expecting me to comment at this stage, are you? I'll be struggling to get any evidence from this body. The rain hasn't done us any favours.'

DC Gail Swann poked her head through the flap in the tent. 'Morning, sir.' She smiled at Nell. 'Morning, Dr Forrester.'

Both of them gave a silent nod.

'The witness who found her was panicking about getting to work, so I told him he could go, and we would catch up with him later. Hope that was OK? He's only round the corner. He's a mechanic at the garage there.'

'I'll have a word with him now,' Drummond said, striding out of the tent. 'What's his name?'

'Liam Stiller. It was his dog that found the body.' Gail tugged her hood closer as the rain lashed down. They splashed through the mud to get to the far pavement. 'It's him again, isn't it, sir?'

'Him? Who?' Drummond frowned.

'The strangler.'

'I hope not.'

'But it is, isn't it?'

'Well, let's just see,' Drummond said, narrowing his eyes against the driving rain.

Brockett's Garage was less than a five-minute walk away. A balding man in a dirty blue boiler suit lifted his head from the engine of a Ford Astra as Drummond and Gail approached. 'Police?' he asked, before they had even produced their warrant cards. 'Liam told me about the body.' He grabbed an oily rag and wiped his hands. 'I suppose you'll be wanting to speak to him.'

Drummond nodded.

'Liam,' the man yelled. 'You've got visitors.'

Liam Stiller's head appeared from the pit under the raised vehicle he'd been working on and nodded to Gail as he hoisted himself up.

'This is DI Drummond,' she said. 'He needs a few words with you.'

Liam Stiller grimaced. 'Just so long as you don't ask me to look at it again.'

'You must have got a shock,' Drummond said.

The man shivered. 'Doesn't bear thinking about. Those eyes...I'll never forget those staring eyes.'

'I understand you were walking your dog. Did you notice anyone else on the waste ground?'

Liam stared at him. 'You mean he could have been there hiding...watching us?' Drummond saw the shiver shoot through the man again. 'I don't know, it was dark.' He paused. 'No, I didn't see anybody, but then the head torch isn't that brilliant.'

'Was it raining?'

'A bit, but then it came in a downpour. I was running late, and Sabre wouldn't come back to me. I could hear him barking and cursed him for ignoring me. The ground was squelchy, and I didn't appreciate having to go and find him.' He paused again and Drummond could see in the man's eyes that he was reliving the event. 'In the torchlight I could see Sabre pawing the ground and kind of whining. When I got to him, I bent down and grabbed his collar to clip the lead on.' He swallowed. 'That's when I saw her...those eyes staring up at me. It was horrible. I couldn't get out of there fast enough.'

Drummond and Gail exchanged a look. The heavy rain wasn't the only thing that had destroyed evidence. There was no telling how much the dog had contaminated the crime scene.

Nell had recovered the victim's handbag and sealed it into an evidence bag when they returned to the scene. She held up another plastic bag containing a letter. 'According to this our victim is a Bernice Brennan and she has a son in care. We have an address in Trongate.'

It was the other side of the city and explained why Drummond knew very little about the woman. 'The forensic officer has a set of keys that were in her bag,' she said. 'They'll have to be dusted for prints before you can take them.'

Drummond narrowed his eyes against his thumping head. 'You get more like one of us every day, Nell,' he said, standing back as the victim was zipped into a body bag and carried away by the undertakers.

'D'you think the dates have anything to do with it?' Gail Swann asked.

'Dates?' Drummond frowned.

'Well, the strangler's last victim died on the last shopping day before Christmas and this is St Valentine's Day.'

Drummond looked at her. 'Is it?'

Nell heaved an exaggerated sigh. 'Does this mean I shouldn't expect a Valentine card then?' She shot Gail a mischievous grin, amused by Drummond's embarrassment.

'We'll check it out,' he said gruffly. 'There might be something about the locations too.'

'I don't see how. The bodies weren't found anywhere near each other,' Nell said.

'That's exactly my point. That might have been intentional.'

'It's not much to go on,' Gail said.

Drummond agreed, flicking his attention back to Nell. 'Well let's hope the PM comes up with something more promising.'

The pathologist picked up her bag. 'Don't hold your breath,' she called over her shoulder as she ducked out of the tent.


Bernice Brennan's bedsit was in the close of an old Glasgow tenement. A card bearing her hand-printed name had been taped to the door frame. Drummond had no confidence that anyone would respond to his knock but knocked anyway. He thought about putting his shoulder to the door. There was no telling when they might get their hands on the keys.

'Bonnie's not in. Who are you?' The woman had appeared from the back court, a bucket in her hand and a cigarette dangling from her mouth.

They produced their IDs. 'Police,' Drummond said. 'DI Drummond and DC Swann. Can I ask who you are?'

The woman nodded to one of the two doors in the close. 'I'm Nancy. Bonnie's a mate. I live there. What do you want with her?'

'Can we have a few words, Nancy?' he said as a man

and woman, dripping wet and carrying heavy shopping bags, pushed past them. The man muttered something about them blocking the close. The woman drew Nancy a look. It wasn't friendly. 'You'd better come in.' She raised her voice. 'Too many nosey auld biddies here that want to know your business.'

The woman with the shopping tutted and shook her head as she and the man puffed up the stairs.

Nancy pushed her door open. It hadn't been locked. 'Come in. You better tell me what Bonnie's been up to now.'

'What makes you think she's been up to something?' Gail asked.

'Because it's what she does. She's always banging on about social services taking her boy. She doesn't realize that chucking bricks at their windows isn't helping her.'

'I don't suppose you have a photo of Bonnie?' Drummond said.

'No. The pictures are all next door.' She began to look anxious. 'What's she done?'

Drummond paused. 'We've found a body,' he said. 'We believe it might be her.'

Gail shot him a look as Nancy's hand went to her mouth and she collapsed onto a chair. 'Jesus. What happened?'

Drummond's expression was grim. 'That's what we're trying to find out.'

What colour there had been in Nancy's face had drained away as she stubbed her cigarette out in a dirty ashtray. 'I've got a key,' she said, getting up and crossing the room to rummage through a drawer. 'You'd be surprised how often she locks herself out.'

Drummond and Gail exchanged a look as they got up and followed her next door.

'We'll give you a shout if we need anything,' he said as

Nancy unlocked the door to Bonnie Brennan's place and handed him the key.

The bedsit was chaotic. At first the detectives thought the place had been turned over, but it soon became apparent that this was how their victim had lived. Drummond's eye fell on the framed photo by the unmade bed. The woman had frizzy blonde hair, challenging green eyes and she balanced a baby on her knee. 'It's her,' Gail said. 'And this must be her son. I wonder why he was taken into care?'

Drummond looked around him. 'Do you really need to ask?' He'd seen for himself how Bonnie solicited from street corners. She probably brought some of her punters back here. He paused, frowning. Could she have brought her killer here? He thought it unlikely, but they needed to get the forensic team out to check anyway.

He took the mother and child photo from its frame and slipped it into his pocket.

Nancy was still hovering about outside the door. 'You didn't say how she died. Was it an accident?' She locked eyes with Drummond.

'I'm afraid not,' he said. 'We'll need a formal identification.'

'You must have known Bernice quite well,' Gail said.

'Bonnie,' she corrected. 'She hated being called Bernice. She was my best mate.'

'Can we go back into your place?' Drummond asked.

# FIVE

THAT MONDAY DCI JOEY BUCHAN had fired her usual caustic words at them. They still hadn't caught the bastard strangler. As if every man and woman on the team wasn't already busting a gut trying to do just that. Somebody was murdering women right under their noses and he was getting away with it. Joey Buchan wasn't the only one raging with guilt and frustration. Traces of DNA were found on the bodies, but until they could match it up with the killer it was useless. They had the scarfs he'd used to strangle the women, but Drummond wasn't holding out much hope they would be helpful. The cat and mouse cards left with the bodies were devoid of fingerprints and could have come from any number of online printers, or the killer's own computer.

Buchan was tapping her finger angrily on the Murder Wall where pictures of Maggie Burns and Bonnie Brennan took centre stage. A stark reminder of their failure...Drummond's failure. He stared at the images. Pictures of Annie Bishop and William McDade had also been added, together with Big Mal McKirdy and Benny Saul's ugly mugs. Drummond narrowed his eyes. What was it they were they missing?

The top brass had brought in criminal psychologist, Francine Janus, a thin, serious-looking woman with cropped black hair and the shadow of a moustache. She had told them the killer was analytical in his approach to the murders. Each woman had been brutally attacked and as the PM reports on the bodies indicated, they had been choked to death probably in the act of being raped.

'He probably cruises the city streets, choosing his victims with precision,' Francine Janus told them, adding what they also already knew – that he was targeting blonde, middle-aged women, all of them with heavily made up faces.

'So, what are you telling us?' Drummond had sighed. 'We should be looking for a nut-case who's killing his mother?' The mother fixation about killers was the usual rubbish trotted out by these psychologists.

'That's exactly what I'm telling you, Detective...?' She raised an eyebrow. 'I'm sorry, I don't know your name.'

'DI Jack Drummond,' he said stiffly, aware of Joey Buchan's deep scowl, but he continued anyway. 'Why prostitutes?' he asked. 'Why not secretaries or hairdressers, or any other ordinary women going about their business?'

Francine Janus was still staring at him. 'In our killer's mind he probably sees himself as ridding the city of filth. He'll believe he's doing a good thing. He'll be on a crusade. He sees these woman as deserving their fate.'

'A religious fanatic,' Drummond muttered. 'That's all we need. Why can't we just be honest and say he's a crazy bastard who kills women?'

'We can,' Francine came back at him. 'But it's my job to delve deeper into that crazy mind and find a reason why he is doing what he's doing. It's supposed to help you.'

Drummond looked away, frowning.

'What happens when he runs out of middle-aged blonde prostitutes?' Gail Swann asked.

The psychologist shrugged. 'He might transfer his interest to another city.' She paused. 'Or he might move into the rest of the community.'

DCI Joey Buchan unfolded her arms. 'So, no woman is safe?'

'That's about it I'm afraid,' Francine said, sliding her thin backside off the desk she had perched on.

Watching her leave, Drummond wondered how long it had taken her to reach a conclusion that was already obvious to anyone with half a brain. None of it helped them catch their killer.

Joey Buchan was looking around the room. 'Any of you got an idea you'd care to share?'

Gail Swann was staring at the Murder Wall. 'I'm still wondering about the places where he's dumping his victims.' She paused, looking about her.

'Go on,' Buchan said.

Gail shrugged. 'The psychologist said our man was meticulous. I just wondered if the disposal sites were significant.'

Drummond's eyes went back to the wall. She could have a point.

Buchan turned to him. 'Have we looked at this, Jack?'

'Only as far as questioning anyone whose property overlooked the sites. We checked surrounding roads and put out requests for anyone who might have been out and about in the area at the time. A few people came forward, but none of them saw anything.' He was still staring at the wall.

Something was missing and then it clicked. 'We need pictures of the witnesses who found the bodies,' he said.

Joey Buchan's eyebrows went up. 'You're not suggesting the killer could be one of them?'

'No, but it's not out of the question. It would be a way for him to get an insight into the police investigation. He's probably arrogant enough for that.' He nodded to Gail. 'DC Swann is right. We should be looking for connections.'

Joey Buchan's face stretched into an expression that indicated she thought the whole theory was far-fetched. But they were in no position to ignore anything. 'OK,' she said. 'You've talked yourself into a job, DI Drummond. You check that out yourself and get those photos up on the wall.' She glanced around the room. 'The rest of you have been briefed. Get out there and catch this bastard.'

The phone on Drummond's desk rang and he grabbed it.

'Is this a bad time?' PC Pete Mullen was the old-fashioned kind of cop everybody trusted. He had been a community bobby pounding the city centre streets since before Drummond joined the Force. He was also his best friend.

'It's fine, Pete. We'v just finished a briefing. How are you doing?'

'Great, yeah. Just wondered if you fancied grabbing a bite to eat tonight?'

Drummond hesitated. The Four Crowns was one of Pete's local pubs, but Drummond wasn't sure how welcome he'd be there, not after last week's fracas. He hadn't thrown the first punch but there was no way he was going to let a lowlife like Wattie Bremner get away with yelling abuse at him across a crowded bar just because he was the polis. In the end they had both been thrown out.

'Where were you thinking of meeting?' he asked.

'Come over to the house. I'll cook,' Pete said.

Drummond's eyes went to the ceiling. 'You heard about the stramash then?'

'Everybody has, Jack. You need to curb that temper of yours.'

'It wasn't my fault, Pete.'

'Even so. You're a DI. People need to respect you.'

'Are you inviting me over for a lecture?'

Pete laughed. 'Would it do any good?'

'Probably not,' Drummond said. 'What are you cooking?'

Drummond loved the city at night, but it felt like a different place since this psycho had started murdering people. So far, he had confined himself to attacking prostitutes, but they had no reason to believe his next victim would be another hooker.

Drummond felt sorry for the women. What life did they have selling their bodies to any passing male willing to pay the price to subject them to God knows what degradation? Most of them weren't even earning a living, only financing a drug habit. They had enough to contend with without being preyed on by some sick maniac.

The first time Drummond spotted Evie in the red-light area he thought she must have innocently strayed there returning home from some city centre nightclub. She looked like she should be getting an early night for school next day, not loitering about with the city's prostitutes. His heart sank when he saw her get into a car and be driven away.

Whatever circumstances in this girl's young life had driven her onto the streets, she was on a downward spiral unless somebody stopped her.

Normally he turned a blind eye to the hookers' activities, but while this killer remained at large none of them was safe. The ones he'd spoken to had ignored his advice to stop hanging about street corners. Maybe now was the time to get tough with them.

Maidie Gemmell was as hard as they came. She'd been plying her trade on the city streets long before Drummond joined Glasgow's finest. She tossed away a fag butt and rolled her eyes as he approached. 'Give us a break, Mr Drummond. Business is bad enough without you turning up and frightening the punters away.'

'Your next punter could be your last. Think of this as me doing you a favour.'

'You're not going to nick me?'

He lowered his brows and stepped closer. 'That's exactly what I'll be doing unless you stay off the streets. Pass the word on.'

Maidie sighed and rummaged in her bag for another cigarette. 'It's the kid you want to be chatting up, not me. She's the one getting all the tricks.'

'What about her?'

Maidie shrugged. 'Nothing. But if you're looking for a soul to save you could look in her direction. Mark my word, that one's heading for trouble. I've told her to watch herself and got a load of shit for my trouble.' She sniffed. 'She thinks she knows best.'

Drummond doubted if Maidie's concern was as well intentioned as she'd have him believe. Getting rid of the competition was more like it. 'Do you know where she lives?'

'She's got a room next to mine. Of course, you could just hang about here. She'll be back,' she said. 'Evie specializes in quickies.'

Drummond levelled a frown at her. 'You still here?' he said.

'OK, I'm going. Just make sure you chase her too.'

Drummond moved into the shadow of a doorway. He didn't have long to wait for Evie to put in an appearance. He stepped forward. 'You and I need to have a chat, Evie.'

The girl drew back, her eyes flicking over the warrant card Drummond held up. 'What do you want?' Her tone was huffy. 'I haven't done anything wrong.'

'You have, actually, but I'm sure you know that.' He nodded towards his car. 'Let's have a chat over there.'

The girl flashed him a disgusted look. 'You want a freebie?'

'I want a chat, but if you have any objection, we can do this back at the station.'

Evie threw up her arms in a gesture of defeat as she walked with him to the car. She flounced into the front passenger seat and folded her arms. 'Is this going to be a lecture?'

'Would it make any difference?'

'No.'

'So even if a detective police inspector offers you a second chance if you stop soliciting on the streets you will ignore it? Is that what you're saying?'

Evie wriggled uncomfortably. 'I'm not doing any harm. The men like me. It's not my fault if the old hags are jealous.'

Drummond sighed. 'You're not getting it, are you, Evie? It's not about *you* doing any harm. There's a killer out there and he's targeting girls like you. It's not safe for you, or any of the other women, to be out on the streets at night. You have no idea what you're getting yourself into when you go with these men.'

Evie's expression was still mutinous. Drummond glared at her, trying to control his growing frustration at the girl's blatant defiance. 'How old are you, Evie?'

'Twenty.'

'I'll ask again. How old?'

Evie looked away. 'Seventeen...and don't ask if my parents are trying to find me because they're not. I don't want them to. I don't need them. I can look after myself.'

Drummond's laugh was incredulous. 'This is how you look after yourself? How long do think it will be before the pimps move in on you? You do know what a pimp is?' Evie stared stubbornly ahead. 'Once you're in their clutches they don't let you get away,' Drummond said. 'Where are you staying?'

'I've got a room.'

Drummond nodded. 'OK, here's the deal. I drive you there and you collect your things and I put you on the train home.'

She turned furious brown eyes on him. 'I'm not going back there. I told you.'

Drummond shrugged. 'The other alternative is that I arrest you for soliciting in a public place. Your choice.'

Evie kept up her angry stare. 'No wonder they call you lot pigs. You're a bully.'

Drummond smiled. 'You'll thank me for this one day.'

An hour later they were in Queen Street station waiting for a train to Edinburgh, where Evie assured him, she had family. Drummond felt uncomfortable about not escorting her all the way, but he was a copper, not a social worker. He'd done all he could for the girl. He thrust one of his cards into Evie's hand together with a couple of £20 notes. 'Any problems just ring me. OK?' She gave a grudging nod, but there was no backward glance of gratitude as she boarded the train.

Drummond watched as it moved off and wondered, as he turned towards Pete Mullen's place, if he had just relocated the girl's life of prostitution to Edinburgh.

# SIX

'How much longer do you think you'll get away with using your fists when you should be using your brain?' Pete's words were cutting.

'I thought you said this wasn't going to be a lecture.' Drummond frowned, lifting a lid off one of the pots simmering on the stove and taking a sniff.

'I lied,' Pete said. 'Sit down, Jack.' He slung a tea towel over his shoulder. 'We're mates, aren't we?'

Drummond squinted at him. 'Not if this is going to be one of your good advice sessions.'

Pete Mullen was the best friend Drummond was ever likely to have, next to his old man, who ran a corner shop in Garnethill and complained that he never saw him. Nobody cared as much as Eddie Drummond whether his son lived or died, with the possible exception of Drummond's brother, Daniel, and his family. But then they were just that...family. And family didn't count. They *had* to love you.

Pete was still talking. 'You have to start trusting people, Jack. Some of us are on your side, you know.' He paused. 'Do you regret joining the polis?'

Now, there was a question. Did he regret it? He would never have been a copper if it hadn't been for Pete. He'd been well on his way to becoming a young thug when Pete yanked him up by the scruff of the neck and made him listen to a few home truths. They both knew he'd planted the evidence that got the Blades gang banged up in Polmont, Scotland's young offenders' institution. They deserved it. They killed his boyhood pal, Jemmie Khan... callously knifed him because he was black.

Drummond sighed. 'Do I regret becoming a copper?' He was still thinking about that. 'I don't really know...maybe.'

'Your trouble is you can't walk away. You take it all personally when you should be standing back to get some perspective on things.'

Drummond pulled a face. 'Maybe, but it's different for me. You're a community copper on the beat, Pete. I'm a DI on the murder squad. And right now, there's a nutcase out there murdering people.' He looked up, frowning. 'It's my job to stop him and I can't bloody do it.'

'That's not all on your shoulders,' Pete interrupted. 'Quit beating yourself up. You'll catch this guy; you know you will.'

'Yeah, but when? He's already killed two women, maybe more. He's out there doing whatever he likes and I...we... don't seem able to do a bloody thing about it.'

'Is that why you punched Wattie Bremner?' He frowned. 'I know he's got a face that just begs to be slapped, but you're the polis, Jack, and we're supposed to be above stuff like that.'

'He picked a fight.' Drummond held up his hands. 'OK I know I should have walked.'

Pete was shaking his head. 'What was it he said that got your dukes up?'

Drummond grimaced. 'He was taunting me, shouting about how useless the polis were. He said a five-year-old bairn was more capable of catching the strangler than me.'

'You punched him for that?'

'His cronies were all there egging him on. He was loving it; said he was thinking of giving the strangler a hand killing the prossies because with me on the case there was no chance of them ever getting caught.' He looked up. 'That's when I punched him. He made a swing back at me and there was a struggle. We were both put out the pub.'

'And did the fisticuffs continue out in the street?' Pete asked.

'No, Bremner didn't have his mates with him out there. I grabbed him by the scruff of the neck and told him what would happen if he ever tried to pull a stunt like that on me or any police officer again. He got the message.'

Pete pulled a face. 'So, you threatened him?'

Drummond grinned. 'You might say that. I couldn't possibly comment.'

Pete shook his head and turned to the cooker, tipping the pasta into a colander.

Drummond produced the beer he'd brought and took a couple of glasses from the drainer.

'What you need is a steady relationship,' Pete said, pointing his fork at him. 'And I don't mean one of your chaotic affairs with some poor woman who lets you treat them like a doormat.'

Drummond looked away. The memory of being uncere-moniously bundled out of the lovely Megan's flat, followed by two black bin bags of his clothes, was flashing through his mind. His feelings were still bruised about that. She was nobody's doormat, but she had wanted a steady relationship, *he* hadn't.

'What about that nice lassie you work with?' Pete wasn't giving up. 'Now she would be a good influence on you.'

'Gail Swann?' Drummond stared at him. 'I don't think so.'

'What's wrong with her?'

'She's a colleague. She's ambitious. She has a son. And besides, we don't fancy each other. Need I go on?'

Pete pressed his lips together. 'Doesn't stop you fancying that Nell Forrester.'

Drummond blinked. His old friend's ability to see right through him never failed to surprise. There was no point in denying it, but how did he know? He had to admit that he did fancy the delectable Nell, even if she showed no signs of reciprocating the feelings.

'Stop trying to play Cupid,' he said, pointing a forkful of spaghetti at him. 'It's not sorting out my love life that I need. It's a breakthrough in these murders.'

'That might take more thinking about,' Pete agreed.

When they'd finished eating it was Pete who suggested a trip to the pub. Drummond needed no persuasion.

'Mine's a dram,' Pete Mullen said as they walked into the Hauf and Hauf public house.

Drummond signalled the barmaid to give them both a double Famous Grouse.

'You've had a face like a slapped backside all night. My cooking's not that bad, is it?' Pete said.

They moved away from the bar and sat down. 'You take me too seriously, Pete. Misery is my middle name.'

'Yeah, I know. You have to do something about that. Why are you letting this case worry away at you? Things will get better; it's bound to start going well soon.'

Drummond sat back, sighing. 'I wish I had your confidence, but this guy just seems to disappear into the ether.

I've never known a case like this.' He took a swig of whisky. 'Two women murdered and we're no closer to catching him.'

'That's not true. Every killing takes you closer to catching him. You need to stand back and look at it all from a different viewpoint.'

Drummond laughed. Pete Mullen was the cop who pounded the beat and listened to locals' problems over cups of tea in their kitchens. The cop who dished out sound advice instead of threatening people. The cop who had saved him from a life of crime and thuggery on the streets of Glasgow. 'Are you telling me to think outside the box, Pete?'

'I'm telling you that you probably know a lot more about this killer than you realize.'

Drummond drained his glass. 'I'm listening.'

'The first question to ask is why he's killing prostitutes, blonde prostitutes.'

'The criminal psychologist woman Buchan has drafted in tells us he's basically killing his mother.'

'Is she suggesting the mother is a prostitute?'

'Who knows? I'd trust a witch doctor's mumbo jumbo before believing anything a psychologist said.'

Pete shook his head and tutted. 'Still that chip on your shoulder. Don't be so hard on psychologists. They're just a tool the polis use. Sometimes they help, sometimes they don't.'

Drummond gave an impatient glance to the bar. 'This must be one of the times when they're useless then.'

'What if it doesn't point to the mother being a hooker? What if she just had an affair and that affair split up our killer's happy home? Maybe he's never forgiven his mother and now he's taking his revenge on her by killing these other women?'

'And there are fairies at the bottom of my garden,'

Drummond said, collecting their glasses and making for the bar. He watched his old friend as he stood there, wondering how he coped on his own. It wasn't something he'd considered before. Pete and his wife, Rose, had split up years ago. The demands of the Force did that to so many couples. Their daughter had gone to live with her mother and although he knew the divorce had been amicable and Pete regularly saw them both, it was obvious how desperately he missed his family. That wasn't going to happen to Drummond. Serious relationships were not for him.

'So, what else have you got?' Pete asked, when he got back with the drinks.

'Not a lot. We don't even know if the killer lives in Glasgow, although he does seem to know his way around.'

'What about the time between the murders? Why isn't he being more consistent with the killings?'

'I'm not sure what you mean.'

Pete leaned in closer. 'Maybe he once worked here in the city and then moved away but returns to Glasgow for meetings, or whatever.'

'It's a theory, Pete. I don't see how it helps us any. The killer's clever, too clever to leave clues. We got some DNA from the scarf he used to strangle the first victim, but it didn't match anything on our database. The second time it was raining, so we lost what evidence there might have been.'

Pete was thinking. 'Do you suppose that was on purpose? Maybe he knows water washes away clues.'

'I considered that,' Drummond said. 'Even if it's right, it doesn't help. I've also been wondering if he likes to hang around the body until it's found.'

Pete looked up. 'Why would he do that?'

Drummond shrugged. 'No idea. Maybe in his mind he's

looking after the body, making sure she's found and treated with respect.'

'Respect?' Pete blinked. 'If he cares that much then why is he killing these women in the first place?' He took a long, slow sip of his Famous Grouse. 'Although thinking about that, what does it suggest? Who treats women badly but likes to believe he respects them?'

Drummond closed his eyes and let the possibilities scroll through his mind. Were they looking for a professional man? Doctor? Teacher? Police officer?

Pete nodded to the clock behind the bar and finished off his drink. 'Sorry, Jack. I need to get off. I need my beauty sleep.'

Drummond got up too. 'Thanks for everything tonight, Pete,' he said as the older man put an encouraging hand on his shoulder. They parted outside the pub and Drummond walked back to his flat with the word 'respect' rattling around his head. He was wondering if he'd done the right thing bundling young Evie off on the train. As far as he knew, the killer hadn't murdered anybody in Edinburgh, not yet.

# SEVEN

THERE WAS an urgency about DC Gail Swann's stride as she crossed the incident room to where Drummond and Joey Buchan were talking. He looked up. 'What?'

'It's a body...in the River Kelvin. Uniforms are there now.' They were both giving her a hard stare and she nodded. 'Looks like she's been strangled.'

'Shit!' Joey Buchan whirled round. It had been months since the last strangling and they were no closer to nabbing the bastard. Now here they were again. 'You two better get over there.' She was punching out a number on her phone. 'And don't think you're off the hook, Inspector!' she called after him as he strode off, Gail Swann hurrying along beside him. 'We'll talk about this again.'

He gave her a backward wave.

'What have you done now, sir?'

'Nothing. It's just the DCI getting her knickers in a twist again.'

'Maybe if you didn't wind her up so much...' She was running after him down the stairs.

Drummond scowled. 'There would be no fun in that,'

he called back, tossing her the keys of a pool car. 'You drive. I need some thinking time. What else did uniform say about the body?'

'Only that it was spotted by a jogger. They managed to get it up onto a bank.'

'How did they do that?'

'Don't know. I think they found a branch or something.'

It was just after nine and the city centre traffic was beginning to ease off slightly as they sped along Dunbarton Road.

They pulled in behind the patrol car on Kelvin Bridge as a middle-aged PC hurried to meet them.

'She's just there, sir,' he said, leaning over the bridge and pointing.

Drummond looked down and cursed. Another blonde! And the black scarf she'd been strangled with was still tight around her neck. They would have to pull her further up the bank before any initial forensic examination could be carried out, although he doubted how much, if any, useful evidence that would throw up. Having been in the river wouldn't help.

DCI Buchan had called out the troops. Other police vehicles were arriving, but there was no sign of Nell Forrester. A stern-looking young man he didn't recognize had been pulling on his whites at the rear of a vehicle and was now walking towards them with the familiar bag.

'Martin Sinclair, forensic pathologist,' he said. 'What have we got?'

Drummond stopped himself asking where Nell Forrester was. The stab of disappointment that this man had turned up in her place had surprised even him. 'It's a body in the river,' he said. 'Down there where all the activity is. You can't miss it.'

Martin Sinclair gave him an unamused sideways look. Gail said nothing as they followed him down to where the body lay.

'What about this one, sir? Do you recognize her?' Gail asked as they stood looking down at the scene.

Drummond pursed his lips and tilted his head. 'Not sure.'

'But she's a prostitute? Right?'

'We don't know that, not yet.' But he knew everything was pointing in that direction. Unless, of course, this was the work of a copycat killer, which was highly unlikely unless there was a mole on the team. No details had been released about the scarfs. He turned away; his face tight. What kind of twisted bastard killed women like this? And why prostitutes? Why blondes? It looked like a pattern. The choice of victims couldn't be a coincidence. So many questions, so few answers. He needed time to think.

He caught Gail's eye. 'Wait here and get the genius down there–' he nodded to the pathologist '–to tell you all he knows. Tell him to check the pockets. I want to know if the killer left his calling card. And have a word with that jogger who found her. I'll catch up with you later.'

'Where are you going?' Gail asked.

Drummond wished he knew. He'd seen all he needed to for now. He had to get away from the crime scene. It was doing his head in. 'I have a few things to check out. Let me know if anything turns up here.'

He climbed back up the slippery river bank. He needed to find a pub.

Whisky at this early hour was not a great idea, but he ordered the traditional Glasgow 'hauf an' a hauf' anyway. He watched the blonde, middle-aged barmaid hold the glass to the optic and fill it with a double measure of Bell's. She put it on the bar beside the half pint she'd poured and took the money from him. Then she disappeared to the far side of the bar to continue her conversation with a guy in a tweed jacket and a polo shirt.

He picked up the whisky glass and threw back half the contents, thinking about where the strangler could have dumped the body in the river. Until they knew that there was no chance of any CCTV. Perhaps this time the killer would be unlucky? Perhaps somebody saw him disposing of it? A witness would be good.

Drummond drained his glass and held it up for a refill. If the strangler had been acting true to form, he'd killed his victim that morning, sometime in the early hours after having picked her up from a location in Glasgow's red-light district. He went over what they knew.

He believed the killer had studied how forensic officers retrieved evidence from victims and crime scenes. Could he be a police officer, or just clever enough to do his homework?

Witnesses had given different descriptions of the cars used to pick up his first two victims. Were they different vehicles? Had he hired cars to hide his tracks? Hiring a car required a valid driver's license and credit card. They were still trawling through every car-hire company in the city for details of who had a hired a car on the relevant nights. But as the hirer could have rented the vehicle for any number of days or weeks – or even months – it was a slow and painstaking job. So far it hadn't thrown up anything useful.

Drummond sighed. They didn't even know if the strangler was from Glasgow. He certainly knew his way around. The disposal sites where he dumped his victims hadn't been chosen at random. They were diverse, far apart, and appeared to have nothing in common.

Maggie Burns had been dumped at The Barras, one of the busiest places in town, Bonnie Brennan had been found miles away on open waste ground in Pollockshaws. And now this third woman in the River Kelvin. Why the river? He was missing something.

His phone buzzed in his pocket and he fished it out. DCI Joey Buchan! 'Where the hell are you, Drummond?' No friendly 'How are things going, Jack?' She was on the warpath.

'You should be here at the crime scene!'

'Has something happened?' He felt his heartbeat quicken.

'We might know where he dumped this body.' He could hear the urgency in her voice. 'Somebody has rung in reporting a fly-tipper. He says he witnessed a bloke heave a heavy bundle into the river upstream from our crime site.'

'You think this was our man getting rid of the body?'

'I'm making no assumptions, but it needs checking out. We've already got a couple of uniforms on the way there. Get Gail to pick you up. She has all the details.' He heard her sigh. 'And, Drummond,' she said. 'Stop bloody disappearing!'

Less than three minutes after telling his DC to meet him at the art galleries he spotted the pool car approaching.

Gail's nose wrinkled and she shot him a look as he slid in beside her. She was clearly disapproving.

'What?' Drummond snapped.

'Am I allowed to mention that you smell like a distillery?'

'I was working. I do my best thinking in pubs.'

'I'd still give the DCI a wide berth for a couple of hours,' she said.

'Just watch the road,' DC Swann. 'Nobody's asked for

your opinion.' But he saw her grin as he rolled down the window.

'You were right, by the way,' she said. 'There *was* a cat and mouse card in our victim's pocket.'

A police patrol car was already there when they pulled up and one of the two uniformed officers was talking to a man on the bank of the river. 'This is Mr Fenning. He reported seeing a man fly-tipping here last night.'

Jason Fenning was a fit-looking thirty-something dressed in a grey tracksuit. 'I hate people who dump their rubbish just anywhere. It's us mugs who have to pay for it,' he complained. 'I tried ringing the council to report it, but I couldn't get through to them last night. I rang you lot because I thought you'd pass it onto them. I wasn't expecting all this fuss.'

Drummond kept his distance. 'Where did you see this rubbish getting dumped?' The man pointed. Drummond nodded to the other officer. 'Go and help your colleague look for it.'

Gail pulled a notebook and pen from her bag. 'Can you describe the man you saw?'

Jason was slipping his phone from his pocket. 'I can do better than that,' he said, bringing up a video he'd made of the incident.

Drummond shot out his hand. 'Can I see?'

The man handed over the phone. 'Be my guest.'

Drummond played the short video several times. It showed a man in a hoody heave a large plastic sack into the river. Their victim hadn't been in a bag when she was found. His spirits sank. Whatever was in this sack he doubted if it was a body. He emailed the video to his own mobile before handing the man's phone back.

'There's something here, sir.' The call came from the river bank. 'I think we've found it,' the PC shouted.

Drummond hurried down. The officer was using a long branch he'd found to make a grab for the bag that had become tangled amongst the weeds. Drummond helped the two officers pull the thing from the water.

'What d'you think it is?' The younger of the two officers looked unsure about finding out.

'Untie it,' Drummond ordered. They had been joined by Gail and Jason Fenning. The officer untied the bag at arm's length as though he thought it might explode.

'What is it?' Fenning said as the contents spilled out over the bank. Gail clapped a hand to her mouth and turned away, retching.

'Jesus Christ. It's a dog and puppies.' Fenning looked up at Drummond, frowning. 'Did that bastard drown them?'

The sight disgusted Drummond too, but it had nothing to do with the strangler. They went back to the pool car and he reached for his phone to pass the depressing news on to Joey Buchan. He heard her mutter a curse. 'I was hoping we had something there. You'd better turn it over to the council. Let them deal with it now.' There was a pause. Drummond could hear her speak to someone in the room with her. She came back to him. 'The forensic boys recovered an address from the body,' she said. 'You and DC Swann can check it out. The mobile phone we recovered was registered to a Lena Murray. I'll message you the details.'

'Fine,' he said, as she clicked off the call. The name meant nothing to him, but then he hadn't recognized the victim. He turned to Gail. 'Who found the body?'

She flicked through her notebook. 'An Olivia Ryder. She was out jogging when she spotted the body in the river.'

'Have you taken a statement?'

'Not an official one. To be honest she didn't really have anything useful to tell us. She jogs around the park every morning. The body caught her eye as she came across the bridge. It was tangled in weeds by the bank.' Gail looked up. 'That's about it. She's going to call in at the station later today.'

'How about an address?'

Gail flipped through her notes. 'She has a flat in South Woodside Road, but she'll be at work now. She's an auctioneer for an antiques centre in Dumbarton Road.'

He gave a thoughtful nod as Joey's message buzzed in.

'We'll try this one first,' he said. Gail reached for the satnav on the dashboard of the pool car waiting for him to tell her the postcode, but he shook his head. 'We won't need that. It's Hill Street. I could take you there with my eyes closed.'

'Of course,' Gail said, remembering what he'd once let slip. 'You were brought up around there.'

'Let's just get going,' he said. He had no intention of discussing his upbringing or sharing small talk about his family with his detective constable. Not that he'd had a difficult childhood, but it had been tough. It had shaped him into the man he now was, he just wasn't sure that was a good thing. He knew he still had anger issues. He had never fully dealt with his obsession for revenge on the hit and run driver who had killed his beloved mother less than twenty yards from their close. That driver had never been found, had never been brought to justice. No ten-year-old should have to deal with that.

# EIGHT

DESPITE THE DRAMATIC changes in the city's topography over the years, Glasgow's Garnethill area was still recognizable from Drummond's stamping ground days. The corner shop where local people bought their morning rolls and newspaper was still run by his father. It was only a stone's throw from the address they had for Lena Murray.

Gail parked in front of the new flats and gazed up at the glass frontage. 'Are you sure you've got the right address.'

'Nope,' Drummond said. 'But for the moment it's all we've got.'

Doing the death knock was probably the worst job any officer had to do. He tried to harden himself against the experience but how could telling someone that the person they loved was now dead not affect you?

And here they were, about to do it all over again.

The door was opened by a middle-aged man in a grey cardigan and needlecord trousers. The look of dread that filled his eyes as he stared at them made Drummond want to reach out for him.

They produced their warrant cards and the man bit his lip. 'It's Lena, isn't it? What's happened to her?'

'May we come in, sir?' Drummond said quietly.

The man stood back, and the detectives followed his directions to the front room. The flat was smart and clean. There was no sign of children but that didn't mean their victim was not a mother.

'Can we ask who you are, sir?' Drummond said.

'I'm Derek Murray, Lena's husband. Just tell me what's happened.'

Drummond swallowed. No point in beating about the bush. 'We've found a body. She had this address in an envelope in her bag.'

The man looked like he was going to faint, and Gail rushed forward to guide him to a chair.

'Is it my Lena?' He was gazing from one to the other as though imploring them to tell him they'd made a mistake.

'We won't know that for sure until she's been identified.'

Derek Murray stared at them. 'You want me to identify her?' He sounded horrified.

'There's no hurry,' Drummond said, but he knew this wasn't true. No proper investigation could begin until they had an ID on the victim.

'You haven't told me what happened to her. Was she in an accident?'

Drummond glanced away. 'The body we found this morning was taken from the River Kelvin.'

'She drowned?' Derek blinked.

'There's no easy way to say this, Mr Murray. The woman we found had been...' He hesitated. 'We believe someone put her in the river.'

The man stared at them with horrified eyes. 'You mean Lena was murdered?' He let out a wail and began rocking his head in his hands. Drummond and Gail watched him uneasily. They were both aware of the statistics that most murders were committed by someone who knew the victim. If this man was putting on an act of grief, then he was very good at it.

'Can you tell us where your wife was last night?'

Derek Murray was now wringing his hands. He began pacing the room. 'I warned her to stop, but she wouldn't. We could manage on my wages, there was no need for her to do that...not that.'

Drummond shot Gail a look. 'What are you talking about, Mr Murray? What did Lena do?' But he already knew what the man was going to say.

Derek Murray gave an almighty sob. 'Lena was selling her body,' he said miserably. 'Prostituting herself to buy this stuff.' He opened his arms and gestured around the room to the stylish furniture. 'As if we needed stuff like this.'

Gail frowned. 'You weren't able to stop her?'

'You didn't know Lena. When she made her mind up about something there was nothing that would stop her.'

'Have you been married long?' she asked gently.

'Ten years.' He gave a hopeless sigh. 'If we'd had children things might have been different. Lena really wanted children, but it didn't happen.' He looked up. 'My fault. I couldn't even do that right.'

Drummond suppressed his own sigh. If their body really was Lena Murray and she had been soliciting, then she fitted the profile of the strangler's other victims. It didn't really take them any further though.

'You mentioned your wages. What do you do, Mr Murray?' Gail asked.

'I'm a bus driver.'

'And Lena? Did she have a job?'

'Lena worked in a cafe in Sauchiehall Street. The Tea Cosy.'

Gail scribbled the name into her notebook.

'Will you be all right?' Drummond asked. It was a ridiculous question because the man clearly wasn't. 'Can we call anyone for you, a member of your family?'

Derek shook his head. 'There was only Lena...' His voice trailed into silence.

'If you can give us a telephone number, we'll contact you about coming in to identify your wife,' Gail said, and jotted down the number she was given.

'Are you sure we can't call someone?' Drummond asked again. 'We have specially trained support officers to help at times like this.'

Derek Murray shook his head and slumped onto the expensive brown leather sofa. Drummond felt uneasy about leaving him on his own, but he couldn't make the man accept help.

'What now, sir? That cafe?' Gail asked as they left the building and went back to the car.

'Yes, the cafe. Can you check that out?' Drummond said. 'It's just around the corner and you can walk back to the nick from there. I'll go and see our jogger friend. What's she like?'

'Pretty level headed I would say, not that I questioned her in detail.'

Drummond nodded. He suspected interviewing this witness would simply be ticking another box, but it had to be done and didn't require two detectives wasting their time.


Drummond's nose twitched as he stepped into the antiques

centre. The place smelled of wealth. He looked around him. Everything was old, and expensive. There were no antiques in his flat, only second-hand furniture and none of that came with the kind of price tag he suspected the pieces here would fetch at auction. From the reception window he could see into the office. It was a frenzy of activity. He pressed the brass bell and a grey-haired woman in a cherry red cardigan approached. 'Sorry about all this. It's not really as chaotic as it looks.' She smiled. 'How can I help you?'

Drummond gave his name and showed his warrant card. 'I'd like to see Olivia Ryder.'

'Olivia? She's on the rostrum at the moment, but I think they're coming to the end of the list. Can you wait?'

He nodded. The woman indicated a customers' bench, but Drummond ignored it, following the signs to the auction room. He'd expected Olivia Ryder to be spectacled and bookish, but the young woman brandishing the gavel was a Titian-haired beauty who appeared to have the audience in her thrall. He had no problem standing there watching her.

The silver box she was currently auctioning was displayed on a screen. 'This is the one you've all been waiting for, ladies and gentlemen. Can I start at £100?' Her green eyes searched the room. 'How about £80 then? Just think how beautiful this would look on your dressing table, madam.' Her lovely face broke into a dazzling smile. 'A gift for your lady, sir. Just imagine how popular you would be.'

Hands began to shoot up: £80...£90...£100...£110. The gavel came down at £210. Two more items sold equally well, and the room began to clear as the auction came to an end. Drummond approached Olivia Ryder as she left the rostrum and again produced his ID. She looked surprised. 'I told the officer this morning that I would come to the station to give my statement.'

'You can still do that. This is just an informal chat.' He smiled. 'I promise not to keep you long.' Her eyes lingered on him as she returned his smile. 'I'm about to go on a break. There's a pub around the corner.'

Drummond was trying not to be mesmerized by those emerald eyes. 'Good idea,' he said. He went with her while she collected her jacket and they walked together to the Rope and Anchor. She ordered a glass of white wine and a prawn sandwich. Drummond stuck to beer.

'You found the body, I believe,' he said, not taking his eyes from her.

She broke off a piece of her sandwich and dropped it on her plate. 'It was horrible.' He saw her shiver and wanted to put an arm around her. 'I jog over that bridge every morning and the scene never changes. That's why I spotted the thing.' She looked up at him. 'It was out of place, you see.'

He nodded. 'Go on.'

Olivia lifted her glass and took a sip of her wine. She had abandoned the sandwich. 'It was caught up in something by the bank and the current was tugging at it, making it move about. I was in two minds about going to the side of the bridge for a closer look or jogging on.' She paused, her gaze darting about as she remembered the horror of what she'd seen that morning. 'I thought at first that it was rubbish someone had dumped in the river.' She turned to Drummond. 'Why do people choose the loveliest places to fly-tip their junk?'

Drummond's shoulders lifted in a shrug.

She carried on. 'It wasn't rubbish. I took out my phone and punched in 999.'

'What time was that?'

'Let me see.' Olivia's brow wrinkled as she worked it out.

'I left the flat at 6.30 and it takes me about ten minutes to get to the bridge, so 6.40.'

'Did you see anyone else about at that time of day?'

She thought about that. 'You mean like another jogger?'

'Not necessarily,' he said. 'Just anyone else out and about.'

'I didn't see who put the thing there, Inspector, if that's what you mean.'

Drummond finished off his pint. That would have been too much to hope for. Despite how much he was enjoying this woman's company he'd been right in the first place. It was a box-ticking exercise.

Olivia was leaning in closer. 'Look, I can't go on calling you "Inspector". What's your first name?'

Jesus, he was flushing! Her directness unnerved him. He cleared his throat. 'It's Jack,' he said.

'Like I said, Jack, I didn't see anyone, but you've made me think. There was a car.'

'A car?' He was instantly a policeman again.

She nodded. 'Through the trees. It was a dark saloon car. I didn't give it much thought at the time. I was so traumatized by seeing that body in the water.'

'Did you get a look at the driver?'

'That's probably what made me dismiss seeing the car. He was in a tracksuit with the hood up. He looked like a jogger. Most people who jog around the park so early come in their car and park up.'

Drummond's mind flashed back to when they'd found Maggie Burns at The Barras. The CCTV image they'd watched of the killer dragging his victim's body along the lane was scrolling through his mind. He'd been wearing a tracksuit – and the hood had been firmly pulled up. It was hardly a connection though. Everybody wore tracksuits these days. But still...

'Does it help?' Olivia was still leaning in close. He wondered how she would react if he should reach out and touch her cheek. He'd probably get a slap. She might even report him for sexual harassment.

'Do I still have to come into the police station to give a statement?' She was sitting very close.

'That would be helpful.' He was glad she couldn't see this funny lurching his heart was doing.

'Will you be there, Jack?'

His body was responding to her closeness in a way that was not strictly professional. He swallowed. 'Possibly not, but we have other officers who can take your statement.'

Her fingers stroked the stem of her glass. 'That's a shame,' she said.

'It doesn't mean we couldn't meet up again. Maybe we could have a drink some time?' He couldn't believe he was inviting her on a date.

'I'd like that, Jack.' She smiled into his eyes as she took a card from her bag. 'My mobile number is on the back.' She slid the card onto the table and stood up. 'Call me,' she said. He watched her leave the pub, his hand trembling as he picked up the card and put it in his pocket.

# NINE

THOUGHTS of the delectable Olivia Ryder were still filling Drummond's head as he sat at his desk next day. His phone rang and he grabbed at it, irritated at the interruption to the pleasing fantasy forming in his mind.

'There's someone down here to see you, Inspector,' the voice said. Drummond gave a disgruntled sigh. He was on the point of barking he was too busy, but he knew whoever was asking for him would only come back.

'Two minutes,' he said, grabbing his jacket as he strode out of the incident room and made for the stairs.

Three faces glanced up at him as he burst into the reception. He didn't recognize any of them. The desk sergeant caught his eye and nodded to the street door.

'Sorry, Jack, you just missed her.'

Drummond cursed, battering through the glass door and squinting up and down the street He spotted her slumped against a parked car. He hardly recognized her. The long dark hair had been chopped and dyed blonde, she had a black eye and there was an angry cut on her cheek.

Judging by the way she was holding herself she'd also had a kicking.

She looked like she had acquired a nasty new habit since he'd last seen her – one that would be expensive to maintain. The stupid girl had got herself involved with drugs. He could feel the anger searing inside him.

Evie Walker tried to smile but it came over as a grimace. 'You said I could contact you if I needed a mate. I think I...' She didn't need to finish the sentence. Drummond sprang forward to catch her as she started to slide to the ground.

'You need a doctor,' he said.

She grabbed his arm. 'No doctor. Please!'

But he was in no mood to argue. 'You're going to A&E.'

An hour later, with a dressing over the cut on her cheek and a dose of methadone inside her, Evie hobbled by his side across the hospital car park.

Drummond got her into his car and then sat back frowning. What was he supposed to do with her? He couldn't just bundle her off on a train this time. 'Maybe now you'll consider going home,' he said.

The look of horror in her eyes told him that wouldn't be happening. 'Well what then? Is there a friend you could stay with?' She shook her head.

He sighed. 'What about those relations in Edinburgh? Couldn't they take you in?'

The look she gave him told Drummond there had been no relations in Edinburgh. He rolled his eyes. No need to wonder how she'd been supporting herself there. She'd been back soliciting on the streets. It left him with no option.

'Right,' he said wearily. 'You can stay at my place for a few days until you get yourself sorted, but there will be rules.'

Evie's face broke into a crooked grin and he was

reminded again of his young niece, Sarah. But she'd grown up in a loving family. He suspected it had been very different for Evie.

Trusting this young woman with the free range of his flat was madness, but what choice did he have? He felt responsible for her.

Evie glanced about her as they walked in, her surprised expression clearly indicating that a man on his own would live in such order. Drummond followed her gaze around the small sitting room, taking in the two grey sofas he'd bought second hand, the coffee table, bookcase and the TV in the alcove. It was minimal and orderly, just the way he liked it.

'You're very tidy,' she said.

'That's because I don't choose to live in a pig sty.'

'I won't mess it up, I promise,' she said, looking up at him.

'You'd better not or you'll be out on your ear just as soon as I get back.'

She frowned. 'You're going out?'

'I have to work.' He nodded to the kitchen. 'There's food in the fridge and the TV controller is just there.'

She touched his arm as he turned for the door. 'I really appreciate this Mr Drummond. I won't let you down. I promise.'

He nodded. 'I might be late back. You can sleep in the bed. I'll have the sofa.'

'Thank you,' she said. He thought he caught the glint of a tear in her dark eyes as she looked away.

On the landing outside his flat he stood shaking his head, not quite sure what he'd been thinking to allow a young hooker with a drug habit to stay with him. He could imagine what DCI Joey Buchan would say about it if she found out. But she wouldn't find out, nobody would. This was one part of his private life he definitely needed to keep quiet.

He went back to the nick and sat at his desk, trying to focus on the various lines of enquiry he'd assigned to his team of detectives. There was one way he could distract himself from worrying about Evie Walker. He took the smart business card from his pocket and flicked it over, staring at the mobile number Olivia had written on the back. He felt the stir of excitement as she answered.


Olivia Ryder's flat was as stylish as he'd imagined. The silver-framed modern art on the white walls wasn't to his taste, but here the paintings somehow looked right. Two low-slung armchairs flanked an impressively large fireplace. Apart from a black leather sofa, coffee table and drinks trolley there wasn't much more furniture in the room.

'Do you like what you see, Jack?'

He wasn't sure if she was referring to how fabulous she looked in the slinky black dress or the minimalist style her flat had been furnished in. It was 'yes' to the first, 'no' to the second. She looked good enough to eat in that figure-hugging dress. It wasn't what he'd been expecting given they had only been meeting for a drink, but maybe Olivia had always had other plans for them that evening. He was in her flat, so he was hopeful.

From where he sat on the sofa he could see into the gleaming white kitchen. There not a single item of clutter on the granite worktops. He thought of his own basic kitchen and the coffee pot, mug stand, toaster, kettle, jars of spices and all the other essential things that were practically to hand. This was a different world.

'You like my apartment?' Olivia asked, returning with a bottle of wine and two stemmed glasses.

He nodded. 'Very smart.' He wasn't sure what he was supposed to say. He thought there'd be more old paintings, some antiques maybe, or did she get enough of these things at work?

She put down the tray and invited him to pour. They sat, sipping their wine and eyeing each other. 'Tell me about being a policeman,' she said.

The remark took him by surprise. He'd joined the force because a savvy old copper had saved him from a life of crime, but he wasn't about to tell her that, so he batted it back with his own question. 'Why did you become an auctioneer?'

'Because I'm good at it,' she said. 'I was brought up in an antique shop in Edinburgh and went to all the auctions with my father. By the time I went to university I knew as much about the business as he did.'

'University as well? I'm impressed,' Drummond said. 'What did you study?'

She gave him a slow smile. 'I studied law,' she said, beck-oning him to join her across the room.


Drummond had a skip in his step as he breezed into the incident room next morning. Only Gail Swann raised an eyebrow that he was still wearing yesterday's shirt. He didn't care. He was seeing Olivia again that weekend...and he couldn't wait.

He wondered how Evie had got on alone in his flat all night. She'd looked worried when he'd dashed back to tell her he'd either be home late or not at all. He hoped she wouldn't have gone out looking for drugs. He should have checked up on her before coming to work but DCI Buchan was already on his case and there hadn't been time.

She was looking particularly stormy when the team got together for the morning briefing. 'Three bloody murders and we're no further forward,' she said icily. 'This strangler bastard is bloody playing with us.'

She swung her attention to Drummond. 'What've we got on this last one, DI Drummond?'

He stepped forward so he could address the room. 'DC Swann and I interviewed her husband and according to him she's not a full-time hooker. She has a job in a local cafe.'

Joey Buchan gave a heavy sigh. 'I'm guessing it wasn't her waitressing skills that attracted our killer. If she had this cosy respectable life, why the hell did she turn to prostitution?'

Drummond pulled a face. 'The money. According to her husband, Derek, our victim liked nice things and the prostitution paid for them.' He turned to DC Dale McQueen, who had been detailed to pay Benny Saul another visit. 'What did Saul have to say about her?'

Dale flicked through his notebook. 'According to him, Lena Murray was a freelancer. He says she was definitely not one of his girls.'

'So, he admits he does have girls?' Gail Swann said.

Dale nodded. 'But I wouldn't celebrate too soon. Knowing what a worm the man is, he'll have another story today.'

'We need to speak to Derek Murray again. What kind of man allows his wife to go out soliciting? We didn't push him too much yesterday. He looked genuinely devastated when we told him we'd found his wife's body.'

He flicked his attention back to the whiteboard and the pictures of the murdered women. 'Do we need to look at the dates again?' Gail came forward and stood by the wall. 'The first victim was murdered on the Saturday before Christmas, the next on February 14th.'

'Valentine's Day,' Dale said.

Gail nodded. 'And now this current victim, Lena Murray on April 1st.'

DCI Buchan shook her head and slid her bum from the table she'd perched on. 'April Fool!' she hissed. 'He is bloody playing with us.'

Drummond blew out his cheeks. 'Maybe the dates have some other significance, something only he knows.'

Joey Buchan blinked at him. 'Great work, Sherlock. But how does that bloody help us?'

She was right. He felt the dates were significant, but he had no idea why. He was remembering what Olivia had told him about seeing that car cruising through the park when she spotted the body. Was that the killer? They suspected their killer hung around to make sure his victim was discovered before leaving the scene. His mind went back to their first victim at The Barras. Had the killer been there watching when the stallholder Alec Millburn found Maggie Burns' body? Had he been hanging around the waste ground when dog walker, Liam Stiller, found Bonnie Brennan?

Where CCTV was available, they had concentrated on scanning it over the early hours of the morning when the strangler was likely to have dumped the body. They hadn't been particularly interested beyond that, certainly not when the body had been discovered. They had to go back to those tapes.

# TEN

NUMBER 87, Hilton Street was bathed in a pool of yellow light from the street lamp. Drummond shifted his position and squinted along the row of terraced houses. His face had settled into a permanent frown. This surveillance was a complete time waster. He should be out on the streets looking for the Glasgow Strangler. At this very moment another poor woman could be having the life choked out of her while he sat here waiting for a non-existent burglar to put in an appearance.

Beside him, Gail Swann stifled a yawn, trying not to look terminally bored. 'I suppose we're sure about this intelligence, boss?'

He knew she really wanted to ask how much longer he was planning to drag out this pointless stakeout. Slimy Sammy Turk had given him duff info and to make matters worse Drummond would now have to face the music back at the nick. He could see the DCI's sneering face. She was going to love this. Nothing gave Joey Buchan more pleasure than tearing strips off him when he'd messed up. And he had definitely messed up...again. He was imagining aiming his fist at Sammy Turk's stupid pock-marked chin.

The man was the most unreliable of Drummond's informants and yet he still used him.

It had been a couple of years since Turk first sidled up to Drummond in Mungo's Bar, off Trongate, but he remembered it like it had been yesterday. Turk had offered him a Gucci ladies' gold watch. He'd sneaked it out of his pocket, surreptitiously revealing it to Drummond. 'You look like a bloke who knows a good thing when he sees it,' he'd said. 'Nine hundred quid's worth of watch. It's yours for a monkey.' The man was moving restlessly from foot to foot. Drummond had taken an involuntary step back trying to avoid the drift of BO that was wafting in his direction.

Drummond remembered he'd chosen this pub because it was off the beaten track and he'd be unlikely to meet any of his police colleagues there. But he couldn't hide the fact that he was a cop and drinkers who frequented these backstreet Glasgow pubs could smell the polis from a mile away. This idiot must be desperate, either that or he was blind. Drummond was sensing a collar here if he played along. He glanced at the watch and shrugged. 'Too glittery for me, mate.'

'It's no fur you, but just think how much the missus would love tae have this strapped tae her wrist.' He tilted the watch and it glinted in the stark light of the pub. He nudged Drummond's arm. 'You'd be on wan hell of a promise if you gave her this,' he said, winking. Drummond had fought the urge to laugh out loud at the man's audacity. He nodded to the door. 'Not here. Too many eyes. Let's step outside.'

A few heads came up as they left pub, but Drummond

ignored them. He knew what he was about to do. The street was deserted. He gave the man a cold smile. 'You didn't expect me to have 500 notes in my pocket, did you?' The man had given him a cocky look. 'I'm prepared to negotiate,' he'd said.

'I'm not.' Drummond's grin widened as he took out his ID. 'And you're nicked, mate,' he'd said, pinning the man to the wall as he'd seized the watch. 'What's your name?'

'Turk...Sammy Turk and this isnae ma gear. Have a heart, boss, I'm only doing somebody a favour selling it for them.'

'Who?' Drummond's voice had been sharp.

'What's in it fur me if ah tell you?'

'You don't have a choice, sunshine. You've already admitted trying to sell stolen goods.'

'Ah didnae say it was stolen.'

'But it was, wasn't it? No point in lying. You know we can trace exactly where this came from. I'm giving you the chance to come clean. Who gave you the watch?'

'He'll come efter me if he knows Ah snitched on him. Ah need protection.'

Drummond pursed his lips and tilted his head at the man. 'OK, here's what we'll do. You give me this name and I don't arrest you for fencing.'

Sammy Turk looked unsure. 'He'll know it wis me that shopped him.'

Drummond shrugged. 'No reason why he should. We'll be discreet.' The man still didn't look convinced. 'Of course, if you really want an assurance that you won't be dropped in it with your friend we could come to a further arrangement.'

Turk's wary eyes narrowed. 'And whit wid that be?'

'You could join my little band of helpers.'

'You want me to be your snitch?'

Drummond raised an eyebrow. 'Your choice, but it could be in your interest. Every time you give me a good tip-off you get a backhander.'

The man's brow had creased. He still wasn't sure. Drummond waited. They'd both looked up at the click of high heels as a woman walked towards them. 'OK, OK, Ah'll dae it. Let's just get away fae here.' They moved along the pavement, keeping an eye on the woman as she'd disappeared into the pub.

'You were saying?' Drummond was losing his patience.

'It's Jesse Dunn.' The man's voice was rasping. 'He's got a lock-up full of this stuff.'

Drummond headed the team that raided the lock-up and arrested Dunn. He earned himself a stack of brownie points that night.

And so, Drummond's dubious relationship with Sammy Turk had begun. In the beginning, his information had been good, but it very much depended on how desperately he needed a fix.

He'd approached Drummond this time with information that might, if true, lead to the arrest of the bastard who had been preying on vulnerable elderly people. But things weren't looking hopeful.

Beside him Gail sighed and moved her feet, kicking aside the discarded plastic coffee cartons on the floor before settling back into the cramped space of the passenger seat. Drummond avoided her stare. His own patience was at breaking point too. 'We'll give it another ten minutes,' he said. Adding silently, 'Then I'm off to find the little bastard, Turk, and string him up by his balls.'

They'd sat in silence for another few minutes when Drummond's head suddenly jerked up. He sprang forward, peering into the dark at the far end of the street. There it was again! 'Did you see that?'

'What?' Gail said.

'Out there!' Drummond's chest tightened, his eyes darting about, searching for another movement in the darkness. 'Just there!' He pointed. He could feel the adrenaline pumping. 'Three lamp posts along, look!'

Gail squinted into the distance. 'Got it,' she said as they both instinctively slid down out of sight. Someone was pushing a bicycle along the pavement. And they were coming in their direction.

'Sit tight,' Drummond hissed as the figure got closer. Both of them held their breath, watching the biker as he stopped in front of number 87. He propped his bike against the low wall and looked around him. Apparently satisfied there was no one in sight, he took a bag from the cycle's pannier, dipped into it and pulled out a balaclava and a pair of gloves.

'Wait!' Drummond put a warning hand on Gail's arm as she reached for the door handle. 'Let him get inside.' They watched, fascinated as the man tugged on the balaclava and took a tool from his pocket. He approached the front door and began to poke at the lock. The door opened. The man paused, took another look around and entered the house.

'Now we go,' Drummond said. 'And if there's any justice in the world we'll catch this wee bugger in the act.'

And they did.

Colin Urquhart was now locked up in a police cell having admitted five counts of burglary that night and asked for a further thirty-five offences to be taken into consideration.

Drummond found himself in the novel situation of being flavour of the month at the station. But there was no time for complacency. The strangler was still out there and until he was caught no woman in the city was safe.

# ELEVEN

It was almost light when Drummond let him himself into his flat. His feeling of satisfaction that events had gone so well for them that night was beginning to be tinged with growing disgust for the way Colin Urquhart had persuaded vulnerable old people to trust him while his only intention had been to rob them.

He knew the girl had gone even before he entered the flat. Evie never had a lot to say for herself at the best of times, but it was never this silent. Glancing into his small sitting room it was clear she hadn't taken time to tidy up before she left. But it was the state of his bedroom that pissed him off most. It looked as though it had been ransacked. Drawers had been turned out and their contents left in heaps on the floor. The jackets and shirts that had been on hangers in his wardrobe were strewn about the bed. It looked like Evie had gone through every pocket she could find. He cursed. The emergency stash of £500 that he'd kept zipped into the inside pocket of his leather jacket had gone. His own fault for leaving any money at all about the place, but still he swore. So much for trying to help her. He shouldn't have fallen for her hard-luck story when he found her waiting for him after work that night. Her disrespect for his home and his property was like a physical slap in the face.

He'd done his best to look out for her and now this. When would he learn that you can't help people who don't want to be helped? Well, damn her. She was on her own now. He wasn't going out to search the Glasgow streets for her.

Drummond thought she would have used his money to score by now anyway and had probably been robbed of the rest of his money. He tried not to think about the state she would almost certain have got herself into. He poured himself a stiff whisky and threw it back before crashing out on the sofa.

It was 6 a.m. when the buzz of his mobile woke him. He squinted at the name of the caller as he reached for it. DCI Joey Buchan. Shit! This wouldn't be a social call, not unless she'd been hitting the gin bottle. She had a habit of turning up at his door when she was pissed and feeling sorry for herself. But his boss sounded stone-cold sober. 'We've got a body, Jack,' she said. 'Gail Swann's already at the scene. She says it looks like another hooker. You'd better get yourself down there.'


So much of Glasgow had changed over the years, most of it for the better. The crumbling, insanitary tenements, where three families shared a single toilet on the stair head, had gradually been replaced with new flats, green spaces and flower displays. But here and there the old city could still be found if you knew where to look. The cobbled lane at the bottom of Buchanan Street was one of those places. Drummond had a bad feeling as he approached it. The girl's body was sprawled amongst the overspill of rubbish from a pub bin, her sad slim frame discarded like just another pile of trash. Drummond could feel the bile rising in his throat. Before he even looked at the victim, he knew who she was. The last time he'd seen her she was smiling up at him from the sofa in his front room. It was Evie.

'What d'you think, boss? There's no scarf. Maybe our man ran out of stock,' Gail Swann said.

The look Drummond gave left her in no doubt he didn't appreciate the comment. 'We have no evidence that she was a hooker,' he said sharply, but he knew that's exactly what Evie had been.

It had been weeks since they'd pulled Lena Murray out of the River Kelvin. Like Maggie Burns and Bonnie Brennan, before her she had been strangled with a scarf. There were no obvious signs that Evie had been strangled. Maybe this was a tragic accident after all, but Drummond didn't think so.

Gail had gone back to watching Nell Forrester working with the body. The pathologist shook her head and stretched her back, turning to Drummond. 'These street girls get younger all the time. This one looks like she should still be in school.'

Drummond swallowed back the lump in his throat. He was aware of her curious glances. No doubt she was wondering why they weren't sharing their usual flirty banter, but he was in no mood for wisecracks. He looked away. This was his fault. If he hadn't left that money for Evie to find she would still be safe back at his flat. He stepped back, trying not to throw up in front of Nell and his DC.

As he moved away, something at the back of the lane caught his eye. He pointed. 'What's that? Look! Over there!'

A scene of crime officer in his white forensic coveralls moved carefully to the object Drummond was indicating and raised his camera. He snapped a number of pictures in situ before bending to pick it up. Drummond's insides made another alarming lurch as he recognized the cheap red simulated leather shoulder bag. It was Evie's. He'd seen it often enough lying around his flat. He said nothing as the forensic officer opened it and took out the roll of notes. His heart skipped a beat. Seeing his cash made Evie's killing all the more sinister. Why had the killer not taken the money? If his first thought had been right and Benny Saul was involved, then he would definitely have taken the money. Even so, it didn't let him off the hook.

Drummond glanced back to the body. He didn't know why he had singled out Evie Walker to take under his wing, except that she hadn't been much older than Sarah, his brother, Daniel's sixteen-year-old daughter, and he felt responsible for her.

Evie wasn't a real hooker. She was educated enough not to be plying her trade in a seedy city backstreet. He'd also credited her with enough sense not to have got involved with Saul – and yet she had. She'd snatched her phone away one day when it rang, but Drummond had already seen the caller's name. It was Benny Saul. Drummond was furious with her. She'd let him down. The only reason he'd allowed her to stay was her assurance she was living on benefits, and not turning tricks.

Saul specialized in getting his girls hooked on drugs. Their dependence was what kept them in line. They needed him and he exploited that. Evie had been doing well in her fight against smack. Maybe not great because she had the odd lapses, but Drummond had been hopeful the real Evie would win through. No chance of that now.

Nell Forrester was gathering her things together and standing up. Her eyes were still on the body.

'Anything for us yet, Nell?' He'd been expecting her usual cocky answer, telling him to be patient until the PM, but she looked up at him.

'Don't quote me, but there are marks around her face and neck. I don't think she was strangled, Jack. I think she was suffocated to death.'

Drummond stared at her. 'So not our serial killer?'

'It's far too early to say. This one looks different.' She glanced back to Evie's body. 'She also has needle marks on her arms.'

'You mean it could have been an overdose?'

'Don't push me, Jack. I've already given you too much information. You know as well as I do that nothing is definite before the post-mortem is completed.'

'But you think she was murdered?'

Nell gave him another look and sighed. 'We'll see.'

Drummond's eye was on the CCTV camera he'd spotted at the back of the pub. 'Find out who the key holder is for this place, Gail, and get him out of bed. I want to see those CCTV tapes.'

Gail moved away, her mobile phone at her ear.

Drummond's gaze went back to Nell, who was taking one last look at the body. His face was a grim mask. Seeing a scene like this was never easy, but it was even worse to see a young woman's life thrown away, especially one he'd been trying to help.

He was thinking back to the last time he'd seen her. She'd been curled up on his sofa watching some rubbish quiz show when he'd walked in. He'd asked if she had eaten. 'I'm fine,' she'd said, hugging a cushion, her eyes still fixed to the TV screen.

'That's not what I asked.' Drummond had looked down at her, frowning. 'When was the last time you had a decent meal?'

'I've had cornflakes. I'm not hungry.'

He'd taken the fish suppers he'd bought into the kitchen and put them on plates and then carried one through to her on a tray. 'Don't expect this kind of service all the time.' He'd grinned down at her.

She had made an effort to sit up, but the look she gave the fish and chips was disinterested. 'I said I wasn't hungry.'

Drummond had collected his own tray and sat on one of the two armchairs, tucking into his chips. 'Starving yourself is not negotiable. If you want to stay here, you eat. It's a rule of the house,' he'd said through a mouthful of food.

Out of the corner of his eye he'd seen her pick up a chip and put it into her mouth. It was a reluctant gesture, but at least she'd been eating, and he'd wondered if this was progress.

Letting her stay at the flat was meant to be a strictly temporary arrangement but he'd seen no signs that Evie was planning to move on. He'd been planning to give her one more day and then she would have had to find somewhere else. She hadn't been his responsibility.

But he'd known she was heading for disaster. Why hadn't he taken her to a professional, someone who could have helped her? Why had he been so arrogant to assume that she only needed a roof over her head and a kind word now and again? He was just as much responsible for Evie's death as the bastard who gave her the drugs. But who had that been? The first name that flashed into his head was Benny Saul. He needed to speak to his informer.

Slimy Sammy Turk had got himself a job as glass washer and general dogsbody in exchange for a meal and a bed in a dingy back room in a pub off Gallowgate. Hostelries in this area opened early and a couple of drinkers were already at the bar when Drummond walked in. He ordered a whisky and looked around him. There was no sign of Sammy – and then he spotted him through the back of the bar. The look of shock when he spotted Drummond left him in no doubt that he shouldn't openly approach him. The man jerked his head towards the back of the pub. Drummond finished his whisky and went out. Sammy was already in the lane behind the pub. He looked twitchy.

'If anybody sees us, I'm a dead man, you do know that, Drummond?'

'I needed a word.'

'If you're here to thank me for tipping you off about the pensioner robber, you shouldn't have bothered. The cash will do.'

'It's not about that,' Drummond said. 'I need information about something else.'

Slimy Sammy was throwing uneasy glances around him. 'Well, say it fast and get yourself the hell out of here.'

'What do you know about a young hooker called Evie?'

'Nothing. Who's she?'

'Think again, Sammy. She's about seventeen, had long dark hair until she chopped it all off and dyed it blonde. She might have been in trouble with Benny Saul.'

Sammy was hopping nervously from foot to foot. 'Jesus, Drummond. You don't mess about.'

'What is it?' Drummond hissed. 'What do you know?'

'I heard there was a wee lassie trying to do her own thing.'

Drummond moved his face closer. 'Yes?'

'She was what you might call an entrepreneur, you know, working on the streets but not handing all her earnings on to Saul. They don't like that.' He glanced at Drummond. 'What's happened to her?'

'She's dead.'

'The strangler strikes again, eh?'

'We don't know that, not yet.' Drummond had a strange feeling. Evie's body hadn't looked right. She hadn't looked like the strangler's other victims. There was no scarf, and no taunting cat and mouse card. And her body hadn't been moved.

Sammy blew out his cheeks and looked back to the pub door, still anxious to make sure no one was showing an interest in them. 'I don't know any more than that. I can't help you, Drummond.'

Drummond pushed a £20 note into the man's hand. 'Find out what you can. There'll be something more in it if you dig anything up.'

The man stuffed the note into his trouser pocket. 'Clear off now. If I'm seen talking to the polis I'll be for the chop.'

Drummond pulled a face, watching him as he scurried back into the pub. His phone buzzed and he snatched at it.

'Bad news, sir,' Gail Swann said. 'The pub's CCTV is broken.'

Drummond's initial feeling of despair was being replaced with a growing rage. He wanted to throw Benny Saul against a brick wall give him a good kicking. But for the moment he would settle for just finding the man. He knew Saul was only a link in the chain of evil, the go-between before you got to Big Mal McKirdy - and it was him, the main man, not the monkey, that Drummond was after. However, he would have to start somewhere, and the monkey would do.

# TWELVE

THE CALL CAME in as Drummond and Gail were heading back to the station. It was DCI Joey Buchan. 'We've got another one, Jack,' she said. 'At a church in South Portland Street. The strangler has had a busy night.'

Drummond swung the car round and they sped off in the direction of the Gorbals. 'All we need now is a drive-by shooting,' Gail said.

'That's exactly what we don't need,' Drummond hissed. His head was not in a good place for investigating another strangler killing. His mind was still hovering over Joey's comments. She had clearly decided Evie was also one of the killer's victims. Drummond thought otherwise.

A woman was in the back of the police patrol car that was parked outside the church. She stared at them as they passed.

'She's the church cleaner. It was her who found the body,' the young uniformed officer who met them said.

'We'll have a word with her in a minute,' Drummond said. 'Where's the body?'

'It's round the back. Forensics are on their way.' The PC

pulled a face. 'The cleaner was emptying the rubbish and says she almost tripped over it.'

'Poor woman,' Gail said, glancing back to the patrol car.

Even though it was now well past 8 a.m., the sky was heavy with rain clouds and daylight was still in short supply. A single lamp bolted to the building, presumably to illuminate the bins' area, cast a pool of depressing yellow light over the scene. The woman was on her side, her long ash blonde hair spread across the damp concrete path, a crimson-coloured scarf twisted around her neck. They kept their distance from the body, mindful of the need to preserve any evidence. Drummond averted his glance from the horror of the woman's staring eyes.

'Has the body been touched?' he asked.

The uniformed officer shook his head. 'Not by us. I don't know about the witness back there; she says not but she's in such a state I don't think she knows what she did.'

They all looked up as two vehicles arrived in convoy. Forensic officers jumped out of the first and Nell Forrester's cocky sidekick, Martin Sinclair, got out of the second car. 'Good morning, Inspector.' He nodded to Gail. 'Busy morning, eh, folks?'

'So it would seem,' Drummond said flatly, watching as the pathologist crouched beside the body. He could see the corner of a calling card in the top pocket of the victim's red jacket.

Sinclair glanced back to Drummond before carefully sliding it out. He held it up between gloved fingers so they could see the familiar silhouette images of the cat and mouse. 'We seem to be amassing quite a little collection of these,' he said, dropping it into an evidence bag.

The killer was getting his message home loud and clear. He was playing with them. But five killings and only four cat and mouse cards. There was a sick feeling in the pit of Drummond's stomach as he turned to his DC. 'Stay here, Gail. I'm going to have a word with our witness.'

Gail raised an eyebrow. Drummond knew she was surprised that he wasn't delegating the task to her, but he needed to be personally involved in every aspect of this investigation now. Psychopaths like this killer just kept pushing the envelope, taking more brazen risks with each victim, but that's how they got caught. The cat and mouse cards wound him up, but their man was getting too cocky. Eventually he would run out of luck.

The woman in the police car was still visibly shocked as Drummond got into the front seat and swiveled round to face her.

'I suppose she *is* dead?' she said flatly.

'The pathologist is with her now,' Drummond said.

The woman was shaking her head. 'Poor Carol. She didn't deserve that. What will her two wee bairns do now?'

Drummond blinked. 'You know her?'

'Aye, I do – and her mother. They live in the next block tae us.'

Drummond pulled out a notebook and pen. 'What's her name?'

'Carol Nicholson. She's a barmaid at the Drouthy Duck. My Sam and I go there every Wednesday for the quiz night. We like a good pub quiz.'

'You said you also know her mother?'

'Aye, that's right. Moira. Carol and the bairns live with her.'

'Is there a Mr Nicholson?'

'No, Moira's been a widow for years.' She looked at him and frowned. 'Oh, I see what you mean. You're asking if Carol has a husband. She doesn't. I don't know anything about her men, except that the bairns had different fathers.' She shrugged. 'But they are long gone. Carol never talks about them.' She met Drummond's eyes. 'She was a lovely lassie. Who would do such a terrible thing to her?'

'I wish I knew, Mrs...?' He raised an eyebrow, inviting her to give her name.

'Agnes Somerville,' she said. 'Everybody calls me Aggie.'

'How long have you worked at the church, Aggie?'

She screwed up her face, thinking. 'About ten years. It's only a couple of hours a week, but the money comes in handy when you've only got a pension. And it's right on my doorstep. I live at the bottom of the road – Norfolk Court. Carol and Moira are in Portland Court, number 10.' She filled up and produced a crumpled tissue from her pocket. 'Poor Moira's going to take this bad. How is she going to tell the bairns that their mammy is dead...murdered?'

'That's where we'll need your help, Aggie,' Drummond said. 'We'll be going to see Carol's mother, but in case we don't manage to see her immediately can we depend on your discretion?'

'You mean I shouldn't talk about this?'

Drummond nodded. 'Things will be bad enough for that family. We don't want them – especially the kiddies – hearing about what's happened through local gossip, or from Facebook or Twitter.'

Aggie Somerville looked shocked. 'I won't be doing any gossiping about poor Carol, if that's what you're saying.'

Drummond smiled. 'Of course, you won't,' he said.


They took the lift to the tenth floor and stood outside Carol Nicholson's door. Gail rang the bell, hesitating slightly as she lifted her hand. Telling a family that their loved one was dead would never be easy. And yet they could never close their minds to the possibility of that family having been involved in the victim's demise.

Moira Nicholson was a short, plump, friendly looking woman whose initial expression of apprehension turned to disbelief as she realized what she was about to hear.

'It's Carol, isn't it? What's happened?' She stared at them with wide fearful brown eyes.

'Moira Nicholson?' Gail asked quietly.

The woman nodded, her hand covering her mouth.

'Can we come in?'

Moira Nicholson moved aside as the two detectives stepped inside the flat and into the front room. Even on a dismal morning like this the place felt bright and cheerful. Drummond's eyes went to the picture on the mantelpiece. It looked like a professional studio photograph of Carol Nicholson and her two young children.

Moira followed the direction of his gaze and smiled fondly at the picture. 'Rosie and Joe, they're five and six now.'

The officers exchanged a look. 'Would you like to sit down, Mrs Nicholson?' Drummond said.

'Something's happened, hasn't it? Just tell me!'

Drummond cleared his throat. 'We found a body this morning...'

Moira Nicholson began to sway. Gail rushed forward and they both grabbed her as she collapsed. They guided her to the sofa and Gail pulled a box tissues off the coffee table and put them beside her. They waited for her to regain her composure.

'It's Carol, isn't it? I knew something terrible had happened when her bed hadn't been slept in. Was it a road accident? I hated her staying out late.'

Drummond paused for a beat. 'It wasn't a road accident,' he said quietly. 'We're treating this as a suspicious death.'

'What?' The woman was on her feet, her look of disbelief going from one to the other. 'What d'you mean, suspicious?'

'We can't say more at the moment. We'll know better once the post-mortem's been done.'

'Post-mortem?' Moira Nicholson's head was in her hands and she was shaking. 'I can't take this in.' She sank slowly back onto the sofa.

Drummond cleared his throat. 'You said Carol stayed out late?' His voice was gentle. 'Can you tell us about that?'

Moira turned distressed glistening eyes on him. 'She had to work late Friday and Saturday nights when the pub was busier. She never got home before the early hours.'

The witness had told him their victim was a barmaid at a local pub, but he needed her to verify this.

'Where did she work, Moira?'

'At the Drouthy Duck. All the customers know her. Carol is very popular...and the money's good.'

'When you say she had to work late. How late did you mean?' Gail asked.

Moira shrugged. 'I don't know. It was always the early hours. I never sat up waiting for her.' Tears were rolling down her cheeks now. 'I get the bairns their breakfast at the weekends so Carol can have a long lie.'

'Where are the children now?' Gail asked.

'They're at the pictures. One of the neighbours takes them to a children's matinee with her own bairns on a Saturday morning.'

'I know this is a really difficult thing to ask but the sooner we can get an ID–'

She didn't let him finish the sentence. 'You haven't identified her?' she said sharply. 'You mean it might not be her?'

Drummond saw the hope leap into her eyes and put up a hand. 'I mean an official ID,' he said quickly. 'We're pretty certain the body we found is Carol.' He saw her shoulders slump. 'I'm so sorry,' he said quietly.

'What do I have to do? I don't know where to go.'

'Don't worry about that,' Drummond said as he and Gail got to their feet. 'We'll collect you and make sure you get home afterwards. It will only take a few minutes.'

Moira Nicholson shuddered. Identifying her dead daughter might take only a few minutes but Drummond knew the images she would see this day would haunt her for the rest of her life.

The smell of disinfectant hit them as they walked into the Drouthy Duck. The floor was glistening wet as a dumpy woman in a floral overall sloshed a mop over it.

'We're shut,' the barman called across to them as they approached. 'Come back in half an hour.'

'We need to speak to the manager,' Drummond said, showing his warrant card.

'That would be me. It's my pub,' he said, slinging the towel he'd been wiping the bar with over his shoulder. 'What can I do for you good people?'

'We didn't catch your name,' Drummond said.

'It's the same as the one over the door, Graham Bell.'

Gail scribbled in her notebook.

'We're enquiring about a member of your staff, Carol Nicholson,' he said.

'Carol? What about her?'

'When was the last time you saw her?'

The barman's eyes narrowed. 'She's not in any trouble, is she?'

Drummond frowned. 'Why would you think that?'

'Well you two are here,' Graham Bell said. 'Something's up. What's going on?'

The dumpy woman, having clearly decided this conversation was infinitely more interesting than floor washing had abandoned her task and was now leaning on the handle of her mop following their every word.

Bell saw Drummond glance at her, and he nodded to the woman. 'Thanks, Gracie. You can get off now.' The woman gave him a protesting look. 'I haven't finished it yet.'

'It's fine. Just go.'

The cleaner gave a disgruntled mumble as she clattered off through a side door and Drummond returned to his questions. 'How long has Carol worked for you?'

'I don't know...a year, maybe more.'

'You'll have records though?' Gail cut in.

He was looking at them with suspicion now. 'They're in the back.'

They followed him through and watched as he flicked through a hard-backed notebook. He looked up. 'Eighteen months,' he said.

Drummond held out his hand. 'Can I have a look?'

There was a moment's hesitation before the man handed it over. Drummond cast his eyes over the pages. He didn't recognize any of the names.

'What time did Carol leave last night?'

Graham Bell looked confused. 'Carol wasn't working last night. She's got some other part-time job Fridays and Saturdays. And before you ask, the answer's no, I don't know what it is. She was quite secretive about it.'

'Aren't those your busiest nights?' Gail asked.

'Tell me about it. I did try to persuade her to come in at weekends. I even offered her more money, but she was adamant. The other job paid more.'

Drummond met the barman's eyes as he handed back the staff book. He suspected he wasn't nearly as innocent as he would have them believe. It was looking more than likely that Carol was supplementing her income by doing a bit of private soliciting. She was another prostitute strangled with a scarf, another victim of their serial killer, another episode in his twisted game of cat and mouse.

Evie hadn't been strangled and there had been no cat and mouse card. Maybe her death had been a tragic accident after all, but Drummond didn't think so.

## THIRTEEN

'WE FOUND VICTIM NUMBER FOUR TODAY,' Drummond said over a deep sigh.

Pete tilted his head at him. 'I thought it was five?'

'What? No. Isn't four enough?' And then Drummond realized Pete had heard about Evie. They weren't crediting her killing to the strangler, not yet.

'I take it you're no nearer nabbing this guy?'

Drummond shook his head. 'Unless we get a break they'll be moving in the big shots to take over the investigation.'

Pete's face stretched into an expression of concern. 'It's not your fault, Jack. Stop blaming yourself.'

'Of course, it's my fault. We should have caught this bastard after he killed Maggie Burns. Instead I let it drift and now three more women have been murdered.' Drummond narrowed his eyes, staring at the barman who was filling a glass from the Bell's optic.

Pete was watching him. 'There's something else, isn't there? What are you not telling me?'

Drummond had not intended talking about Evie, but

this was Pete. He sighed. 'The other body...the one you thought was the killer's fifth victim.' He paused. 'I knew her.'

'I'm sorry, Jack. I didn't realize.' Pete's voice was full of sympathy. 'It's hard when you know a victim.' He met Drummond's eyes. 'So, she wasn't one of the strangler's?'

'We don't know, maybe not.' He glanced away, narrowing his eyes. 'It's my fault she's dead, Pete. I was supposed to be looking after her.' He swallowed. 'She was staying in my flat.'

Pete blinked. 'Jesus, were you in a relationship with this woman?'

'I wasn't screwing her if that's what you mean. She was only seventeen for God's sake. I was just helping her out... not very well obviously.'

Pete sat back, folding his arms. 'You'd better start at the beginning.'

Over the next ten minutes Drummond described how he'd found Evie soliciting and packed her off to what she'd told him was family in Edinburgh. He recounted his shock when she'd later turned up battered and bruised and appealing for help.

'She'd nowhere else to go, Pete. I had to take her in.'

'You have to tell DCI Buchan about this. Do it now! Don't wait. You haven't done anything wrong.'

'Evie's dead, Pete. How is that not my fault?'

'You've lost me now. How is that your fault?'

'If I hadn't interfered, she might still be here.'

Pete leaned forward, lowering his voice. 'OK, you should have come clean straight away, but it's not too late. Tell Joey.'

'You know I can't do that. She'll suspend me.'

'You don't know that.'

'Of course I do. Joey won't have any choice.'

'She'll do what she can to protect you.'

Drummond stared at him. 'Protect me? I don't want any protection. You haven't understood any of this, have you?'

'Enlighten me,' Pete said.

'If I get suspended, I'll be off the case. How can I find Evie's killer if I'm off the case? And what about all those women the strangler murdered?'

Pete gave a disbelieving laugh. 'You're such an arrogant little sod, Jack. You're not the only committed cop in the world. You should trust your colleagues.'

Drummond put his head in his hands. 'I don't know what to do. If I go to Buchan and tell her all this then I'm dead. She won't do anything to help me, that's for sure.'

'You've got to talk to her, Jack. Throw yourself on her mercy if you have to.'

'What if they think it was me who supplied the drugs that killed her? Can't you see how this is going to look?'

'I can see how it will look if you don't come clean now. You have to tell Joey Buchan.' He picked up the mobile phone Drummond had put on the table. 'Call her. Tell her you're coming in. Tell her it's urgent. You need to speak to her.' He offered the phone across. 'Like now, Jack!'

Drummond shook his head. 'No, I need to get this straight in my head before I do anything I might regret.'

'OK,' Pete said. 'Let's rewind. You said you put the girl on a train to Edinburgh, so how did she end up staying at your place?'

Drummond pursed his lips, the memory still emblazoned in his mind. 'She was waiting for me outside the nick one night. I hardly recognized her. She'd chopped off her long dark hair and dyed it blonde, but that wasn't it.' He swallowed. 'She'd been badly beaten. Her face was a mass of bruises. She said the man who attacked her was still looking for her. She was terrified, Pete. She asked me to help her.' He bit his lip. 'There's something else.' He paused. 'Evie was a user. What was I to do? I couldn't just walk away and leave her there.'

Pete blew out his cheeks and rolled his eyes. 'So, you took her home with you?'

Drummond hung his head and nodded. 'I let her have my bed and I took the sofa.'

'I believe you, but nobody else will.'

'I know,' Drummond said. He waited a beat. 'There's more.'

Pete waited.

'Evie had £500 in her bag when she was found.'

'I'm not sure I want to hear this,' Pete said.

'The money was mine. I kept a roll of notes hidden in my wardrobe for a rainy day.' He looked up. 'When I got home that night, the flat had been ransacked. Evie had found the money. She was gone.'

## FOURTEEN

DRUMMOND WAS DREADING GETTING BACK to his flat and yet he knew it could possibly throw up the only clues he would get about how Evie had lived her life. He had provided a roof over her head, even if he had set a timer on how long he would let her stay at his place, but they hadn't ever really talked. His fault again. The job and the kind of life he lived meant he spent hardly any time at his home and when he was there, he was usually flat out. He might have given Evie a safe shelter, however temporary, but apart from that they had hardly spoken to each other. He should have been more supportive, taken more interest in her.

How could he have been so arrogant as to believe he'd been helping the girl? He didn't know anything about her. Why hadn't he sat her down and asked a few basic questions about her family and why she had run away from them? There had been the twang of a Highland accent, but that hardly helped. The Highlands covered a wide area. Evie's family home could have been anywhere.

He let himself in and stared gloomily about him. The place still looked like it had been ransacked, which is exactly what Evie had done to the place before she left. It didn't feel like his home any more. His first instinct was to pour himself a stiff whisky, but he left the bottle untouched in the kitchen cupboard. It was about the only thing Evie hadn't chucked about. With a sigh he replaced the tins and packets she had swept from the shelves and went to straighten up the rest of his flat. In the bedroom he put his shirts and jackets back on their hangers in the wardrobe and roughly folded his jeans and underwear before stuffing them back in their drawers. He wasn't fanatical about being tidy, but he did need some semblance of order..

Drummond had given up his bed to the girl and some of her clothes were strewn about the floor. He was loath to touch them, but he couldn't leave them there. Going back to the kitchen he found a plastic carrier bag and swept the flimsy garments into it.

The phone was under the bed, hidden under a grubby white T-shirt. He sat back on his heels and stared at it. Maybe Evie hadn't been searching for money after all. Could she have been looking for her lost phone?

He pulled out the plastic evidence gloves he always kept in his jeans' pocket and snapped them on. His hand shook slightly as he picked up the cheap black phone and tapped into the contacts and began scrolling down the list. This little phone could be dynamite!

He went back up the list and his heart gave a lurch. There it was: "Mum". There was no number for her father.

Drummond took the phone into the kitchen and put it on the table, staring at it. He needed to think. Evie's mother had a right to know what had happened to her daughter, but how could he explain having the phone? He screwed up his face. He knew he had to hand it over to the techies, but not before he did a bit more checking. He wanted to know who

Evie was emailing. He tapped the mail icon and his heart lurched as "Mum" came up. There was an almost daily list of emails from Evie's mother and the first thing he learned when he opened a few at random was that Evie's name was actually Emily.

He steeled himself to read what her mother had written. He was a hardened cop, but it was difficult not to feel the poor woman's distress. In message after message she appealed to her missing daughter to come home.

"My darling Emily – where are you? You're breaking our hearts. Please! Please! Come home. We can talk, we can listen, we can do whatever you want. Just ring me.

I don't know what else to say. I don't even know if you're reading this. I cry every day just thinking about you being out there all alone. You're my little girl, Emily. I love you... we all love you! You know that.

The twins miss you. Little Archie misses you. They don't understand why you're not here with us. None of us do."

"Iona came by again yesterday. She's as worried as the rest of us. You must have received her texts and emails? Why are you not answering them? She's your best friend for pity's sake, Emily. At least if you don't feel you can speak to us, speak to her...PLEASE!!!"

"The rowan tree is still full of red berries and that little pink rose you planted at the end of the garden is starting to flower. I stand beside it staring out across the firth with the tears streaming down my face wondering where you are. You need to come home, Emily. You should be here with us."

"Angus and I prayed for you again yesterday. We prayed that you won't be punished for this terrible thing you've done. He's angry that you've deserted us. I just want to know why. Tell us why, Emily. Why? Why? Why?"

Drummond sighed and shook his head. That's what he'd like to know too. Evie had refused to say why she'd run away from home, but surely, she wouldn't have been running from her mother? This woman sounded genuinely desperate. He could almost hear the emotional fatigue in her words. He read on.

"I was looking at fiddles in that music shop in Church Street today. They're so expensive. Angus wants the twins to learn to play. He wanted to let them have a go on your fiddle, Emily, but I said no. It wouldn't be right. It's your fiddle and it's up to you who does or doesn't touch it. Angus wasn't pleased. He doesn't see the sense of it lying in your room if Logan and Daniel could be encouraged to show an interest in playing it, but I said that won't be happening without your permission."

Drummond was trying to scan through the messages with a more professional eye now. He could see there were many possible clues to where Emily's mother lived.

A music shop in Church Street, a view of the firth from the garden. It was something, but how many Church Streets were there in the Highlands? Drummond's brow wrinkled. But maybe not so many music shops with an address in Church Street?

It took only a few minutes on Google to track down Ghillie's Music, Church Street, Inverness. He stared at the name. Could this be the shop Emily's fiddle had come from? Inverness? He thought about it. Her accent would probably fit. The shop might have a list of customers who had purchased musical instruments from them.

On the other hand, he could simply reply to one of the woman's emails using Emily's phone. But that would be too cruel. If this really was Evie/Emily's mother, then she was about to suffer enough grief without him adding to it.

It crossed his mind that the family might be known to social services. But what could they do when he couldn't give them a name? And then it hit him. Of course, why hadn't he thought of that immediately? Emily's parents must have reported her missing. It took only seconds to get through to Inverness CID. The officer who picked up the phone sounded terminally bored.

'Missing persons? You've got the wrong department,' the man said.

'No, hang on. Give me a minute.' Drummond identified himself and explained the situation. 'I just wondered if anything about this girl rang a bell with you.'

The officer sounded like he was stirring himself. 'Emily you say?'

'That's right. There's not much to go on. I know she, or a member of her family, purchased a fiddle from a music shop in Church Street. Does that help track anything down?'

'It might do. Leave it with me and I'll make a few calls.

What was your name again?'

Drummond repeated his details.

'OK, Inspector, I'll ask around about your girl.'

'You didn't give me your name,' Drummond said.

'It's Rougvie,' the officer said. 'DS Nick Rougvie.'

'Can I ask one more favour, Nick? I'm going out on a bit of a limb here with this line of enquiry and I'm not exactly flavour of the month at my nick. Can this be between ourselves for the time being?'

DS Rougvie laughed. 'I've been there myself. Don't worry. I'll keep you out of it.'

'Thanks, Nick. I owe you one.'

Drummond clicked off the call and glanced back to Evie's – he still hadn't got used to calling her Emily – phone. He had no excuse for hanging on to it. But if he handed it in, he would be in all sorts of trouble, not that he was worried about that. He was always in trouble. This indiscretion though might result in him getting suspended. He mulled over the possibility that he could convince DCI Buchan that he had found the thing. His story would have to be good. If she found out the dead girl had been staying in his flat and that he had kept quiet about finding her phone in his bedroom, there would be no half measures. Joey Buchan would see to it that he was marched straight out of the Force. Police Scotland and Detective Inspector Jack Drummond would no longer be together.

He hadn't touched the phone without gloves, so his fingerprints wouldn't be on it. He was toying with the idea of dropping it in the lane where Evie/Emily's body had been discovered. There was no CCTV to record it. Or better still, he could let Gail find it. The crime scene investigators wouldn't be happy at any suggestion they had missed a vital piece of evidence. They would have to deal with it.

## FIFTEEN

Disposing of Evie's phone for Gail to 'find' had been easier than Drummond had thought. He'd deliberately suggested they should revisit the scene. If he was lucky, the CCTV camera would still be out of action. Not that it mattered because as part of the murder investigating team, they had every right to be there. He hung back as Gail walked up the alley, then he dropped the phone in a rubbish-strewn corner. She hadn't suspected a thing when he'd led her there and saw her pick up the thing. Drummond had hated the deception and he hated himself for using a colleague like this, but if he had to distance himself from the phone it was best if Gail should find it.

'We need to get this fast-tracked,' he said when they got back to the station, holding out the phone he'd put in an evidence bag. 'If this belongs to the dead girl, I don't want to waste any more time finding what's on it.'

'Saul gives all his girls cheap mobile phones,' Gail said. 'He probably got a job lot somewhere.'

Drummond turned away, his brow furrowing. The phone he found in the flat wasn't Saul's. It was Evie's own phone, which was why her mother had her number and could send all those emails. But Gail was right, there must be another phone somewhere. If they had it maybe it would help to identify and protect the killer's future victims? Drummond ran a hand over his hair. This was all spiraling out of control. They needed to catch this man.

It was the next morning before he received the transcripts from Evie's phone. He scanned the pages. There was far more information here than he'd been able to get from it himself. 'I'll check up on this,' he said, continuing to flick through the sheets. He couldn't risk Gail making the connection about the music shop in Church Street and contacting police colleagues in Inverness, as he'd done.

As though by telepathy his mobile rang. 'Inspector Drummond? It's DS Rougvie. I think I have something for you.'

Drummond kept his expression bland. He didn't want Gail seeing the flash of excitement in his eyes. 'I'll take this outside,' he said, striding out of the incident room and through the door to the back stairs. He knew she was staring after him with a puzzled frown, but now wasn't the time to share whatever information he might be about to receive.

'Sorry about that,' he said, gripping the phone. 'What've you got?'

'Well, the first thing I did was to check missing persons. Nothing. Your girl has never been reported. So, I called in at the music shop. The business is a one-man band affair. Err, sorry, no pun intended.'

'Go on, Sergeant,' Drummond said impatiently.

'He remembered your girl. Long dark hair and about fourteen years old, he said. She'd got into the school orchestra and her parents were buying her a violin so she could practise at home. Seems they were keen for her to learn, especially the father.'

'Did you get an address?'

'I did. Thankfully our man keeps records. It's 10, Firth View, Balcreggan, Inverness.'

'And the name?'

'Oh, didn't I say? It's McLeod. The name of the person who paid for the violin was an Angus McLeod. I can take a run out there if you like.'

'No, don't do that,' Drummond said quickly. 'The names still don't match. If the girl we knew as Evie really was their daughter then it has to be me who breaks the news that she's dead.'

'Oh, sorry. I didn't realize. You didn't say.' He hesitated. 'You'll be coming up then?'

'Yes, I'll be driving up.'

'You've got my number. If there's anything else I can do just let me know.'

'Thanks, I appreciate your help, but I'll take it from here.'

Drummond had been to Aberdeen on a previous investigation, but not Inverness. He checked out the journey times on his phone as he went back to the incident room.

Gail looked up as he came in. 'Everything all right, sir?'

Drummond smiled. 'Everything's fine.' He went to his desk and began sifting through the details from Evie's phone again. He'd have to bide his time before announcing he'd traced her family to Inverness.

It was approaching noon when he stood up and stretched. 'Any luck?' Gail asked.

He nodded, glancing at his watch. 'I've got an address in Inverness. No point wasting time.' He grabbed his jacket from the back of his chair. 'Tell DCI Buchan I'm driving up there.'

'What! Now?' Gail's eyebrow shot up.

'Yes,' he said, striding past. 'Tell her I'll call her from the road.'

'She won't like it,' Gail called after him as he strode away, raising an arm that suggested the opinions of his superior officer were the least of his worries.

An internet check had confirmed it would be a three-and-a-half-hour drive, depending on traffic. Drummond had already decided not to go directly to Evie's family. He wanted to get a feel for the area first, a sense of Evie's life before she fled to Glasgow. That would involve an overnight stay at a local B&B. He called in at his flat and threw a few things in a bag before getting on the road.

At this time of day, he'd missed the worst of the heavy traffic getting out of the city and onto the M80. An hour later and it would probably be gridlock, Drummond thought. At the big roundabout outside Perth, he joined the A9 and settled down for the next couple of hours driving north. He'd made good time and it was approaching five o'clock when he reached Inverness and joined the teatime traffic going through the Longman Industrial Estate. He had no real idea where he was going so he followed the stream of vehicles negotiating the series of little roundabouts through the estate and out of the city centre.

His second priority was to find a B&B and dump his bag, the first was to find a pub. He spotted the Riverside Inn as he drove across a bridge and headed for it. Traffic was still bumper to bumper on the bridge above but down here it was a different world. Drummond parked in front of the pub and got out of the car, a hand on his back as he stretched his cramped limbs, anticipating the pleasure of the pint of real ale he'd been promising himself.

There was only one customer at the bar nursing a pint. He gave Drummond a nod as he walked in. The barman appeared from somewhere out the back and Drummond ordered a pint of a local brew he hadn't heard of.

'Haven't seen you in here before,' the barman said. 'On holiday, are you?'

Drummond wiped the foam from his mouth. 'Just passing through.' His eyes were on the notice behind the bar advertising accommodation. 'Actually, maybe you could help me. I'm looking for a room for the night.'

The barman gave a nod. 'We have availability tonight as it happens.' He moved to the end of the bar and came back with a black ledger. 'Just the one night, was it?'

Drummond nodded.

'It's fifty quid, including breakfast and payable in advance. Will that do you?'

'Fine,' Drummond said, accepting the pen being offered to sign the book. His fellow drinker watched as he pulled out his wallet and took out his bank card.

'Come far?' the drinker asked as the financial transaction for the room booking concluded.

'Glasgow,' Drummond said.

'Ah, Glasgow. Now that's a hell of a place.' He lifted his beer glass and took a drink. 'You'll know the Horseshoe Bar then?'

Drummond nodded. He did. Intimately – all 104 feet of it. 'They say it's got the longest bar in the country,' the man said.

Drummond had heard it was Europe, but he wasn't

going to argue. He didn't particularly want to be drawn into conversation, but the man persisted.

'You here on business?'

'Like I said, I'm just passing through.'

'Through to where?'

Drummond finished his pint. 'Through to bed.' He beckoned to the barman. 'Can I go up to that room now?'

'Sure,' the man said, moving away to fetch the key. He returned and handed it over. 'It's Room 2 at the top of the stairs.'

Drummond thanked him and nodded to the drinker before going to his car to collect his overnight bag from the boot and heading up the narrow, creaking stairs.

Room 2 turned out to be a basic, but clean, comfortable room overlooking the river. He dropped his bag on the bed and fished out his mobile. There was a missed call from Joey Buchan and another from Pete. He'd stopped on the drive up to phone Joey and explain why he needed to check out the address in Inverness. She hadn't been pleased that he'd gone off without first running the trip past her. Joey liked to be in control. She'd be even more unhappy when she learned he was staying overnight. But that could wait.

He stood by the window watching two swans glide elegantly downstream and wondered if DS Nick Rougvie would like to join him for a drink.

# SIXTEEN

DRUMMOND PULLED up a street map of Inverness on his phone and was surprised to see the address for the Mcleods was within walking distance of the pub. It was in the opposite direction from the town centre, but it was over half an hour before he was due to meet Rougvie.

The traffic had died down and he set off at a steady pace on foot through the backstreets. The house was a semi-detached stone villa set back from the road. Drummond had been imagining a less impressive council house on a busy estate. This property, although not especially grand, had an air of faded elegance, something that spoke of a bygone age. It didn't look like the home of a teenage girl. As he stood on the other side of the road, a car turned into the driveway and parked at the side of the house. A man in his early forties got out and reached back in for a briefcase. Drummond studied the serious expression and the solid upright frame, the dark businesslike suit and the thinning ginger-coloured hair. Was this Evie's father? She hadn't looked anything like him, but that was neither here nor there. He wondered how the man would react when he shared the tragic news. No one had come to the door to meet him and Drummond guessed if Evie's mother was inside, she was probably busy in the kitchen.

He tried to imagine the writer of those emails on Evie's phone. For some reason he was picturing a small, pretty woman with intelligent green eyes and a vulnerable smile – completely the opposite of Evie.

He knew he should cross the road and knock on the door, but still he hesitated. There was a possibility this family had no connection with Evie. What if the music shop owner had given Nick Rougvie a wrong address? Even if it was right, it was only indicating a customer who had bought a fiddle. It was all ifs and buts. He needed to do more digging, he needed to find stronger evidence that these people were Evie's parents before wading in and destroying a family's life. Drummond turned on his heel and was heading into town to meet Rougvie when his phone buzzed.

'It's Nell, Jack. I thought you'd want to know. The girl in the alley died from having pressure applied to her neck.'

'She was strangled?' Drummond felt his heart sink. 'Are you saying she was another victim of our serial killer?'

'I doubt it, unless he was going out of his way to do everything differently. I'd say it was another killer who wrapped his hands around our victim's neck and choked her.' She paused. 'She was also full of heroin.'

'But it was definitely the pressure to the neck that killed her?' Drummond asked.

'Isn't that what I said?'

Drummond felt sick. 'Yes, you did. Thanks for letting me know, Nell.'

'Are you OK, Jack?' She sounded concerned.

'I'm fine, Nell. Look, I have to go. I'll get back to you.' He stared at the phone for a while after he ended the call. Who had reason to want Evie dead?

He walked at a slower pace to the Market Bar in the centre of Inverness where Nick Rougvie had suggested they should meet. It could never have been described as palatial. In comparison to the Horseshoe Bar back in Glasgow it was minuscule.

Drummond prided himself on being able to spot a cop at a hundred yards, but the man at the bar had him guessing. There was a comfortable, stocky look about him. Wide shoulders in a grey tweed jacket and a crop of wiry grey hair. He turned as Drummond walked in and gave him a nod. His smiling face was round and pink, with only the merest stubble on his chin. Drummond couldn't picture this man dealing with the thugs he met on the Glasgow streets, but then Pete was no tough guy either and he had worked on what they called those mean streets all his years in the Force.

Nick Rougvie turned and smiled as he introduced himself and they shook hands.

'What would you like?' Nick said.

Drummond asked for a pint of the local brew he'd had before.

Nick ordered the drink as he reached into the inside pocket of his jacket and pulled out a couple of printed sheets. 'I don't know if you need it or not, but I've been doing a bit more digging about your girl.'

'My girl?' Drummond frowned. 'You mean your girl. We haven't established if they are the same person.'

Rougvie flushed. 'I meant Emily.'

Drummond immediately felt guilty at having sounded

so grumpy. The man had put himself out for him. He should be more gracious. 'Sorry. I know what you meant. It's been a long day.' He put out his hand for the information.

'It's from the school's Christmas show. Emily gave a solo performance on her violin.'

Drummond was staring at the photocopy of the local newspaper article. The girl in the picture was Evie, but the caption read Emily Ross. The date of the article was the first week in December.

Nick was studying his face. 'Is that her, sir?'

Drummond gave a sad nod. The barman moved away to serve a customer at the other end of his bar. Nick lowered his voice. 'You didn't come all this way to find out about a missing girl. What's this all about, sir?'

Drummond took a long swig of his beer and put the glass back on the counter. He looked up and met Rougvie's eyes. 'I'm investigating a murder,' he said. 'Five of them if we include Emily.'

'The strangler?' Nick blew out his cheeks. 'You think this girl was a victim of the Glasgow Strangler?'

Drummond shot him a surprised look. He hadn't considered the murders would be as big news so far north, but why not? Inverness might be distinctly chillier than Glasgow, but it was hardly Alaska.

Nick was frowning at him. 'We're not all bagpipes and tartan shortbread tins up here, you know. Inverness is probably the fastest growing city in Scotland.'

A slow smile spread across Drummond's face. He was being put in his place and Nick Rougvie was probably right. Most Glaswegians regarded the Highlands as a place for the tourists, somewhere to go skiing in the winter and drive around checking out the scenery for the rest of the time. If he was going to get on with this Highlander, he'd have to ditch the notion that locals were simple folks who spoke with a quaint lilt and lived in remote croft houses like the gillies and shepherds.

He was beginning to accept that most Highlanders didn't live like this. This man, Nick Rougvie proved that. From the short time he'd so far spent in the man's company he'd got the impression he was nobody's fool.

Drummond put his hands up in a mock gesture of self-defence. 'Sorry,' he said, beckoning the barman over to replenish their glasses. But Nick put his hand over his. 'Not for me, thanks. I have to get off.'

'Not even another quick one?' Drummond was using his most persuasive voice. 'I'd appreciate a bit more background on Emily Ross.' He could see Nick was relenting.

'Well, just the one, although I'm not sure what else I can tell you.'

Their glasses were filled and both men took a swig. Nick wiped the foam from his mouth. 'I would have done more nosing around if I'd known you were investigating these murders.'

Drummond said nothing. The link to Inverness was so tenuous there hadn't seemed much point in involving the local plods. But he wasn't so sure now.

'What would you do, Nick, if you were investigating this family?'

Nick raised an eyebrow. 'Are you thinking they might be involved?'

Drummond shrugged. 'We can't rule anything out, but no, I have no reason to suspect the family. It would just be helpful to know more about what drove Emily away from home.'

'Maybe she was being bullied at school?' Nick offered.

It was a possibility, but Drummond didn't think so. Since Emily Ross and Evie were the same girl, he knew she could give as good as she got.

'Or a boyfriend,' Nick continued. 'What if she was running away from a bad relationship?'

Drummond thought about that. He supposed it was possible. But would a failed romance turn a seventeen-year-old girl to drugs and prostitution? He turned back to Nick. 'What can you tell me about this school Emily went to? Does it have a drugs problem?'

Nick pulled a face. 'Nothing special that's come to our notice. That doesn't mean it's not happening. Why do you ask?'

Drummond sighed. He'd been wondering how much to share with the man, but he'd quickly decided he could be trusted. 'The girl we knew as Evie had a drug problem...a serious drug problem.' He didn't mention he'd been trying to help her overcome it.

'I see what you mean,' Nick said. 'Our girl was probably on drugs before she left home.' He looked up. 'Maybe that's your answer. She probably thought it would be easier to follow her habit if she moved to the big city. Or she could just have been desperate to hide her drug taking from her parents.'

Drummond nodded. He would no doubt discover more once he'd interviewed the family. He wasn't looking forward to it.

Nick finished the dregs of his pint with an eye on the clock. 'I really do have to go this time.' He produced his card. 'This is my number. Ring me if there's any more I can do.'

Drummond took the card and nodded as Nick left the

pub. He wondered vaguely what the man had to rush off for. There was probably a hot meal and a loyal wife and family waiting for him. It wasn't often that he felt he was missing out on a family life. The only thing waiting for him was a solitary takeaway fish supper and probably several more pints and a few too many whiskies.

# SEVENTEEN

No police officer enjoys making the death call and Drummond was definitely convinced this is what it was. The girl he'd known as Evie Walker was Emily Ross. He had to share the grim news of her murder with her family.

There was a faded prettiness about the middle-aged woman who opened the door and gave him a questioning smile. Drummond produced his warrant card. 'I'm DI Drummond. Are you Mrs McLeod?'

The woman nodded. 'Rachel McLeod, yes.' He saw the flash of hope spring into her eyes as her hand went protectively to her bulging stomach. 'Is it Emily?' She searched his face. 'Have you found her?' A child's cry came from somewhere inside the house and the woman cast an anxious glance back.

'Could we step inside for a moment?' Drummond said gently, his eyes falling to the bump. This was going to be even more traumatic than he'd imagined. He should have brought Rougvie with him. Somehow, he knew the man would deal with this better than him. Drummond was more effective with his fists than dealing with the emotions of bereaved families.

Rachel led him into a spacious back room where two identical-looking toddlers glanced up from the multi-coloured bricks they were constructing into a wobbly tower and stared at him with interest. Another younger child was sitting in a wooden playpen yelling its head off. The woman stooped to scoop the child up. 'There, there, Archie,' she soothed, cradling him close as she lowered herself onto the sofa. There was excitement in her voice. 'You have news about Emily?'

Drummond's glance went around the room. 'Is your husband here, Mrs McLeod?' Rachel shook her head. 'You've found her, haven't you?' she said, her eyes glued to his face. 'Where is she? Is she coming home?'

Drummond swallowed. He'd already seen the framed school photo on the mantlepiece. It was Evie. There was no way he could sugar-coat this pill. 'We've found a body, Mrs McLeod,' he began. 'The body of a young woman...in Glasgow.'

He saw the fear flash into the woman's eyes. 'It's not Emily?' She stared at him, her voice rising. 'Tell me it's not Emily!'

'We haven't had an official identity.' His eyes went back to the photo. 'Is that your daughter, Mrs McLeod?'

Rachel's glance flew to the mantlepiece and back to Drummond, her eyes pleading. 'Please don't tell me Emily's dead.' She was shaking her head. 'She isn't dead!'

Drummond resisted the urge to look away, to glance anywhere other than into the face of this distressed woman.

'Look, can I call someone for you?' he said. 'You shouldn't be here on your own with the children. I can get one of your neighbours to come in.'

'Our childminder, Mandy next door.' Her voice was so distant Drummond could barely make out the words. 'She'll be wondering why we're late.'

'I'll ask her to collect the children,' Drummond said, but as he turned to leave the room the doorbell rang. He glanced back at Rachel, but she didn't appear to have heard it. She was still nursing the child and staring vacantly into space.

The caller had apparently let themselves in, for he could hear the front door opening and closing.

'Only me, Rachel,' a voice called from the hall. 'Is everything OK?' The woman came into the room and stopped, staring in surprise at Drummond. 'Sorry, I didn't realize you had a visitor.'

Rachel turned huge, confused eyes on the woman. 'They've found her, Mandy. They've found Emily.' Her voice broke. 'She's dead!'

'No!' The woman's shocked stare went from one to the other. She rushed forward and gathered Rachel and her child into her arms. 'What happened?' She shot Drummond a shocked look.

'They found her in Glasgow,' Rachel interrupted, her voice trembling.

Mandy was shaking her head in disbelief. 'I don't think the children should be here. Let me take them next door.' She gently eased the child from Rachel's arms.

'Can I help?' Drummond asked, stepping forward.

'No, we'll be fine.' She smiled down at the twins. 'Come on, Logan...you too, Daniel. Let's go next door and play some more.' The idea obviously appealed to the twins for they scrambled to their feet and toddled after the childminder.

Rachel was still in a daze as she stared across the room, a fistful of tissues in her hand.

'Her husband should be here,' Mandy said quietly to Drummond as she passed. She nodded to the mobile phone by the book case in the corner. 'Angus's number will be on it.' She cast a worried look back to Rachel. 'He probably won't like being disturbed at work, but that's his problem.'

Drummond took a couple of strides across the room and picked up the phone as Mandy shepherded the children out. Angus was the first name he found on the list of contacts. He tapped the number and it was answered immediately. An irritated voice was barking at him, 'I've told you not to disturb me at work, Rachel.'

'This is DI Drummond, sir. I'm a police officer. I think you need to come home.'

'What? Why? What's happened?' The man was still sounding more irritated than concerned. 'Has something happened to the children?'

'Your wife and children are all fine,' Drummond said. 'I'll explain the rest when you get here.' He disengaged the call and turned back to Rachel. She was pacing the room.

'How did Emily die? Was it an accident?' Her voice sounded distant.

Drummond hesitated, trying to find the least shocking way of telling her, but there was none. 'We'll know more once the post-mortem has taken place.' He cleared his throat. 'But we don't believe she died from natural causes.'

'Suicide?' Rachel's horrified eyes bored into him as she rose and faced up to him. 'Are you saying Emily took her own life?'

'We don't think so.'

'Not suicide, then what?' Rachel cried, her voice rising.

Her eyes flew wide. 'You think Emily was murdered, don't you?'

Drummond caught her as her legs gave way and he guided her back onto the sofa. She sat there, staring at some distant spot across the room. Drummond watched her, not sure what to do. To his surprise, Rachel squared her shoulders and stood up again.

'I'll make some tea,' she said. 'Angus will want tea.'

Drummond frowned. Grief and shock affected people in different ways. Making tea for her husband was probably her coping mechanism. He still felt a flash of dislike for the man even though he'd never met him.

He followed her into the kitchen. 'Can I help?' There was no response. She was moving around the kitchen like a robot, filling the kettle, putting tea things on a tray – and then stopped, a soft, faraway smile on her face.

'I used to make her a mug of hot chocolate when she came home from school. We'd sit here at this table and she would tell me about her day.' She looked across at Drummond. 'Emily loved school. She played the fiddle in the school orchestra.' Rachel's expression darkened. 'Then everything changed,' she said, her voice almost a whisper as though she was talking to herself. 'Emily would go straight to her room when she came home. She wouldn't talk to me. I knew something was wrong, but it was like I couldn't reach her anymore.'

The kettle boiled and switched itself off, but Rachel didn't notice. She was in another place. 'I let her down,' she said slowly. 'This is all my fault. I should have tried harder.'

'I don't believe for a minute that it was your fault Emily left home. You can't blame yourself,' Drummond said.

'Why not?' She swung round to stare at him. 'I'm her

mother. It's my job to know what's going on with my children.'

The front door opened and slammed closed again. Drummond heard the footsteps in the hall. 'Rachel?' The man's shout was urgent.

Rachel blinked and brushed away sudden tears. 'We're in here, Angus.'

The man who came into the kitchen wore the same smart suit he'd been in when Drummond saw him arrive home the previous night. The glare he flashed to Drummond, as he put an arm around Rachel, was accusing. 'You've upset my wife.'

Rachel raised huge shocked eyes to her husband. 'They've found Emily, Angus.' Her voice was shaking. 'She's dead!'

Angus McLeod's frown went to Drummond. 'Is this true?'

'We've found a body, sir. We believe it might be your daughter.' He held the man's eyes.

'Emily was my wife's daughter, Inspector, my step-daughter. Where was she found?'

Drummond blinked. It wasn't the response he'd expected. Why would the man ask that and not how the girl had died? 'I've come from Glasgow, sir,' he said. 'That's where we found her.'

'Glasgow? What was she doing there?'

'That's what we need to find out. Do you work locally, Mr McLeod?'

'What?' He sounded distracted. 'Yes, in the town centre. Alba Bank. I'm the manager.'

'They think Emily was murdered, Angus.' Rachel's voice was trembling.

Angus McLeod frowned. 'Murdered? Why would anyone murder Emily?'

'I can't confirm Emily was murdered. We're still investigating her death,' Drummond said, meeting the man's eyes. 'When did she leave home?'

Angus McLeod went back to his wife's side and put a protective arm around her again. 'We don't know, Inspector. She'd been acting oddly before she went away.'

'Oddly?' Drummond repeated. 'In what way?'

'She spent a lot of her time in her room,' Rachel said. 'It wasn't at all like her. She always chatted away with me when she came home from school. I looked forward to our little chats. When she stopped doing that, I thought it was something I'd done. She said it wasn't and that she was fine, but she wasn't.'

'We suspected she was being bullied at school,' Angus McLeod broke in.

A picture of the defiant, spirited young woman he'd known as Evie came into Drummond's mind. She was the last person he felt who would have allowed herself to be bullied. But then the girl in the photograph didn't look like someone who would swap a comfortable life here in Inverness with a family who loved her for the unforgiving streets of Glasgow's red-light district.

'Did you ever suspect Emily was taking drugs?'

Rachel's eyes flew open. 'Drugs? No!' She was enraged. 'Emily didn't take drugs! Why would you suggest such a thing?'

'Yes, why, Inspector?' McLeod demanded, his brow wrinkling. 'Is that how she died? First you tell my wife our daughter was murdered and now you're suggesting she took an overdose?' He moved closer to Drummond, a hint of threat in his stare. 'Are you telling us Emily committed suicide now?'

Drummond put up a hand to calm the man. 'That's not what we're saying, sir. We have to check every possibility.'

The man turned his back on them. Drummond could see his shoulders shaking. Rachel put up a hand to touch her husband's arm. 'They'll need us to identify Emily,' she said softly.

Angus nodded.

'I can take you to Glasgow today if it helps,' Drummond offered.

Angus McLeod shook his head. 'That won't be necessary but thank you. We have the car. Just tell us where to go.'

# EIGHTEEN

Drummond knew he was in for a roasting from Joey Buchan next day as soon as he arrived back in the incident room.

'Good of you to join us, Inspector Drummond.' She had interrupted the morning briefing to throw him a sarcastic smile.

Drummond responded with a hard stare. What was she talking about? He'd almost broken his neck rising at dawn and leaving the Riverside Inn without the breakfast he'd paid for to get here this early.

Joey raised an eyebrow and he wondered if she'd regretted the narky comment. Not that he was all that bothered what she thought. He was here for the McLeods, but mainly Rachel McLeod. Her distress yesterday had got to him. He'd accompanied many relatives to the mortuary to identify their loved ones. Why was this one going to be any different?

The McLeods must have left Inverness shortly after him for he'd just been told they were waiting for him down in reception. If anything, Rachel loooked even paler than yesterday. Her dark eyes sparkled with unshed tears and her hair had been drawn back from her face. Drummond could see she was desperately trying to hold herself together.

'Can we do this now?' Angus McLeod said abruptly. 'We have to get back for the children.'

Rachel was staring at the floor.

'Of course,' Drummond said. He'd beckoned Gail Swann to accompany them. 'We can take my car. It's not far.'

Rachel McLeod drew back, her face deadly pale as they approached the mortuary door. 'I can't do it,' she said. 'I can't go in there.'

Angus put a hand on her shoulder. 'Let me, Rachel. You don't have to put yourself through this. That's what I'm here for.'

Drummond turned to hide a frown. It seemed all too clinical between this couple. Why couldn't the man see his wife needed a hug, not a hand on her shoulder? It didn't take a lot of imagination to understand how Rachel would be feeling right now. Drummond was having enough trouble dealing with his own feelings. He should have made a better job of looking out for Evie. The weight of guilt still sat heavily in the pit of his stomach.

He shot Gail a look and she nodded in response, moving to the distressed woman's side. 'We can wait here,' she said gently, guiding Rachel to one of the chairs in the corridor.

As Drummond led Angus into the mortuary, the man turned back to his wife. 'Courage, my love. Remember the whole congregation is praying for us.'

Rachel lifted her tear-stained face and nodded, but it was clear she took no comfort from the words.

Evie's body – Drummond was still having trouble thinking of her as Emily – lay under a sheet. At his nod a member of the mortuary staff lifted the sheet from her face. Viewing bodies was nothing new to Drummond, but he felt himself wincing as he glanced down at the girl. He looked away quickly, reminding himself he was here to study Angus McLeod's reaction to seeing the body of his dead stepdaughter. Until they caught this killer, everyone was a suspect.

Drummond wasn't sure what he'd been expecting from the man, certainly not what was happening now. Angus McLeod was sobbing, loud uncontrollable sobs. He turned away, his shoulders heaving.

Drummond swallowed. 'The death of a loved one affects everyone differently,' he said, not sure if he was expected to comfort the man. He didn't feel inclined to offer more than words. He was wondering how Rachel would have felt if she had witnessed this.

'It's just the shock,' Angus McLeod said. 'She looks so perfect lying there.'

Drummond thought the girl looked far from perfect. She had the haggard pale look of an addict and the angry dark bruises on her neck were more than obvious now.

McLeod was dabbing at his eyes with a white linen hankie he'd taken from his pocket. 'Just give me a moment,' he said.

'I'm sorry but this has to be official.' Drummond stepped forward. 'Is this your stepdaughter?'

The man still had his back to him. He lifted his head and squared his shoulders. 'Yes. This is my stepdaughter, Emily Ross.' He spun round to face Drummond. 'I'd like to take my wife away from here now, if that's all right with you, Inspector.'

'Of course,' Drummond said. 'There are a few preliminaries we need to clear up before you go. Perhaps we could all go back to the police station. I promise not to keep you longer than we need.' He made an attempt at a smile. 'We have a very nice canteen that produces very passible coffee.'

'We don't drink coffee,' Angus said. 'But if you have more questions then let's get them over with as quickly as possible.'

They were moving out of the mortuary and into the corridor. Rachel rose from her chair as they emerged from the door, her eyes bore into her husband's face, willing him to say it wasn't Emily. Drummond could see she'd been clinging to the last unlikely hope that the body on the trolley back there was some other girl. But her face fell as her husband approached. 'It's her, my love,' he said at last, putting his arms around Rachel and patting her back. 'It's Emily.'

Drummond and Gail exchanged a look as the couple stood there embracing. And then Rachel pulled away, swiping angrily at her tears with the flat of her hands. 'Why Glasgow?' she demanded. 'Why did Emily come here? It's not as if she knew anyone here.'

'We don't know, Mrs McLeod,' Gail said. 'We're still investigating everything.'

'She had no money, so how was she managing to support herself?' She turned to Drummond. 'And where was she staying? Somebody must have been helping her.'

Drummond didn't like where this was going. He could see his career flying out the window. There was so much more he could tell this woman, but would that give her any more comfort? He doubted it. Or maybe he was just protecting himself? Whatever it was, it would have to wait until later. There was only one focus on his mind now. He had to find Emily Ross's killer.

· · ·

Gail rang ahead to warn staff at the station to make sure an interview room was free, and they were shown straight there when they arrived. 'I'll find us some coffees,' she said.

'As I've already told your boss, we don't drink coffee,' Angus McLeod said. 'Can we have water?'

'I'd like coffee, please,' Rachel said. 'White and sweet.'

Angus shot her a look, but Rachel had averted her eyes.

Once again Drummond sensed the friction between the two of them or perhaps, he was misinterpreting the normal reactions of a grieving couple.

Rachel had pulled out her mobile phone. 'Is it all right if I check up on the children? We left them with our neighbour, Mandy.'

Drummond nodded. 'Of course,' he said.

They all fell silent as Rachel made the call. Her eyes lit up at her friend's assurance the children were fine. For a few brief seconds she had escaped from the living nightmare that was Emily's brutal death. Her eyes were on her husband. 'Thanks, Mandy. I knew they'd be fine with you. We should be back in a few hours. I'll keep in touch.' The call ended, but the light in her eyes remained.

'Everything OK?' Drummond asked, giving the woman his kindest smile.

'Mandy says they're fine.'

'Will this take long?' Angus cut in. 'We need to get back to our children.'

'Just a few questions,' Drummond said, addressing his comments to Rachel. 'We promise not to keep you longer than we have to.'

'Where was Emily found?' Rachel asked, her eyes challenging.

'We don't need to go into this now, Rachel. The officers

will give us all this information when they complete their investigations.'

But Rachel persisted. 'I need to know the truth.'

Drummond and Gail exchanged a look. He was weighing up how much to say. He didn't want to distress the woman any more than he had to.

'Emily's body was found outside one of the city centre pubs,' he said. No need to mention the poor girl's body had been dumped amongst the rubbish in a dismal alley.

Rachel kept her eyes down, so he had no idea how she responded to this. He waited a second before going on. 'Can you remember the last time you saw your daughter, Mrs McLeod?'

'Of course. I think of little else. I was in the kitchen up to my elbows in flour when Emily came in that day.' Rachel touched her face. 'She said she was off to meet her friend, Iona.' A wistful smile crossed her face. 'She gave me a peck on the cheek. I didn't even turn around. Archie was in his pram and had started to cry. I went to wash my hands to pick him up.' Her head was shaking sadly. 'I didn't even say goodbye to Emily.'

'When did you realize she'd gone?' Drummond asked gently.

'Later that evening,' Rachel said. 'It was the middle of the week and Emily knew we didn't like her staying out late.' She glanced at her husband, who appeared to be struggling to control the tremble in his bottom lip. 'When it got to 10.30, we started to worry. We gave it another hour and then I rang Iona. She was in bed. She said she knew nothing about meeting Emily that evening.'

'We sat up all night ringing everyone we could think of,' Angus McLeod said.

'But we knew it was hopeless,' Rachel interrupted.

'Emily had taken most of her clothes. She must have had a rucksack hidden in the hall or something when she came in to say goodbye...' Her voice tailed off.

'Did she contact you at all?' Gail asked.

'I got a text the next day. Emily said she was fine and not to worry about her. She said she needed to get away for a while and would appreciate if we didn't try to find her.'

Drummond watched Gail scribble notes as the woman spoke. 'The friend you mentioned, did Emily get in touch with her?'

Rachel frowned. 'She said not, and to be honest she looked as shocked about Emily going off like that as the rest of us.'

'What's the friend's surname?' Drummond asked.

'Grant, Iona Grant'

'But she'll be no help,' Angus McLeod said. 'I don't know what Emily saw in the girl. I warned her she was trouble, but you couldn't tell Emily anything.'

Their drinks arrived, but no one picked them up.

'Was Emily raped?' Rachel's stark words hung in the air.

Angus shot his wife a shocked look.

Drummond shook his head. 'We don't believe so.' He saw Rachel swallowing hard.

'Who found her?'

'Oh, for pity's sake, Rachel. We don't need to know this. We should go and let these people get on with their business.'

'Emily is their business,' Rachel burst out angrily. 'She's my daughter and I want to know everything.' Her voice wavered. 'I want to know why she died. I want to know who killed her.'

Gail stretched out a hand to her, glancing at Drummond.

He cleared his throat, not sure if the anger he was feeling was on Rachel's behalf or his own. 'We'll find him. We'll find who killed your daughter. I promise you.' He was aware of Gail's frown, but he'd meant what he said. If he couldn't catch this murdering bastard, then he was done with this job.

Angus was on his feet. 'I'm taking my wife home now.' He put an arm around her. 'If that's all right with you, Inspector.'

There was a scraping of chairs on the floor as they all got to their feet. 'Thank you both for your co-operation. We'll keep in touch.' He accompanied them out to the car park and watched as they crossed to their vehicle. There was a defeated look about the slump of Rachel's shoulders, but her husband walked tall, with only the slightest hint of a limp.

Drummond didn't wait to see them drive off. As he turned for the incident room, he knew he would soon be following them back to Inverness.

# NINETEEN

'It's Jack Drummond, Nick. I'd like to take you up on that offer of help.'

'DI Drummond.' He sounded pleased to hear from him. 'Sure, what can I do?'

'Can we meet?'

'You're back in Inverness?'

Drummond adjusted his mirror to watch a uniformed PC approaching. 'I'm down here in your car park.'

There was a second's hesitation and then, 'I'll come down.'

The PC was now beside him, indicating he should roll down the window no doubt to inform him he couldn't park there. Drummond produced his ID and raised an eyebrow. The young officer looked embarrassed. 'Sorry, sir, just checking.'

Nick Rougvie arrived as the PC was walking away. 'I see you've met Police Scotland's finest. You'll have to over-look our Sandy's enthusiasm. If it moves, he'll try to arrest it.'

'No worries.' Drummond grinned, opening the car door for Rougvie to get in beside him.

Nick glanced at his watch. 'I haven't got long. What's this help you need?'

'I'd like you to accompany me to interview a couple of people.'

Rougvie glanced out across the car park as another police vehicle drove in. He gave the two officers a wave. 'I'm happy to go with it, but this time we need to make it official. You'll have to run this past my governor.'

Drummond frowned. He'd been hoping to avoid that.

Rougvie laughed. 'DCI Fraser's not so bad. I'm sure he'll spare me if he can.' He started to get out of the car. 'Come on, I'll introduce you.'

Detective Chief Inspector Gavin Fraser's dark pinstriped suit would have looked completely out of place in the backstreets of Glasgow that Drummond frequented. He was reminded more of the superior, snotty-nosed advocates he knew so well from the city's High Court. But appearances weren't everything. Maybe the man wasn't as much of a dandy as he looked.

Drummond met his assessing stare as Nick Rougvie introduced him and explained why he was there.

They shook hands under DCI Fraser's continued scrutiny. 'How long will you need the services of my officer, Inspector?'

'Couple of hours tops, sir,' Drummond assured him. 'I need someone with local knowledge and since I already know DS Rougvie...' He let the sentence trail off.

'Has this been cleared with your own superior officers in Glasgow?' Fraser asked.

Drummond tried not to shuffle his feet. 'I wanted to clear it with you first, sir, but there won't be a problem. My governor will be on board with it.'

Fraser's silent stare was making Drummond uncomfortable, but then the man nodded. 'OK, Nick. 'You can go with the inspector, but don't disappear. I expect to be kept in the loop.'

Rougvie smiled. 'Absolutely, guv. I'll keep in touch.'

He waited until he was out of Fraser's hearing before saying, 'We can take one of the pool cars.' Drummond raised no objections.

Down in the car park Drummond briefed Rougvie about the previous day's meeting with Angus and Rachel McLeod.

'Poor devils,' he said. 'Can't have been easy to identify their dead daughter.'

'Emily was Rachel's daughter,' Drummond said. 'She didn't marry Angus until much later.'

Rougvie blew out his cheeks. 'I didn't know that. I tried to do a bit of checking into their backgrounds to see if I could find out any more about Emily.'

Drummond raised an eyebrow at him. 'Did you now.'

'Well, I was interested.'

'So, what did you dig up?'

'Not a lot, but I do have an account at the Alba Bank in the centre of town where Angus McLeod is the manager. I know a member of the staff, so I asked a few discreet questions. It turns out the man isn't exactly popular. He runs the bank with rigid efficiency. I've seen for myself how he orders everybody about.'

Drummond sighed. 'He's a bank manager.'

'That's no excuse for being offensive. The man has no people skills.'

'What else did you find out?'

'Not much, apart from the fact that McLeod is fiercely protective of his family's privacy.'

Hmm, Drummond thought, why didn't that surprise

him? On the two occasions he'd met the man he hadn't exactly been friendly.

'I'd like to interview the couple's neighbour,' Drummond said. 'She's a childminder who seems to come and go as she pleases at the McLeod house, at least when Angus isn't there.' He pulled out a tattered notebook and flicked through the pages. 'Emily had a friend, Iona Grant, and she's another witness I want to meet. We might also have a word with Rachel.'

'Not Angus?' Rougvie asked.

'We'll get around to him all in good time,' Drummond said.

Ten minutes later the detectives were outside Mandy Stranger's front door. 'It's very quiet in there,' Rougvie said, listening. 'Maybe she's out.'

Drummond pointed to a notice telling callers not ring the bell between 11 a.m. and noon, but he did anyway. It was answered immediately by a slightly annoyed-looking Mandy Stranger. Her expression flashed surprise when she recognized him. She glanced quickly back into her house. 'I've just got the children down for their nap.' She pointed to the card and put a finger to her mouth indicating they should be quiet. 'I suppose you'd better come in.'

They followed her into a busy-looking kitchen where a young woman was washing plastic beakers and plates at the sink. 'This is Shona,' Mandy said. 'She helps me. Could you check the children please, Shona, while I have a word with these gentlemen?'

The girl gave a shy nod, drying her hands on a towel as she left the room.

Mandy turned to them. 'Take a seat,' she said. 'I suppose this is about Emily. Rachel told me about yesterday.' She shook her head. 'How do you cope with seeing your child lying dead in a mortuary?'

Drummond glanced at Rougvie as he fished his notebook from his jacket pocket and took out his pen. 'It was Mr McLeod who identified his daughter.'

'Emily was Rachel's daughter, not Angus's, although you wouldn't have thought so from the way he treated her. Talk about ruling with an iron rod. If it had been up to him Emily wouldn't have left the house. He disapproved of almost everything she did and every friend she had. I wasn't surprised when she ran away.'

Drummond frowned. 'Is this what Rachel told you?'

'Rachel? No, she didn't have to. Angus made no secret of his strict regime with the family. I've had Emily in tears in this very room at the way she was treated at home.'

'You said you weren't surprised that she left. Did Emily tell you she was planning to go?'

Mandy shook her head. 'I don't think she told anyone. She just took off. Rachel was distraught.'

'How did Angus take it?' Drummond asked.

'He was furious. He doesn't seem to consider that any of it is his fault. Rachel doesn't seem to blame him either. He rules the roost over that family, and she lets him. Angus's overbearing behaviour might not frustrate her, but it sure as hell makes my blood boil.'

She looked from one to the other. 'Do you know he objects to Rachel leaving the house without his permission? She isn't allowed to go shopping unless he agrees to everything on her list. I'm talking here about groceries, not even personal things.

'And then there's the twins. Angus isn't happy about me looking after them for a couple of hours a week. He says Rachel is their mother and taking care of them is her job.'

'And yet he relented?' Drummond said. 'How did that come about?'

Mandy gave a slight frown. 'Rachel is my friend, but it's been one baby after another since she married that man and now, she's pregnant again. She needed a rest.

'It all came to a head about six weeks ago when Rachel fainted in the kitchen and banged her head on the edge of the table. I found her on the floor with Archie and the twins. They were all screaming their heads off.

'I called for an ambulance and then rang Angus. The paramedics wanted to take Rachel to hospital for a check over, but she refused to go and when Angus arrived, he backed her decision.' She began to assemble the nursery beakers on a tray and took a jug of orange juice from the fridge. 'That's when I suggested again that the twins should come to me. Angus wasn't happy but I stood my ground. I hated seeing how tired and stressed out Rachel always seemed to be. I'm a registered child minder and trained nanny. The twins know me and anyway, they were only going to be next door. Eventually Angus saw sense and agreed.'

Nick Rougvie had been sitting quietly, taking all of this in, but now he had questions too. 'Do you know who Emily's real father is?'

'You'll have to ask Rachel that. We didn't know each other back then.' But her response came too quickly to be believed.

Rougvie smiled. 'It's fine. I just wondered because you seem so fond of Rachel.'

Mandy poured juice into the assembled beakers. 'She's had a bad time. It's not easy being a single parent. Perhaps that's why she turned to the church.'

'Rachel's religious?' Drummond asked.

Mandy shrugged. 'She's not devout if that's what you mean. I guess she was looking for support.'

Rougvie leaned forward. 'Well that was a good thing, wasn't it?'

Mandy spun round and met his eyes. 'It was the Free Presbyterian Church.'

'The Wee Frees,' Rougvie said, shooting Drummond a glance. 'You sound disapproving.'

'They have some strange ideas,' Mandy said, stopping what she was doing. 'We used to live in a village up north. There was a Free Church right on the beach. That strange psalm chanting thing they do used to give me the creeps. I was only little back then, but it scared me. No music, just the voices of the congregation resonating out across the sand.'

Drummond and Rougvie exchanged a look. Mandy was back in her childhood and for the first time sounded vulnerable. Drummond cleared his throat. 'What kind of strange ideas?'

Mandy's brow creased. 'Well, for a start they don't recognize Christmas or Easter or approve of working on the Sabbath.'

'That's not so strange, is it?' Rougvie cut in.

'Perhaps not, but some of them take it to extremes. They won't even take a bus to their church services because the public transport runs on Sundays. Oh, don't get me started on that lot.' She looked at Drummond. 'They treat their women like second-class citizens, you know. They're not allowed to preach in church or be office bearers, or even to wear trousers. And they make women cover their heads in church.'

Mandy Stranger clearly had no time for the Free

Church or its people. Drummond wondered if she had shared these feelings with her friend next door.

'What about Rachel?' he said. 'Did she find the support she needed in the church?'

Mandy's shoulders rose in a shrug. 'It was Angus who persuaded her in that direction. They knew each other from the bank. He was her boss.'

'Angus is a Wee Free?' Rougvie asked.

'Oh, didn't I say?' Mandy gave him a cold stare. 'Angus is an elder in the Free Church.'

## TWENTY

THE TWO DETECTIVES sat in the car looking back at Mandy Stranger's house. 'What did you make of that?' Rougvie asked.

'I detected a wee bit of prejudice.' Drummond smiled.

'Yeah, she really doesn't like Angus, does she?'

Drummond pursed his lips together. 'We don't know how much her opinion of the man affects her friendship with Rachel.' But he was getting a clearer insight into why Emily left home. He had detected no religious streak when the girl had been under his roof, so he could see why she would rebel against Angus McLeod's domineering ways. It didn't explain though why a respectably brought up schoolgirl had turned to prostitution – and drugs.

'Where to now, guv?' Nick Rougvie asked.

Drummond was tempted to suggest the pub, but he knew he wouldn't relax until they'd spoken to Emily's mate. He pulled his tattered notebook from his pocket and ran his eye over the scribbled notes he'd made when he'd first spoken to Rachel. 'According to her mother, Emily's friend,

Iona Gant, is a student at the college here...the University of the Highlands and Islands she called it. Do you know it?'

Rougvie nodded. 'The campus is out on the airport road. Do we know what course she's taking?'

'Beauty? Is there such a course?'

'I know students get offered plenty of choices, so probably,' Rougvie said.

Drummond thought the University of the Highlands and Islands looked more like an international hotel as they walked into the reception area. Judging by Rougvie's purposeful stride to the information desk he clearly knew his way about the place. Both officers produced their warrant cards. The woman behind the desk gave them a cursory glance.

'We'd like to see one of your students, Iona Grant,' Drummond said.

The woman tapped into her computer and looked up at them. 'Is Iona Grant on our Beauty Care and Make-Up?'

'Sounds about right,' Drummond said.

The woman did some more tapping. 'Ah, here she is.' She adjusted her glasses. 'She should be in a class now. Do you want me to contact her?'

'No, it's fine.' Drummond smiled. 'If you could just point us in the right direction.' The woman leaned across the desk and pointed to the lift. 'That department is on the second floor. You can't miss it.'

She was right. They had walked into what looked like an oversized beauty salon. Everywhere they turned there were rows of chairs in front of mirrors, but not many students. In the absence of anyone official looking to ask, they just walked in. Drummond felt distinctly out of place in these female surroundings. A woman approached and asked if she could help them.

'Iona Grant,' Drummond said, giving the woman a polite smile. 'Is she here?'

The woman looked from one to the other. 'The receptionist downstairs told us to come up,' Rougvie explained.

'OK,' the woman said slowly, her eyes still suspicious. 'Who shall I say wants her?'

'Just tell her she has visitors,' Drummond said.

The woman moved away, glancing back at them over her shoulder as she went.

'I don't think she likes us,' Rougvie said, watching as she moved briskly away. They saw her stop and beckon for a young woman to join her. Their heads came together as though sharing a confidence. The newcomer looked up sharply and began to walk towards them.

'I'm Iona Grant,' she said, her clear blue eyes narrowing. 'Do I know you?'

Drummond and Rougvie produced their ID. 'We'd like a few words if that's OK,' Drummond said, doing his best to sound friendly.

'Is this about Emily?'

Drummond nodded. 'Emily's mum told us you were friends.'

'Is Emily dead?'

The detectives exchanged a glance. Drummond indicated they should move to a window where it was quiet. 'You haven't told me,' Iona persisted. 'Is she...is she dead?'

Drummond's face stretched into a frown. 'I'm very sorry. Emily's stepfather identified her body yesterday.'

Two large tears slid down the girl's freckled cheeks and she brushed them slowly away. 'I knew it. Poor Emily.'

'Did you know her well?' Drummond asked.

'She's my best friend.' She paused to correct herself. 'She *was* my best friend. We went to school together.' She glanced back to the beauty department where Drummond could see students involved in various stages of applying make-up to the faces of what appeared to be fellow student volunteers. 'We should have been doing this course together. That was the plan. We were supposed to graduate together.' Her voice broke and she looked away. 'We were going to open a salon in Inverness.'

Drummond suppressed a sigh. What had been going on with Emily? She had a future all planned out for herself here in Inverness and yet she'd turned her back on it for a seedy existence in Glasgow's red-light zone. He wondered what Iona would say if she knew about this, but now wasn't the time to share it.

'Have you any idea why she would go off as she did?'

Iona shook her head and the single plait of brown hair swung. 'I was gutted when she left. She didn't tell me she was planning to do that.'

'So, you had no contact with her after she left? No phone calls, text messages, letters?' Drummond asked.

Tears welled in the girl's eyes as she shook her head. 'Nothing. I tried ringing her, but it sounded like she had disconnected her phone. Why would she go off without telling me? If she'd been in some kind of trouble, we could have talked it out...' Her voice trailed off.

'And she'd never done anything like this before?' Rougvie cut in.

'Emily had never gone off like that before, if that's what you mean. I know it's crazy, but at first I thought she must have been abducted.' She fished a screwed-up tissue from her pocket and dabbed at her eyes. 'I went to see her mother, Rachel. I wanted to know if they had reported Emily's disappearance to the police.'

'And had they?' Rougvie asked.

Iona flashed him a cross look. 'You must know they didn't. Emily's mum told me Mr McLeod said it wasn't necessary as Emily had texted her saying she was fine. Apparently, she told her mum she needed some space. She wanted time to think about her future and she needed to be on her own to do that.' She took a deep breath, steadying herself. 'It all sounded very iffy to me, but Rachel had the text on her phone, so I had to accept it. I was just miffed that she hadn't bothered to contact me too. I was her best friend after all. At least that's what I'd thought.'

'Do you know if she contacted anyone else?'

Iona shook her head. 'No idea.'

'Did Emily have a boyfriend?' Drummond continued. He didn't think so, but he had to ask.

Iona shrugged. 'Not that I knew about, well, nobody special, but after going off like she did, who knows?'

Rougvie glanced at Drummond for permission to jump in again. He got the nod. 'Was Emily normally secretive?' he asked.

Iona thought about that. 'I wouldn't say secretive. We did confide in each other, but if there was something she didn't want you to know she was very good at clamming up.'

'Was there much Emily didn't tell you?'

'How would I know if she didn't tell me?'

Drummond turned his head away to hide his smile. She had a point. 'You said there was no particular boyfriend. Would you have known if there had been?'

Iona gave a slight smile. 'I think I would have known.'

'We'll need the names of the boys she was friendly with.'

Iona raised an eyebrow. 'Emily didn't go for boys. It was older men she was into.'

Drummond and Rougvie exchanged a look.

'Like I said, there was nothing serious.' She slid Drummond a wary glance. 'I don't want to get anyone into trouble.'

'Why would you think that?' Rougvie asked.

'The man I'm thinking of is married.'

Drummond's eyes were glued to her face. 'We'll be discreet,' he said.

Iona was still looking doubtful about whether she should say more. She gave a resigned sigh. 'He's a tutor here at the college.'

Drummond and Rougvie waited, watching the girl swallow. She looked away, biting her bottom lip. 'You've probably already met him.'

Drummond frowned. He hadn't met that many people in Inverness. His mind scrolled through the possibilities. And then he stopped, his insides contracting. Was she talking about Emily's stepfather? He was picturing him at the mortuary, the tears streaking down his cheeks as he stared at the girl's body. He'd thought it was grief, but could it have been more than that? But no, he wasn't a college tutor. The girl was talking about someone else.

He squared his shoulders. 'Who was the man, Iona?'

The girl's fist tightened around the ball of damp tissue. She hesitated, still unsure, before taking an unsteady breath. 'It was Ian Stranger,' she said. 'The McLeod's next-door neighbour...Mandy's husband.'

## TWENTY-ONE

THE COLLEGE RECEPTIONIST showed a bit more interest when the officers returned to ask for Ian Stranger. She didn't need to check for his department. 'I know he's here,' she said. 'I saw him come in this morning.'

Iona had told them she wasn't sure about the man's subject, but Drummond suspected she felt she'd said enough. He didn't push it.

'You'll most likely find Mr Stranger in the cafe. He should be between classes at the moment,' the receptionist said.

The appetizing smell of freshly brewed coffee reached them as they entered the cafe. About half of the tables were occupied. The detectives scanned the room.

'What about that chap on his own over by the window?' Rougvie suggested.

Drummond nodded. It was as good a place as any to start.

The man looked up as they approached. If this was Mandy Stranger's husband, he was considerably younger than her.

'Mr Stranger?' Drummond enquired. The man looked up, frowning. 'Who's asking?'

Drummond and Rougvie showed their IDs. Neither of them missed the immediate flash of unease that crossed the man's grey eyes. He blinked. 'How can I help you?'

Both men sat down. 'It's about Emily Ross,' Drummond said. 'I understand you knew her.'

'Emily?'

'Your next-door neighbour.'

'Yes, I knew Emily.'

'What can you tell us about her disappearance?'

The colour drained from Ian Stranger's face. He looked genuinely shocked. 'I don't know anything about Emily's disappearance. Why are you asking me?'

Drummond gave him a scathing look. 'You know why we're asking you, Mr Stranger.' He paused. 'Did your wife know you were having an affair with a seventeen-year-old girl...with the daughter of her best friend in fact?'

Stranger sprang to his feet. 'What are you talking about? Of course, Emily and I weren't having an affair.'

Drummond waved him back down. 'Please stay calm, Mr Stranger, and tell us just what your relationship with Emily Ross was.'

'We were friends, that's all.'

Drummond and Rougvie exchanged a deliberate look. 'Friends?' Drummond repeated. 'We heard it was a bit more than that.'

'Look, I don't know who you've been talking to but–'

'Emily Ross is dead, Mr Stranger, and we're investigating the circumstances, so believe me it's not in your interest to mess us about.'

Stranger pushed a nervous hand over his hair, his eyes darting around the room. They were attracting attention from some of the other customers. 'Can we take a walk?' he asked.

'Good idea,' Drummond said. 'You lead the way.'

There was a small lake in the landscaped grounds of the university and the three men strolled across to it.

'Emily's parents are already devastated by what's happened. If you suggest to them there was anything untoward going on between us it would kill Rachel,' Ian Stranger said.

'I don't expect your wife would be exactly happy either, knowing you were in a relationship with Emily,' Rougvie said.

Stranger swung round to glare at him. 'This isn't about me. I've done nothing wrong. Why don't you believe me? Emily and I were not having an affair.'

Drummond faced up to him. 'So why do you think people were getting that impression?'

Stranger stared out across the water. 'People like to gossip, but they got us all wrong. Emily and I were friends, that's all.' He nodded back to the building. 'It's impossible for paths not to cross in there. We all use the cafe. If Emily spotted me at one of the tables, she would join me. There was nothing wrong with that. I think she liked the idea of confiding in an older man.'

'Confiding?' Drummond's ears pricked up. 'What did she confide to you?'

Ian Stranger dragged his eyes back to the detective. 'Emily wasn't happy...at home I mean. She didn't get on with her stepfather.' Drummond waited, aware that they might learn more if the man was not interrupted. 'Angus McLeod rules the roost in that family. He imposes his will on them like he's running some kind of army camp.'

Stranger pulled a face. 'And all that praying. It's not right. Emily hated it and I didn't blame her.'

They walked on in silence as the detectives waited for him to continue, but the man seemed to have said all he was going to.

'Did Emily suggest her stepfather was violent?' Drummond asked.

'Not to her. Emily was no shrinking violet. If Angus had touched her, she would have given back as good as she got.' Drummond concealed a sad smile. He was remembering how fiery the girl could be. 'But I think he was abusing Rachel, at least that's what Mandy thought.'

'Do you or your wife have any proof of this?' Rougvie asked.

Stranger frowned. 'No, but then who knows what goes on behind closed doors.'

The more they listened to the man the more Drummond was inclined to believe him. He didn't think Stranger had been having an affair with Emily. 'Did you know Emily was planning to run away?'

Stranger shook his head. 'If she'd said anything, I would have tried to persuade her not to do that, but she didn't.'

'Were you surprised when she left?'

The man screwed up his face. 'Yes and no. I'm not sure. Emily could be unpredictable. She liked to shock people. I wondered if it was a gesture and she'd been trying to teach someone a lesson, her stepfather maybe.'

From what they'd heard, that was a distinct possibility. But Drummond didn't believe the girl he'd known as Evie would have left her mother in a situation of harm. Unless of course she didn't know Angus had been abusing Rachel.

He wondered why Stranger had said nothing about

Emily's drug habit. They'd turned and were heading back to the college building. 'Was Emily taking drugs?'

The man looked genuinely shocked. 'No, of course not.'

'Why are you so sure?' Rougvie asked.

The man paused, thinking about this. He frowned. 'I think I would have known if Emily had been taking drugs. I saw no sign of it.' He pulled a face. 'Anyway, her stepfather would never have allowed it.'

'OK,' Drummond said. 'Thank you for your help. We won't detain you any longer.'

'What happens now?' Stranger asked. 'Will you be going to see my wife?'

Drummond's mouth was a hard line. 'I think it's you who needs to speak to your wife, Mr Stranger, not us.'

Stranger swallowed. 'Yes, you're right. I'll do that.' He met Drummond's stare. 'Emily and I really were just friends, you know.'

Drummond nodded. 'Thanks for your time, sir.'

They watched him walk back through the campus.

'What did you make of that, sir? Did you believe him?' Rougvie asked.

Drummond pulled a face. 'Probably,' he said. 'But he's not off the hook yet. Maybe you could find a reason to pay him another visit after I leave? Nothing heavy, I just want him to know he's still in our sights.'

'Will do.' Rougvie nodded. They'd returned to the car and were heading back to the city. 'Is it back to the nick, sir?'

'Are you kidding?' Drummond gave him a sideways look. 'I'm depending on your local knowledge to find us the best pint in town.'

Rougvie's face split into a wide grin. 'I know just the place,' he said.

. . .

The pub Rougvie took them to was on the edge of Inverness, on the road to Dingwall. It felt homely and just far enough away from the city centre for Rougvie to be confident they were unlikely to bump into any of his colleagues.

'Not bad,' Drummond said appreciatively, taking a sip from his pint. He thought better with a glass in his hand. He liked this place.

Rougvie was watching him. 'We're right on the edge of the firth here. There's an old fishing village just behind the pub on the other side of the railway line. It's another world down there. You'd never think you were still in Inverness.'

Drummond nodded. He was beginning to feel quite mellow.

Rougvie straightened the beer mat under his pint. 'Look, tell me if I'm speaking out of turn, but I've been following this strangler business in Glasgow ever since your first call.' He hesitated. 'Is it my imagination or is there something else going on with Emily Ross?'

'Something else?' Drummond frowned.

'Well, if what I've read is right, the circumstances of Emily's death were different from the other murders. For a start the others were hookers.' He looked at Drummond and when he didn't respond he went on. 'And she was the strangler's second victim that night. He's never killed twice in the one night.'

'Not until that night,' Drummond said. 'It doesn't mean he won't be trying to do that again.'

Rougvie put down his empty glass and stared at it. 'Multiple murders in the same night? It doesn't fit the profile of killers like this.' He shook his head. 'No, I don't buy it.'

Drummond leaned back and his chair creaked. 'OK. Tell me your theory then.'

'I'm still thinking about it,' Rougvie said, standing up and nodding to Drummond's empty glass. 'Refill?'

Drummond handed him the glass. 'Thanks,' he said, watching him going to the bar. He was thinking about what Rougvie had said, his mind scrolling back to the night in the dark alley when he stood staring down at Emily's body. She had been Evie to him back then. He grimaced. What the hell – Emily...Evie? What difference did it make? She was still dead.

Rougvie returned carrying two over-filled pints. The beer slopped on the table as he put the glasses down. 'I'll have to get back after this or my boss will think we've eloped.'

Drummond reached for his pint. 'That's an idea I won't be dwelling on,' he said.

Rougvie grinned and they sat in silence for the next few minutes, each man content to give his pint the reverence it deserved.

'You think there's something different about Emily's murder too, don't you, Jack? That's why you're here in Inverness. Tell me what's going on.'

'It's a fishing expedition, Nick.' It wasn't a lie. He'd felt that by coming here to where Emily had lived might give him a better idea of who she was. It had, but he was no closer to knowing why she'd been murdered.

'But I'm not sure it's taken us any further. We still don't know what made Emily up sticks here and head for Glasgow.'

Rougvie nodded. 'Aye, it's a mystery right enough. I think our young lass has got to you, Jack.'

Drummond looked away. Rougvie was right. Emily had got to him. He felt guilty. He felt responsible for what had happened to her. He wondered what Rougvie would say if he told him the truth, but now wasn't the time for confessions. He didn't know this man well enough to trust him that much. How could Rougvie possibly understand why Emily had been staying with him when she died?

## TWENTY-TWO

DRUMMOND WAS THINKING about the approach they should take when they interviewed Angus McLeod. After what Ian Stranger told them neither of the detectives was in any doubt that McLeod abused his wife, but Rachel hadn't officially accused him. And much as Drummond itched to grill the man about Emily's death there was no scrap of evidence against him, not even circumstantial. They were hunting a killer and found a wife beater.

'McLeod's a bully and he uses people,' Drummond muttered under his breath.

But Rougvie heard him. 'Using people isn't a criminal offence.'

'Murdering them is,' Drummond said grimly. 'Don't lose track of why we're here. I'm not saying McLeod is the Glasgow Strangler, that would be too easy. But there are loose ends that need attention.'

Drummond's head was full of questions as they walked quickly through the town. The Alba Bank was an impressive old building on the corner of the main pedestrian area. It was ripe to be turned into one of those pubs where they did all day breakfasts. They pushed through the heavy glass doors and went in.

A young woman in corporate uniform colours of maroon and black came forward smiling.

Drummond returned the polite smile. 'Could your manager spare us a few minutes?'

'Do you have an appointment?'

'No.'

'He's engaged at the moment. Perhaps there's something I can do?'

As she spoke, the door to Angus McLeod's office opened and he came out, shaking a customer's hand. The smile on his face vanished when he spotted Drummond and Rougvie.

'It's fine,' Drummond said. 'He seems to be free now.' The two detectives moved across the bank. 'Mr McLeod, good morning. Can we have a word?'

The man nodded. Apart from that initial flash of discomfort Drummond registered, the bank manager appeared relaxed. 'Come through please. Can I offer you some tea?' He stepped aside as they entered the room. Both officers refused.

'Please take a seat.' Angus McLeod indicated the two chairs opposite his own place at the big wooden desk.

'Do you have more news about Emily?'

'No.' Drummond shook his head. 'I'm sorry, sir. We're still following enquiries.'

The man narrowed his eyes at Drummond. 'Enquiries that have brought you all the way from Glasgow?' He waited for a response, but the officers said nothing. 'If you have more information about Emily you must tell me,' he said.

Drummond mentioned the date Emily died. 'Where were you on that date, Mr McLeod?'

McLeod stared at him. 'What's this? Why are you asking me this?' His body had stiffened with indignation. 'You're not suggesting I had anything to do with my step-daughter's death, are you?'

Drummond smiled. 'Of course not, sir. But you of all people must expect our enquiries to be thorough. We're speaking to everyone who had any connection with Emily.'

'You think her killer knew her?' McLeod's surprised expression looked genuine. Drummond's heart sank. There was no giveaway guilt in the man's eyes, no suggestion of discomfort. Could he really be such a convincing actor?

'Like I said, sir,' Drummond continued. 'We're just ticking boxes, eliminating people. It's tedious I know but it has to be done. So, if you could just tell us where you were on that date?'

The bank manager rolled his eyes to the ceiling. They knew he was playing for time, probably weighing up whether they had already spoken to Rachel or not.

'I can double-check my diary but I'm pretty sure I was at home with my family that weekend.'

He didn't see the look that flashed between the detectives. The man was lying. Drummond just knew it. Suggesting checking his diary was clever. It was a way out for him if Rachel said he hadn't been at home that weekend. Drummond pursed his lips, nodding. His expression gave nothing away, but inside him his heart missed a beat. Who wouldn't remember what they were doing on the weekend a member of their family was murdered? It would be ingrained in their head. They would remember everything, who they were with, what was said, what they did, that knock on the door when the police called to break the news.

'If you could just check your diary then, sir,' Drummond said. He was already picturing the formal interview when they got the man down to the nick.

Angus McLeod reached into his jacket and produced a small black leather pocket diary. He flicked through the pages and nodded. 'Yes, here it is. That was the weekend we repainted the nursery.' He pushed the diary across the desk, indicating the entry. Drummond's eyebrow arched as he glanced down at the book. The entry was there, but it was hardly proof the decorating had happened on that weekend.

McLeod was already dismissing them. 'I wish I could have been of more help, Inspector. No one wants you to find Emily's killer more than my wife and I.'

'You have helped, sir.' Drummond and Rougvie got to their feet. 'We hope to have more positive news for you and your wife very soon.'

The man's eyes narrowed a fraction, hardly a response but something. 'We'll look forward to hearing from you,' he said, rising as the officers left the room. Drummond wondered how long it would be before McLeod was on the phone to Rachel. He would know they would question her. He'd want them to get their stories right.

Rougvie had to pick up his pace as he strode after Drummond. 'We need to be all over this man's life. I want to know everything about him. Emails, phone calls, social media, the whole shebang.' Drummond sounded like he was breathing fire. 'I want to know every step he takes, every person he meets, every thought that passes through his head. He's a killer, Nick. I know he is!'

# TWENTY-THREE

THE DETECTIVES TRACKING him down to his office like that had unnerved Angus. They made him feel they knew more than they'd said. Rachel was the problem. She was like a loose cannon these days and he was no longer confident he could still exercise his control over her. And that was no good at all. There was no telling what she might accuse him of, or who she might confide in. And now that the police were investigating Emily's murder, he couldn't take any chances.

Elizabeth Begg Guthrie had sparked his interest the first time he'd met her. The fact that she and her husband, the Free Church minister, the Rev Andrew Guthrie, were new to the area was even better.

He thought back to the evening when Andrew and Elizabeth had invited Rachel and himself to have supper with them at the manse.

Rachel had been reluctant to accept the invitation, but they could hardly turn it down. So, she had sat at the table with a disinterested expression, not engaging in conversation and hardly touching the roast chicken.

Andrew and Elizabeth Guthrie were a particularly dull and boring couple, but Rachel could have made an effort.

Later in the evening when they were leaving, Elizabeth Guthrie had drawn Angus aside and lowered her voice to a conspiratorial whisper. 'You must look after your poor wife, Angus. Andrew has told me what happened to your daughter. I can't imagine the kind of nightmare you must both be enduring.'

He'd looked away, making sure she'd think he was blinking back tears. Elizabeth touched his arm. 'If there is anything Andrew or I can do to help, you must tell us. We're here for you, both of us.'

He had swallowed hard so that his voice sounded emotional when he thanked her. But inside Angus was smiling. Elizabeth Guthrie was exactly the kind of gullible woman who could be useful, so long as he played his cards right.

He hadn't imposed himself on Rachel that night. She never wanted to have sex with him, but in the past she would put up a spirited struggle. He sensed there was no fight in her anymore and he didn't like that. Angus had little interest in submissive women. Elizabeth Guthrie's pale, thin face came into his mind. He tried to imagine what she and Andrew did in bed. He couldn't visualize it would be anything erotic, but you never could tell, not that it mattered. He had other plans for Elizabeth.

It was almost a week later before Angus was able to put his scheme into action. He'd paid attention when Elizabeth had talked about her daily routine and the times she went into the centre of Inverness on shopping trips. It had meant keeping an eye on the manse to watch for her leaving in the morning, but that was no problem, as manager of the Alba Bank he could come and go as he pleased, and no member of staff dared question him.

It was Wednesday morning when he found himself trailing the minister's wife into the shopping centre car park. She spent more than an hour wandering around the shops before going into a tea room in Station Road. He had his fingers crossed that she wouldn't be meeting someone there. That would put the skids on his plan. But no one joined her. This was his moment.

Angus deliberately let his shoulders slump and blinked hard as he entered the cafe, assuming the distracted body image he'd been practising. He made for the counter and ordered a pot of tea. Negotiating the occupied tables, he carried his tray to the far corner of the tea room, carefully avoiding making eye contact with anyone. He felt sure Elizabeth had seen him.

He sat with his back to the room. Had he done enough to elicit her sympathy? What if she had seen him and slipped out of the cafe, not wanting to get involved? It was the chance he was taking.

'Angus. I thought it was you.' Elizabeth Guthrie was suddenly smiling down at him.

Angus jumped to his feet, hoping he was looking sufficiently embarrassed. 'Mrs Guthrie! Sorry, I was in a world of my own there. I didn't see you coming in.'

'Elizabeth...please.' She smiled at him. 'I was already here when you came in. I have a table over there.' She hesitated. 'I was wondering if you might care to join me, but of course if you want to be on your own, I would completely understand.'

Angus gave a resigned sigh. 'I'm not very good company today I'm afraid.'

'Andrew told me the sad news about poor Emily. I am so sorry,' Elizabeth said, her blue eyes full of concern. 'Is there anything I can do?'

Angus shook his head. 'Not really, but I thank you for your kindness.'

'We are one family, Angus and our problems are for sharing.' She had slipped quietly into the seat opposite. 'I just want you to know you are not on your own. Andrew and I are here to help.' She glanced at his untouched drink. 'That must be cold. Let me get you another.' She made to stand up, but Angus put a hand on her arm. 'No, please, allow me to do this. You're being very kind to give me your time.' He resisted the urge to turn and smile. 'Things were going exactly as he'd planned, so he kept a stern face as he went to the counter and ordered more tea for the two of them. It was beginning to feel cosy.

The minister's wife gave him another one of her sympathetic looks as he returned with the tray and sat down. She put a hand over his. 'Only when you're ready,' she said softly.

Angus cleared his throat. 'It's Rachel. I'm nearly out of my mind with worry about her.' He paused, blinking. 'She's behaving so irrationally, and I don't know what to do.'

Elizabeth's brow furrowed with concern. 'In what way irrational?'

'It's difficult to talk about. She seems to have no control over her temper. It feels like she's lashing out at me all the time. I know women sometimes have emotional issues after a baby, but Archie is almost a year old now.' He glanced up. 'Surely she should be over that by now?'

Elizabeth squeezed his hand. 'You must be patient with her, Angus, especially now there's another little one on the way. You've both suffered a terrible loss. Your daughter died in a particularly cruel way. It's a dreadful thing to have to live with. Andrew and I admire both of you so much for the way you're coping with it, but maybe your wife needs an extra bit of support.'

Angus frowned. 'What kind of support?'

'I mean counselling. I think Rachel needs to talk to someone.'

'She can talk to me,' Angus snapped back.

'Can she, Angus?' Elizabeth tilted her head, watching him.

He glanced away. 'You think this is my fault...that I'm letting her down?'

'Of course not, but these situations can be difficult, and you are not a trained counsellor, are you?'

Angus's shoulders rose in a shrug. 'No, but I'm a bank manager. I listen to people's problems all the time.'

'That's different though, isn't it? The people you are dealing with are probably strangers. Rachel is your wife, the mother of your children. You can support her, certainly, but you can't give her the professional help I think she may need.'

Angus allowed his shoulders to slump. This was going even better than he'd hoped. He lifted his eyes to meet hers. 'I think Rachel is telling people I abuse her.'

Elizabeth stared at him. Angus swallowed. Had he gone too far? He shook his head as though in despair. 'I love my wife. She knows that. I would never lift my hand to her, or any woman.'

'Of course, you wouldn't,' Elizabeth said quickly. She hesitated. 'What exactly do you believe she accuses you of?'

'Striking her.' Angus drew in his breath. 'The thing is... she has bruises.'

'Bruises?' Elizabeth frowned.

Angus nodded. 'I can hardly bear to even say it, but on top of everything else...I think my wife is self-harming.'

Elizabeth gave him another wide-eyed stare. 'But that's awful!'

'I'm not concerned for myself, but we have three young children and as you say, another on the way,' Angus said. 'Rachel is like a loose cannon at the moment.'

The woman looked genuinely shocked. 'I had no idea. I'm so sorry. You must definitely seek help for your wife.'

Angus reached across the table and took Elizabeth's hands in his. She looked a little uncomfortable, but she didn't withdraw her hands. 'Thank you, Elizabeth. I just needed the courage to take the next step.'

'And you will seek help?'

'Absolutely,' he said, making a show of just having noticed the time. 'I must get back to the bank. My staff will be wondering where I've got to. Will you excuse me, Elizabeth?' He started to rise and then stopped, meeting her eyes. 'Can we keep this just between ourselves for the moment?' He let her slip her hands out of his.

She lowered her eyes. 'Of course.'

'Thank you so much,' he said. But as he turned to walk away Angus McLeod was smiling. He knew the woman wouldn't be able to resist sharing everything they had discussed with her husband. And that was exactly what he wanted. Rachel could do her worst now for he was confident that no matter how much she accused him of abusing her, no one would believe her.

## TWENTY-FOUR

DRUMMOND FEARED that if DCI Joey Buchan had been expecting this trip to the Highlands to throw any new light on the strangler murders, she was in for a disappointment. He now had to justify his reason for coming back to Inverness.

He'd parked up at his digs after leaving Nick Rougvie back at the station and gone for a wander. The pub he found in Academy Street was quiet enough to give him thinking time. Drummond knew he would be facing the music when he got back to Glasgow. He had no good reason to stay on here and yet he was reluctant to leave. Was that because he felt there was more to learn here in Inverness, or simply because he had no Joey Buchan on his back? The DCI was definitely easier to deal with at a distance. He ordered another pint and a whisky chaser as he sat morosely at a corner table trying not to remind himself that Emily's murder might be his fault. But it was no good. The girl *had* been murdered and if it was the last thing he ever did he would find her killer.

Going over each murder in his head hadn't helped in the past, but he found himself doing just that again.

The women's faces scrolled past his eyes. Maggie Burns' body had been dumped in one of the lanes behind The Barras in the centre of Glasgow. The killer couldn't have found a busier spot if he'd tried. They almost missed the card with the silhouette images of the cat and mouse. It had been under the body. At the time they considered it was something that could have fallen from the killer's pocket, but there had been no fingerprints on it, no DNA clues. The card had been put there on purpose. But why?

Bonnie Brennan, the second victim, had been found miles away on open waste ground in Pollockshaws. The discovery of the cat and mouse card confirmed the killer was taunting them, challenging them to catch him. Drummond conceded it was the part of the investigation that wound him up most. The killer was playing with them. And that was personal!

He thought about Lena Murray. She too had been strangled and her body tossed into the River Kelvin. Why the river? Was the strangler smart enough to work out that water destroyed evidence? It hadn't destroyed the killer's cat and mouse calling card that had later been found in her pocket.

And then there was Carol Nicholson, victim number four. As before, the card had been left for them to discover. The body had been found in the grounds of a Gorbals' church, only a few hundred metres from her home. Had that been deliberate? Had the strangler known these women before he selected them for his victims?

The women had all been working as prostitutes. He left their bodies in places where they could be found. And they had all been strangled with similar scarfs. There was a definite pattern to the killings, until Emily Ross. What was different about her? Why had the killer changed tack? Two victims in the same night – and no card found with poor little Emily's body. Why?

The scene in the dank miserable alley where they'd discovered Emily kept flashing through his mind. He frowned, throwing back the last dregs of his whisky. He didn't believe the one the press had nicknamed the Glasgow Strangler had killed Emily. Or had he? Drummond needed to think more logically about all of this.

The strangler planned his killings with precision. He was clever, meticulous. But what if he came upon Emily that night after he'd killed Carol Nicholson? Could he have resisted murdering again, even if he hadn't been prepared for it? Drummond sighed. He supposed it was possible, but he wasn't convinced.

And how did the killer happen to be in that alley? It didn't make any sense. He had already killed that night. Their criminal psychologist Francine Janus could give no good reason why he'd changed his pattern of behaviour. Had he gone looking for another prostitute and found Emily Ross? Maybe she propositioned him for business and he couldn't refuse? But then that didn't fit either because Emily had been killed in the alley where her body had been found and the strangler always removed his victims from the original murder scene and dumped them somewhere else in the city.

His shoulders jerked up and he blinked. They'd thought the reason the killer moved his victims from the place where he strangled them was to eliminate any chance of them finding forensic evidence. But what if he actually murdered his victims in his car? It was a possibility they had considered and although they were ruling nothing out it wasn't

one of their favoured possibilities. Maybe it was worth revis-
iting? Drummond tried to imagine the scenario. There
wouldn't have been much space if the strangler's car was a
regular saloon type. None of the witnesses had mentioned
seeing a van. The victims had been strangled from behind.
According the post-mortem reports the scarf that was used
in each case had most likely been placed around the victim's
throat and twisted violently from behind.

Drummond sipped his pint. What would have induced
that violence? The strangler clearly hated his victims. But
why? Francine Janus would suggest he was murdering the
mother he hated. If that was true, where was this mother?
Was she still living? Had she been their strangler's first
victim – one they didn't even know about? If so, where was
the body? He was trying to put himself in the killer's shoes.
Why did he hate his mother? Was she a prostitute like his
other victims? Had the discovery of that incensed him and
turned an already unbalanced mind into something even
more sinister?

Drummond's thoughts kept returning to Emily Ross.
Again, he considered the possibility that the killer had gone
wandering the city centre streets that night after killing
Carol Nicholson and dumping her at the church. The site
wasn't that far away from the city centre. Is that how he'd
come upon Emily? Had he spotted her by chance and
followed her into the alley? He was forcing himself to
picture the scene. A shiver raced up his back. In his mind's
eye he could see Emily in her short skirt and high heels
looking over her shoulder as she disappeared into the alley
to inject herself.

He frowned into his pint. Emily must have looked like
easy prey. Is that what had got her murdered? Had the
strangler spotted her and been unable to resist taking a

second victim that night? Had the urge been so strong that he'd abandoned his usual planned scenario? They had to go over that murder scene again. If Emily's murder hadn't been planned, then the killer could have left evidence.

Drummond reached slowly for the pint he'd just had refilled. He was still thinking. Emily's body hadn't been moved. Why? Was it because the killer hadn't had time? Most of the night would have been taken up selecting his victim, Carol Nicholson, taking her off and killing her and then dumping her body at the church. His frown deepened. So how did he come to be in that alley?

The ringing of his mobile phone broke his train of thought. He reached into his jacket pocket. It was Nick Rougvie.

'Are you still in Inverness?' he asked.

Drummond's spirits rose. He liked the man. Was he going to suggest they meet up again?

'I am as it happens.'

'Great. Come and have supper with us then.'

Drummond pulled a face. It wasn't what he'd been expecting. 'Thanks, but I'll pass on that if you don't mind. I've got stuff to do.'

'We all have to eat, Jack. It won't be a three-course meal, nothing fancy. Elaine says there's plenty.'

Drummond hesitated. Apart from family gatherings, which he couldn't get out of, and the occasional meal he shared with Pete, he didn't get too many invitations to people's homes. 'Honestly, Nick. I'm fine,' he persisted.

But Rougvie had caught the hesitation in his response. 'My wife will take your refusal as a slight on her cooking skills. Come on, Jack. You only need to stay for an hour. I'll pick you up.'

Drummond gave a deep sigh. He could tell he wasn't

going to get out of this. 'OK, I give up. Tell your missus I'll be there, but you don't have to pick me up. Give me your address and I'll get a taxi.'

Drummond scribbled down the details and went back to his drink. He had no idea why he'd allowed himself to be talked into this. A fish supper from the nearest chippy would have done him, but it was his last night in Inverness and probably the last time he would see Rougvie. The man had gone the extra mile to help him. Having a meal with his family was the least he could do. He picked up his glass again and sighed.

The taxi pulled up outside a smart semi-detached villa, not far from the town centre. 'Is this it?' Drummond said, looking along the street.

'It's the address you gave me,' the driver said as Drummond got out of the car and searched his pockets for cash to pay the fare.

Nick Rougvie must have been watching for him because the front door opened as the taxi drove off and he stood there grinning. He had changed from his shirt and tie of earlier into jeans and a red V-necked sweater. 'Come through, Jack. We're in the kitchen.'

The delicious aroma that greeted him set Drummond's juices going. 'This is Elaine,' he said, as the woman stacking plates into the oven to warm turned and smiled. Her cheeks were flushed from the heat of the oven, which made the green of her eyes even more intense. 'Hello, Jack,' she said, pushing away shiny black hair with the back of her hand. 'Sit yourself down.' She nodded to the table that had been set for the three of them.

'Smells great,' Drummond said, suddenly feeling embarrassed. Elaine Rougvie was considerably younger than her husband...and attractive.

'Red or white?' Rougvie had a bottle of wine in each hand. 'We give ourselves permission to have a glass of wine once the kids are in bed.'

'Red would be great, thanks.'

'You don't mind eating in the kitchen, do you?' Elaine took the glass Nick was offering.

'It's fine by me.' Drummond took a gulp of his wine then reminded himself he wasn't in the pub any more. He needed to watch his manners. Rougvie wouldn't be bothered, but he suspected his wife might be more critical.

'I wasn't sure you'd still be in Inverness,' Rougvie said. 'Are you staying on for a while then?'

Drummond shook his head. 'No, I'll be on my way first thing in the morning. I should really have gone back today but the room's already booked and paid for.'

He was aware of Elaine watching him over the rim of her glass. 'Is this your first time in the Highlands, Jack?' she asked.

'Pretty much. I was here with my folks when I was young. I remember being on a boat but that's about all.'

'That would be Loch Ness,' she said. 'We took the kids out for a trip during the school holidays. They loved it.' A timer went off and Elaine turned back to the cooker.

'Was it worth your while coming up here?' Rougvie asked. 'We didn't exactly discover much.'

'No, but it helps to be able to fill in some background.' He knew more about Emily now, only it had been like people were describing another girl from the one he had known as Evie.

Elaine had been serving out their food on the worktop beside the cooker and was now placing Drummond's plate in front of him. 'Only mince and tatties I'm afraid,' she said.

If he had been in any doubt about how famished he was, that had long gone. The mince and tatties looked fabulously appetizing.

'Tuck in, don't wait for us,' she said.

Drummond took her at her word. This kind of homely food beat what was served in the high-class Glasgow restaurants any day. It reminded him of school dinners and sitting around the kitchen table at home when he was a kid. His mother had prided herself on her mince and tatties. She got no complaints from him or his older brother, Daniel. Elaine's cooking matched up to that just fine. He'd cleared his plate in no time and accepted second helpings.

'There's an apple crumble in the oven if you have room for it.' Elaine smiled.

'You're spoiling me.' Drummond sat back feeling pleasantly full.

'I'm glad you enjoyed it,' she said, collecting their empty plates. 'Nick doesn't often bring colleagues home.'

Drummond threw Rougvie a look, watching him sip his wine. 'He's been a great help today.'

The man shrugged. 'Just doing my job.'

'And the rest,' Drummond said.

Elaine had put the dishes on the worktop and was busy stirring a pan of custard to go with their crumble. Rougvie leaned forward. 'Can I have a word before you go, Jack? I want to run something past you.'

'Of course,' Drummond said, his curiosity stirred.

The pudding Elaine produced was as delicious as it looked. 'That was just great. Thank you, Elaine,' Drummond said, not sure if he should offer to help with the washing up. But Rougvie came to the rescue.

'You go through and put your feet up, love. Jack and I will clear up.'

'I was going to make coffee,' Elaine protested.

'We'll do that too,' he said.

'Well, if you're sure.' She left the room with a backward glance.

Rougvie began clattering plates into the dishwasher.

'So, what's this thing you wanted to run past me?' Drummond asked, scraping a pot into the bin before handing it over.

'It's about Ian Stranger. He made out he was shocked when you asked if he suspected Emily Ross had been taking drugs.'

Drummond gave him a look. 'You thought he was acting?'

'I don't know, but we should take another look at him.'

'Fine by me,' Drummond said. 'What did you make of Angus McLeod?'

Rougvie stacked the final plate into the dishwasher and turned it on. He straightened up. 'Nasty man. After what Stranger told us I wouldn't be surprised if he was the reason Emily left.'

'Do you think he could have killed her?' Drummond raised an eyebrow.

'It's possible I suppose, if we've definitely ruled out the strangler. Maybe Angus tracked Emily down to Glasgow and lost the rag when she refused to return home with him.' He caught Drummond's expression. 'I take it we *have* ruled out the strangler?'

'Not entirely,' Drummond said. 'What if we've been looking at this the wrong way round? We've been thinking the strangler killed the four prostitutes and that Emily's murder was different and therefore we had a different killer.

What if it was the strangler who killed Emily and it's the other murders that are different?'

Rougvie screwed up his face. 'You think it might be the same killer? Are you saying the first four murders were just a cover-up for the killer's real intention to kill Emily Ross?' He flashed a look back to Drummond. 'You still suspect Angus McLeod is our man, don't you, Jack?'

# TWENTY-FIVE

When Drummond rang DCI Joey Buchan next morning she wasn't buying his reasoning for why he should stay on in Inverness. Not even when he told her his theory about Angus McLeod.

'You're fanaticizing, Jack,' she spat at him. 'Get yourself back here. This is where the killer's operating, not up there in the highlands.'

'I have a gut feeling about this man, Joey. You have to let me stay on here and do some more digging.'

He could hear her irritated sigh over the phone. 'Didn't you hear me? I said come back and that's my last word on it.'

Drummond stared out across the fast-moving River Ness for a few seconds after Joey cut the call. The water looked black and angry this morning. Joey Buchan was wrong, but it wouldn't help to be ruffling her feathers, not when he was still planning to turn up the heat. He would do as she said. He would return to Glasgow, but only for now. Angus was still a person of serious interest in this case. He just needed to convince his DCI of that.

He left Inverness after a hearty breakfast at the River

Inn, pleased that the road out of town was quiet. His last conversation with Rougvie kept circling through his mind. He was sure Angus McLeod was their killer, but as he'd told Joey, it was a gut feeling and you didn't get convictions on that. He needed evidence. He needed to speak to Rachel again.

Drummond was scowling as he strutted into the incident room early that afternoon. A few colleagues looked up from their work and nodded as he passed.

'Nice of you to join us, Inspector,' Joey Buchan said over his shoulder as he reached his desk.

'Anything new I need to know about?' Drummond asked.

Joey shook her head. 'That's why I need you back here. I expect you to dig out something new for us.' She glanced at his desk. 'There's also a bit of paperwork to catch up on.' Her smile wasn't warm. 'I should get started if I were you.'

Drummond stared sullenly at the papers spilling from his in-tray and cursed. As far as he could see, the team had made no headway on the case since he'd been away, but at least the killer hadn't been busy again. There had been no new murders.

DC Gail Swann was smiling as she walked up to his desk. 'Good trip, sir?'

'Feels like I've never been away,' he said. 'Actually, if you've got a minute, I'd like to run something past you.'

'Go on,' she said.

'Not here. Come on, I'll stand you a coffee.'

The lunchtime rush was over, and the canteen was quiet as they walked in. 'Grab a table,' he said, heading off to buy their drinks.

He came back with them and watched Gail reach for one and take a sip, screwing up her nose.

'Horrible, eh?' he grinned.

She nodded, leaning in towards him. 'So, what's this thing you wanted to run past me?'

'What was your impression of Angus McLeod?'

'McLeod? Domineering, a bit of a bully I suppose.'

'Do you think he could be the strangler?'

She stared at him. 'Well, no. I don't see how he could be. Surely our killer is right here in Glasgow?'

'It's only a four-hour drive,' Drummond said.

'Well, yes, but why McLeod? Is there any evidence that points at him?'

'None whatsoever,' Drummond said. 'But it's him. I feel it in my bones. The man's a killer – and he's done it more than once.'

Gail put up a hand. 'Wait, let me get this straight. You're saying Angus McLeod is the Glasgow Strangler because you have *a feeling* he is?'

'OK, I know it won't stand up in court, but I'll get the evidence. What I really want from you, Gail, is support. I want you to back me up when I try to impress on Joey the importance of going back to Inverness. It's up there I need to be digging.'

'Well, yes, I agree. If you're right about McLeod, you need the evidence.' She paused, thinking. 'The girl in the alley didn't fit the profile though. Surely that had to be a completely different killer.'

'Or the same one trying to throw us off the track,' he said, meeting her eyes. 'So, what do you say? Are you with me on this, Gail?'

She shrugged and pushed the remains of her coffee away. 'Why not? What do you want me to do?'

'Just back me up when I speak to Joey.'

The DCI was waiting for them when they got back to the incident room. 'A word please,' she said, beckoning Drummond over. 'If Mohammed can't go to the mountain, we bring the mountain to Mohammed.' She smiled as though she was enjoying herself. 'I know this isn't maybe what you had in mind given this fixation you have about the strangler living in Inverness, but it's the best I could do.' She called out to the door. 'You can come in now, DS Rougvie.'

Drummond's mouth fell open as he watched the big man approach. Rougvie's expression was sheepish.

'I warned DS Rougvie not to tell you he had been seconded to the team, DI Drummond.' She smiled. 'Surprises are always better, don't you think?'

Rougvie raised his wide shoulders in a shrug. 'Sorry, sir. I was under orders.'

Drummond got up and offered his hand. 'No, it's fine. Good to have you on board.' He raised an eyebrow at Joey. She smiled.

'Right, if everybody is happy then maybe we can get on with some work.'

The morning briefing didn't throw up any new leads. It seemed to Drummond that they were all floundering in the dark. 'What about the killer's calling cards? Still nothing on them?' Drummond asked.

Joey looked at DC Dale McQueen.

'Nothing,' the man said. 'The cards are on sale all over the UK. Every branch of Tesco sells them. The ink the killer used to draw the silhouettes is just a cheap marker pen, also available everywhere.'

'Still no fingerprints or DNA?' Drummond interrupted.

The detective shook his head. 'Nothing. Our strangler is too clever to leave evidence like that.'

'He'll slip up. They always do,' Gail said.

Joey moved her bottom off the desk she had perched on. 'Well he needs to do it pretty damn quick because right now he's making us all look like charlies.'

A murmur went around the incident room as the briefing came to an end. Rougvie came up to him.

'Are you pissed off with me for not telling you I was coming down?'

'Don't worry about it. The DCI's just playing games. How long are you here for?'

'Days rather than weeks. Truth be told I could be called back at any time. As soon as work picks up again in Inverness, I'll be off.' He glanced around him at all the empty desks.

'They're all out on enquiries, or skiving, depends how you look at it,' Drummond said.

'No progress on McLeod?' Rougvie asked.

'Still working on it.' He screwed up his face. 'I should be back in Inverness. We both should. That's where all the answers are.'

'I'm guessing your DCI saw bringing me here as the best of a bad deal. I know Inverness, so if the case does start to point in that direction, I might have some insider knowledge.'

Drummond laughed. 'And you're going along with that?'

'Don't be daft. I just didn't want to get cut out of the case. We work well together, don't you think?'

Drummond rolled his eyes and then grinned at Rougvie. 'OK, if you're that keen you can come with me tonight.'

'Where are we going?'

'To the red-light district. It's time to further your education, young man.'

'What? You mean surveillance?' Rougvie sounded surprised.

'Not exactly surveillance. The thing is we have no idea where the strangler is going to turn up, or when. No, I just want to have a saunter about, keeping my eyes open.'

'I take it this is not official?'

Drummond gave him a sideways look.

'You'll have to watch you don't get nabbed for kerb crawling.' Rougvie grinned.

'They wouldn't dare. Anyway, that's what I'll be doing tonight. You're welcome to join me, but you'll have to choose your own beat. If we both turn up in the same place it might look like a parade.'

'Fine. I'll sort myself out.'

'No heroics mind,' Drummond said. 'Even if you do spot something suspicious, you'll have no backup.'

'Same applies to you too, Jack.'

'Don't worry about me. I'll be looking after myself. Just make sure you'll be doing the same. And remember, pull out if you think you've been spotted.'

Rougvie had no intention of placing himself in any danger. Elaine would have too much to say about that. Anyway, he wasn't that brave. It was just before 11 p.m. when he parked up in the dark side street. He was aware that he would stick out like a sore thumb to the working women if he began wandering about their patch. They'd know immediately that he was a cop. But it wasn't the women he was here to watch. He found a doorway that gave him a good view of the area without announcing his presence and settled in to watch. Plenty of punters seemed to be cruising around. Some slowed, looking cautiously around them and stopping when one of the women stepped forward. Rougvie watched as the car doors opened and the woman got in and the car sped off again. Other vehicles slowed but went on their way without stopping.

He blew out his cheeks. This was not one of Drummond's best ideas. Any one of these drivers picking up the hookers could be their man and there was absolutely nothing he could do about it.

He was about to call it a night when a dark vehicle cruised slowly past him. He must have made a movement in his doorway because the driver glanced briefly in his direction, but Rougvie had pulled back quickly. He didn't think the driver had seen him. His own glimpse had been only for a split second, just long enough to register the dark-rimmed spectacles. He watched the car cruise slowly along the road, but it didn't stop, even though a couple of the women had stepped forward expectantly.

Rougvie hung on, curious to know if the vehicle would return, but after another thirty minutes there was no sign of it. A clean, warm bed was waiting for him back at his B&B. He had no motivation to hang around any longer, so he turned, making his way back to his car and left as unobtrusively as he had arrived.

## TWENTY-SIX

THEY MET in the police canteen next morning to compare notes about the previous night's surveillance. 'Sounds like we both wasted our time.' Drummond sighed.

Rougvie's mobile buzzed and he picked it up. 'What, today? I've only just got here.' He frowned at his phone. The other person seemed to have ended the call. 'They want me back in Inverness,' he said.

Drummond shrugged. 'Our man's killing spree hasn't finished,' he said. 'He's just biding his time.'

'You can't know he'll kill again.'

'Oh, I do. Believe me, he's not done.'

'I'm sorry, Jack. I wish I could have done more.'

Drummond rubbed his fingers over his face trying to ease away the tiredness. He hadn't been sleeping. Five women were dead, but it was Evie – he would always think of her as Evie – who was really obsessing him. She might not have gone out that night if she hadn't found his cash. If he hadn't allowed her to stay in his flat in the first place things might have worked out differently. The guilt he felt sat like a heavy anvil on his shoulders.

'Don't apologize,' he said. 'It's hardly your fault we haven't caught him. When do you have to head back?'

Rougvie drained his coffee. 'Pretty much straight away.'

Drummond was about to finish the dregs of his own drink when his mobile buzzed in his jacket pocket. He fished it out and squinted at the ID. 'It's Her Majesty. She doesn't get the principle of personal time. We're not on duty for another twenty minutes.' He tapped the phone. 'DCI Buchan. Hi, what can I do for you?'

Her answer had Drummond jerking bolt upright.

'He's back, Jack!' she said. Every muscle in Drummond's body tensed. 'But it's not all bad news. This time his victim got away.' She paused for him to take this in. 'We've got a witness, Jack.' He could hear the excitement in her voice. 'We've only got ourselves a bloody witness.'

Drummond's body was pulsing. This had to be the break they were waiting for. 'Where is she?'

Rougvie was on the edge of his seat, his eyes fixed on Drummond's face.

'She managed to stumble back to Blythswood Square. One of the other hookers called an ambulance. She's at A&E in the Western Infirmary.'

'I'm on my way.' Drummond was already on his feet, striding out of the pub with Rougvie at his heels. 'What's her name?' he barked into the phone.

'Joanna Flugg,' Joey Buchan said.

They took Rougvie's car and headed across the city. Drummond could feel the urgency throbbing inside him. Would they finally get a description of their man? Maybe even DNA?

The two detectives were heading for the curtained cubicle

at the far end of hospital's A&E department. Drummond already knew what the woman would look like. All four previous victims had been the same – artificially blonde, about five foot four, and brassy. And then there was Evie. For all her bravado Drummond knew it had been an act to hide how vulnerable he was sure she really was.

Joanna Flugg was on a trolley, her knees drawn up to her chin. Her face and neck were badly bruised, and she was trembling uncontrollably. Her eyes flew to Drummond as he pulled back the curtain. "Ave you got 'im?' she demanded, her voice shaking. 'Have you caught 'im? Have you got the bastard?' Her cockney accent sounded seriously out of place here.

'We will.' Drummond tried to sound reassuring. 'Half the force is out there now combing the streets.'

'I'll take that as a "no" then. He's probably out there right now with 'is 'ands around some other poor cow's throat.' She raised her hand to her neck and fingered the bruises.

Drummond shot Rougvie an uneasy look. 'We will catch him, Joanna. I promise you.'

Her eyes went from one to the other. 'I'd like to see your IDs before I say another thing.'

Both men held up their warrant cards. He was trying to conceal his impatience. 'Can you tell us what happened?'

The woman shivered and looked away. 'Take your time,' Rougvie said more gently. 'We know how difficult this must be for you.'

'I thought 'e was a regular punter. I got into 'is car and 'e took off across the city. We parked up in a back lane off Sauchiehall Street and 'e told me to get into the back.'

'What kind of car?' Drummond interrupted.

'Don't know.' She screwed up her eyes, 'It was big and

dark. It could have been old. I could smell leather upholstery.'

Both men nodded.

'I got in the back and 'e climbed in beside me. I wasn't happy about that. Usually if it's just a blow a job the punter wants to get on with it. 'E don't faff about wanting to get in the back.' She swallowed. 'It was weird. 'E just sat there staring at me.' She touched her long, straggly blonde hair. 'Then 'e moved me 'air off me face. 'E was staring into me eyes. That's when I decided to run.'

'You realized he could be the strangler?' Rougvie said.

Joanna shook her head. 'No, not that. Believe me, I'd 'ave kicked the balls off him if I'd thought that. No, I just didn't feel comfortable. I mean there's weird and there's weird. I just wanted to get out of there. I reached for the door 'andle, but 'e grabbed me arm and forced it up behind me back. The pain was excruciating. I yelled, screaming at 'im to let me go.

'We struggled. 'E was trying to yank me other arm back but I wasn't going to let that 'appen. I just kept lashing out. I remember scratching at 'is face. That's when 'e punched me. 'E was trying to force this rag thing round me neck. 'E kept calling me Jezebel...an evil Jezebel. Jesus – who the hell is Jezebel?'

Rougvie was about to answer but Drummond held up a warning hand. 'Go on,' he urged.

Joanna Flugg shrugged. 'That's about it.'

'Can you describe this man?' Drummond asked.

She shook her head. 'I didn't see 'is face. 'E was big though, bigger than me.' She looked at Drummond. 'I don't suppose you've got a fag?'

Drummond signalled for the uniformed cop at the door to find cigarettes.

'You're doing great, Joanna, anything else about him strike you as odd?'

'Is that not enough?' The door opened and the officer came in carrying a packet of Marlboro. The woman held out her hand for them. 'Thanks, mate. Did you bring the matches?'

The man pulled out a lighter as Joanna slid out a cigarette. He lit it for her, and she took a deep drag, dropping her head back, apparently enjoying the feel of the smoke in her throat. Her eyes closed to slits as she blew out the smoke.

''E talked funny,' she said.

Rougvie and Drummond exchanged a look. 'Talked funny? You mean he had a stammer, something like that?'

'No, it wasn't it stammer. It was the way 'e spoke.' She took another drag on the cigarette and the tip burned red. 'But then all you Scotties talk funny.'

'You mean he had a Scottish accent?'

She shrugged. 'I suppose so.'

'OK,' Drummond said, his eyes on her face. 'When you say accent, do you mean a Glasgow accent like mine?'

Joanna pursed her lips, thinking. 'No not like you.' She raised her arm and pointed to Rougvie. 'More like 'im.'

Rougvie and Drummond stared at each other. 'Sergeant Rougvie is from Inverness. Are you saying your attacker sounded like him?'

Joanna Flugg nodded. 'Suppose I am.'

They were out of the cubicle when she called after them. ''E had glasses. Did I mention that? Bloody great black-rimmed spectacles.'

Rougvie was first back by her side. 'Black-rimmed spectacles? Are you sure?'

The woman shrugged. 'I said so, didn't I?' She took

another deep drag of her cigarette. 'Like some kind of professor 'e was.'

Drummond was on his phone before they'd even got out of the unit. 'We need to get people down here ASAP. I want samples taken from our witness. She says she scratched her attacker's face. We might have his DNA.'

There was a light in his eye when he finished the call.

'Are you thinking what I'm thinking?' Rougvie said.

'I'm thinking what we've just been told narrows the field, that's supposing we can believe her.' He gestured to the PC on watch outside the A&E, calling him over. 'I want you to check everyone entering or leaving this unit, and that means the staff too. I don't want any unauthorized person anywhere near here, which means I don't want our witness having any visitors we don't know about. On no account is she to be allowed to leave the ward. If she attempts to go, you will tell her we're keeping her here for her own protection. If it was our man who attacked her then he might come back to finish the job.'

A worried look flashed across the officer's face. Drummond put a hand on his arm. 'Don't worry, son. Just do your job and stay vigilant.'

He marched off, turning to Rougvie. 'I'd feel more confident if it was you that was posted here at the hospital, Nick.'

Rougvie glanced back to the officer who'd now adopted an officious-looking stance. 'He'll be fine,' he said. 'So what's our thinking about what Ms Flugg says? Are we looking for a Highland man?'

'Could be,' Drummond muttered. 'I just don't know how much we can trust her instincts. We only know for sure that she was attacked by a man who tried to choke her. We don't know it was our killer.'

Rougvie screwed up his face. 'Well what about the

Inverness accent? Why wouldn't the killer be from the Highlands? I'll bet there's plenty Highland folk in Glasgow.'

Drummond was frowning. 'He called her a Jezebel. Does that suggest some kind of religious fanatic to you?'

Rougvie gave him a sideways glance. Drummond went on. 'A Highland accent, a religious nut, a big bully who hates women – does that description fit anybody we know?'

Nick Rougvie blew out his cheeks. 'You're thinking about Angus McLeod, aren't you?'

Drummond said nothing.

Rougvie sighed. 'He doesn't wear dark-rimmed specs, and his hair's not black. He's also four hundred miles away in Inverness.'

'It's only a four-hour drive. I keep telling folk that but nobody's listening.'

'Why would McLeod come here when he could kill just as easily on his own doorstep?'

The thought sent a chill through Rougvie. They were back in the hospital car park. 'One of the kerb crawlers I saw last night was wearing the kind of spectacles Joanna Flugg described.' he said.

Drummond watched an ambulance scream past them and come to an abrupt halt at the entrance to A&E. 'It's hardly evidence, Nick.'

Rougvie shrugged. 'It was the right area.'

'Do you remember anything else about him?'

'No. I'm doubting now if he was even wearing those specs. It was dark.'

'I don't suppose you got a reg number?'

'No. Sorry. It was just somebody who drove past me. He was alone in the car though.'

'I doubt if this bloke had anything to do with this, but we can keep him in mind if you like. I'd much rather concentrate on Angus McLeod. As far as we know there were no victims before Maggie Burns was strangled and her body dumped at The Barras.'

'No victims we know about,' Rougvie said.

'I know that, but just stick with me for a minute. If Maggie was his first victim then something must have triggered that killing.'

Rougvie nodded. 'We could check up on him, find out if he was away from home on that date. That would be a start.' He turned to Drummond. 'Does this mean you'll be coming back to Inverness with me?'

'I'll need to do a bit more digging here first, but yes. I don't see any other options. We need to speak to Rachel McLeod.'

Back at the incident room things were quiet. Everyone was out on enquiries. Joey Buchan came out of her office. 'What've we got?' she asked as she came up to them.

Drummond gave her a quick résumé of their brief interview with Joanna Flugg.

'How is she?' Joey enquired.

'She'll live,' Drummond said.

'We need to get her in here for a proper interview.' She turned to Drummond. 'What's your gut instinct, Jack? Was this the strangler?'

'Could be. We might know more when we get the DNA results.'

'How's that going to help when we don't have our killer's DNA?'

'No, but if we can match our suspect up with the DNA.'

Joey Buchan's head snapped up. 'We have a suspect?'

Drummond slid Rougvie a look. 'It's all circumstantial at

this stage but there are a few things we need to check out with Emily Ross's stepfather.' He met her stare. 'The murders started around the same time as Emily left home. Maybe he came to Glasgow to find her.'

Joey pulled a face. 'It's a bit of a long shot, isn't it?'

Drummond described their brief interview with Joanna Flugg. 'Our man was giving her some religious speak – and he had a Highland accent.'

'And you think that's enough to focus on the stepfather?' She turned to Rougvie. 'What's your call on this, DS Rougvie?'

'We need to speak to McLeod, Ma'am.'

'OK,' Joey said, pulling out a chair and sitting down. 'Convince me.'

Drummond and Rougvie gave a detailed account of the information people had given them about the man. 'According to one of Evie's friends, she hated her stepfather. He believes she ran away to get away from him.'

DCI Buchan listened, not interrupting until he'd finished. She slowly got to her feet. 'OK you can go there in the morning, but no messing about. Speak to this McLeod and get back here.' She turned her attention to Rougvie. 'You can get yourself back to Inverness now too. I'll ring your boss and explain why you've been delayed.'

## TWENTY-SEVEN

IT WAS 4 a.m. and the quiet streets glistened from the overnight rain as Drummond drove out of the city. Being about at this hour always felt unreal. The late-night clubs had emptied, but some of their hung-over clients were still making their unsteady way home.

Few other vehicles were on the roads at this hour and the closed shops Drummond drove past looked lonely and forlorn as they waited for their workers to arrive and start the new day. He was looking forward to the drive. It would give him time to consider and weigh up the possibilities that yesterday had thrown up.

Could Angus McLeod really be their man? They would have to be careful how they approached him. The killer was clever. He knew all the tricks. But the fact that he'd allowed his latest victim to get away showed he wasn't invincible. He wouldn't like that. He would know she was giving them information that could lead to him being caught.

Once again Drummond tried to put himself in the man's shoes. What would he do? The strangler could go to ground. He mulled over that possibility, but he'd need to be a loner without any family ties to do that. And if Angus McLeod was their killer, he couldn't afford to behave differently. Or could he?

Would he be taking his frustration out on wife Rachel even now? What if he was still in Glasgow trying to find a way to silence Joanna Flugg? Had they jumped in at the deep end with absolutely no evidence that McLeod was involved in these killings?

Drummond frowned. He would have to keep reminding himself that this was just another exercise to cross a potential suspect off their list. Even thinking of the man as a suspect was a shot in the dark.

It was easily resolved though. If Rachel McLeod could verify that Angus had slept with her all night and never left the house, then he wasn't their man. And he had to admit that this was the most likely scenario.

He made good time and Drummond's spirits rose as the soaring parapets of the Kessock Bridge came into view.

He'd acted on impulse leaving Glasgow so early, insisting on taking his own car. He didn't fancy being left high and dry in Inverness without transport. For the first time he wondered where Rougvie was. They should have convoyed, but he'd been too impatient to get there. He'd ring Rougvie and arrange for them to see Angus McLeod together.

He checked his dashboard clock. It was almost 8 a.m. and the traffic was building as he drove through the Longman Estate. It was almost a reflex action to head for the McLeod house. He didn't need to actually knock the door but keeping the place under surveillance until Rougvie turned up would be no bad thing.

As soon as Drummond turned into the road, he could see the car in the drive. It all looked so normal. His heart sank. Could McLeod really have driven to Glasgow the previous day, attempted to murder Joanna Flugg and then calmly returned to Inverness in time for work that morning? What had felt like a possibility in Glasgow yesterday was now looking highly unlikely.

His phone rang just as the man emerged from the front door, businesslike as always in a grey pinstriped suit and carrying a black leather briefcase.

He didn't look like a man who strangled women.

Drummond raised the instrument to his ear. 'Hi, Nick. Sorry, I should have called you.'

'No worries,' Rougvie said. 'I'm having a bacon roll at a cafe. Where are you?'

Drummond watched Angus McLeod carefully reverse his car out of his drive. 'I'm here at the McLeod place,' he said. He could almost imagine the face Nick Rougvie was pulling at the other end.

'I thought we were going to do this together?'

'We are, if you stop feeding your face and get a move on.'

'It sounds like you might feel better if you fed your face. Didn't you even sleep last night, Jack?'

'Not a lot. I just wanted to get here.'

Rougvie sighed. 'OK. Well, why don't you relax and grab a bit of breakfast. I should be with you in an hour and a half.'

Drummond slid down out of sight as Angus McLeod drove past him. 'Yeah,' he said. 'Maybe I will.'


The barman at the River Inn didn't look in the least surprised to see him walking in. 'So, you're back,' he said. 'The bar's not open yet.'

'It's breakfast I'm after, Colin, the biggest and best you've got.'

Colin Ridley nodded to a table. 'Sit yourself down I'll see what we can do.'

Drummond watched him go off to the kitchen and smiled. He was looking forward to this. While he waited, he texted Rougvie to meet him here, suggesting he called in at home first. The anticipation of food was mellowing him. "Say hello to Elaine for me."

The reply pinged back immediately. "Will do. Thanks Jack."

Drummond had demolished a huge Scottish breakfast right down to the fried tattie scone and was outside the pub staring thoughtfully at the fast-flowing river when Rougvie arrived. 'I should call in at the station and let them know I'm back,' he said, coming to stand beside him.

'If you do that, they might not let you out to play. Ring your guv and put him in the picture. I'll call him later and explain I need you for this morning's investigation. I need your local knowledge.'

Rougvie got out his phone. 'Let's hope Joey Buchan has persuaded him to let me stay on board this case,' he said as he tapped the number.

Drummond watched his body language as he strolled off, talking into his phone. It didn't appear to be going well. Rougvie came back, frowning. 'Your DCI rang him, but I don't think he was listening. He's told me to get back to the station.'

Drummond pulled a face. Shit! He'd called Joey Buchan earlier to let her know he and Rougvie were both back in Inverness and about to visit Angus McLeod's wife. 'I'm not sure this isn't going to turn out to be a wild goose chase, Jack, but keep me informed,' she'd said, adding. 'And keep it tight. I don't want you two going off-road on this.' Drummond assured her this wouldn't happen.

But now he was back with Rougvie and nodding to his car. 'You drive. Let's see what Rachel has to tell us.'

Rougvie stared at him. 'Did you not you hear what I just said?

'Don't walk out on me now, Nick. I'll clear it with your DCI Fraser. This visit won't take long. Trust me.'

Rougvie sighed. 'An hour then, I'll give you an hour.'

The McLeod house was only minutes away. They drove there and sat outside, each man with his own thoughts. If Rachel gave her husband an alibi and said he'd been at home all the previous night, then Angus McLeod was off the hook and the investigation was back to square one. Drummond took a deep breath, making a conscious effort to calm his rising nerves. 'If I've got the family routine right, the twins should be next door with the neighbour by now,' he said, hoping baby Archie would also be settled in his play pen and Rachel free to talk to them. He could hear Rougvie's intake of breath and knew the man shared his nerves.

They got out of the car and approached the front door. Rachel must have spotted them as they came up the path, for the door opened before Drummond knocked.

'You've got news?' she said, her eyes lighting up expectantly.

Drummond put up a hand. 'Sorry, no. Just more routine enquiries. May we come in?'

Rachel McLeod's shoulders slumped. 'Of course,' she said flatly, stepping back to let them pass her into the house. 'I'm in the kitchen. I suppose you'll want coffee.'

Drummond and Rougvie exchanged a look. 'That would be great,' Drummond said, following her into the big homely room. The radio was playing and he recognized the phone-in programme. His father always had it on in the shop.

The kettle had already boiled and both detectives sat at the table as Rachel spooned coffee from a small jar of Nescafé.

'Angus doesn't like me drinking this stuff. He says we should only have tea, but that's just because he prefers tea.'

'How are you two coping now?' Drummond asked.

Rachel's shoulders rose in a huge shrug. 'How d'you think? It doesn't get any easier.'

'Couldn't you all take a family break?' Rougvie suggested.

She swung round to give him a disbelieving stare. 'A break? We never take any breaks. Angus doesn't like family holidays. He doesn't see the point.' She turned back to pour boiling water into the mugs. 'Besides,' she said, sighing. 'He's never here at weekends, at least not on Friday and Saturday nights. He's always back for church on Sunday though.'

Drummond's heart quickened. He cleared his throat. 'What does Angus do at weekends?'

Rachel took a long, deep sigh. 'My husband is a very private man. There are things in his life that he doesn't share with anyone, especially not me.'

Rougvie frowned. 'You mean your husband goes away every weekend and you've never asked him where he goes?'

Rachel put a hand on her swollen belly as though the unborn child inside brought her comfort. 'I didn't say that. Of course, I've asked him.'

'And?' Rougvie went on.

'And nothing. Angus tells only what he wants us to know. He goes off walking during the night, you know. I hear the front door closing.'

Drummond stepped forward, flashing Rougvie a look. 'Do these nocturnal walks happen often?' he asked.

'Probably. I don't really know. We have separate rooms these days.'

'So Angus could be going out at night and you wouldn't necessarily be aware of it?' Drummond was trying to keep his voice steady.

Rachel nodded. 'I don't think he sleeps very well. Sometimes he goes out in the evening and hasn't returned when I go to bed.'

'You must have your own ideas about what's going on though,' Rougvie said gently.

Rachel passed their coffees across the table and sat down cupping her hands around her own mug. She shrugged. 'I believe Angus has another family somewhere,' she said quietly, unaware of the look that shot between the two detectives.

Drummond waited a beat. This conversation was turning explosive. He needed to keep calm. 'What makes you think that?' he said quietly.

Rachel gave a resigned shrug. 'I suppose it was the toys that got me wondering.' She looked up at Drummond. 'I found a pink rabbit in his briefcase one day. I thought it was strange. I mean we have three sons. Why would Angus give any of them a fluffy pink rabbit? I waited to see if he would mention it, but he never did.'

'It could have been a gift for the child of one of the church parishioners,' Rougvie suggested.

Rachel shook her head. 'No, Angus doesn't do things like that. And even if he did, why would he not mention it?'

The woman's theory was fascinating even if it did seem a bit far-fetched.

'And then there was the letter,' she said.

'Letter?' Drummond made no attempt to hide his interest now.

'I found a letter in his bureau. He normally keeps it locked but one day he went off to work and left the key in the lock.' She lifted her coffee and took a slow sip, apparently remembering the incident. 'I know I shouldn't have opened it, but I did. The letter, well just a note really, was under some bills. I picked it up and read it.' Her hand went to her throat. 'I could hardly believe what I was seeing. I know it by heart.'

"*Darling Angus,*" she recited, her voice shaking. "*I know you said not to, but I needed to write this.*

*The days without having you here with us are torture. The weekends are never enough. Forgive my impatience. I know how hard you are trying to find another job so we can be together all the time. Having Grace after all these years is like a miracle and I can't bear that you're missing so much time together.*

*Read this often, my darling. I know you miss us as much as we miss you.*

*With all my love, Judy.*"

Rachel slumped wearily back in her chair. 'If that doesn't sound like he's got another family tucked away somewhere then I don't know what does.'

Drummond prided himself in not being surprised at anything the public threw at him, but he hadn't been expecting this. 'Did you tackle your husband about the note?' he asked.

Rachel rubbed her arm and Drummond glimpsed the bruise on her wrist as her sleeve rode up. 'No,' she said. 'Angus doesn't like being questioned.'

He was aware of Rougvie's concerned glance. His brow wrinkled. 'Why do you stay with him, Rachel?'

The woman stared at him. 'You make it sound like I have an option.' She cupped her baby bulge in her hands. 'I have three young children and this one to think of. Angus would never allow me to leave.'

'If you want to go, he can't stop you,' Rougvie said. 'There's a place here in Inverness where you and the children would be safe. We can help you.'

Rachel laughed. 'A women's refuge in Inverness? It would take Angus five minutes to find me. He'd haul me out by the hair, you don't know him.'

Drummond's anger against the man was flaring. He knew he didn't treat his women well, but he would never raise a hand to any of them. Men who beat women were the scum of the earth. 'You could charge him with assault. We would support you.'

Rachel shook her head. 'I've already told you too much. If Angus suspects I've been going through his bureau or even criticizing him to you he would make my life hell. Please don't ask him about this.'

'But if he's abusing you...' Rougvie protested.

'You don't understand. No one would believe me.' She rubbed her hands over her face but there were no tears. 'The minister's wife came to see me when Angus was away on Saturday. She wanted to help me too.' She looked up from one to the other. 'Apparently I need help because I've been telling people Angus is violent towards me. She said the mind can play tricks when you're pregnant.' Rachel gave an incredulous laugh. 'Like a woman who's never actually been pregnant would know that. Anyway, it appears that Angus has had a word with her, confided in her she said, about the problems he's having with me.'

'She said that?' Rougvie frowned.

'Oh yes. Apparently, Angus is very worried about me...

worried about the stories I might be spreading about him. She said it was all in my mind. She actually offered to counsel me.' Rachel got to her feet and began collecting the empty coffee mugs. Rougvie jumped up to help but she waved him back down to his chair. 'It's what Angus does. He's very clever you see. He gets people on his side.' She paused. 'Believe me, he can be very convincing.'

Drummond rubbed his chin, thinking. 'How did Emily get on with your husband?'

Rachel clattered the mugs into the sink. 'She hated him. I didn't understand at the time. Angus likes to control people, but he couldn't do it with Emily. Nobody told Emily what to do. I know how much that would have frustrated him, but they kept all that hostility under wraps, at least as far as I was concerned.

'At the time I put Emily's dislike of her stepfather down to jealousy. Before I married Angus it had been a struggle being a single mum. Money was tight so all I could afford was a pokey little flat down by the harbour. But we were happy together, Emily and me.

'When Angus arrived on the scene I worked at the bank and he was my boss. He made no secret that he was attracted to me and I was flattered. I suppose Emily felt threatened when he started coming to visit us at home.'

Rachel bit her bottom lip. 'I should have seen it coming. I should have known Emily was never going to get on with Angus. She saw through him from the start. She tried to tell me what he was like, but I didn't believe her. He was still being kind to me back then. But now, thinking back. I know Angus was the reason Emily left. He drove her away.'

'Does Angus know how you feel about this?' Drummond asked.

She nodded. 'Oh yes. I've never actually accused him,

but I'm sure he suspects what I think. It's probably one of the reasons why he treats me like this now.'

The detectives stood up together.

'You won't tell Angus what I've said, will you?' Rachel's voice was pleading. 'He would kill me if he thought I'd been talking like this to you.'

'I don't want you to worry about this,' Drummond said grimly. 'Leave Angus to us. We *will* have to speak to him, but we'll leave you out of it.'

Her look suggested she wasn't at all confident about that.

'Inspector Drummond is right, Rachel.' Rougvie's voice was full of compassion. 'You can trust us.'

Drummond turned back as they reached the door. The woman looked so forlorn sitting there that he wanted to wrap his arms around her, but that would hardly be appropriate. And besides, he was a hard-bitten Glasgow cop and he didn't make gestures like that. He met her eyes. 'We won't be telling your husband that we visited you. That's a promise.'

She mouthed a shaky 'thank you' but he could see she was on the verge of tears.

# TWENTY-EIGHT

'Well?' DCI Joey Buchan demanded. 'Is this bank manager our man?'

'Give us a break, Joey, we've only been here five minutes. He's a strong candidate, but I need to do some more sniffing around.'

'We need results, Jack.'

'And we'll get them. Things are starting to unravel around Mr McLeod. He wasn't at home in Inverness when Joanna Flugg was attacked, although I know that's what he'll claim.'

'So, he has no alibi?'

'Exactly, but he doesn't yet know that. If he thinks he's out of the woods he might get careless. He's cocky enough.'

He could hear Joey's sigh at the other end of the phone. 'We need to get things moving. I'm having to explain what you're doing in Inverness again. Give me something posi-tive, Jack, or I'll have to pull you back to Glasgow.'

'Nobody wants to catch this monster more than me. You know that, Joey, but I need another day, maybe two.'

'Jesus, you don't want much, do you?' There was a

pause. 'OK, but keep me in the loop, eh? And that means me knowing everything you know. Do you understand?'

'Yes, boss. I'll keep in touch.'

He threw Rougvie a grim smile. 'Right, it's your turn now, Nick. We have to put your governor in the picture.'

'That should please him,' Rougvie said.

'We need to do some digging into the charming Mr McLeod's background,' Drummond said. 'And for that we need to get out of this car and get access to computers and phones that don't run out of charge.'

Five minutes later they were speeding past Inverness railway station and heading for Rougvie's nick on the Longman Estate.

Drummond fancied he spotted a trace of relief in DCI Gavin Fraser's expression when they walked into his office and guessed Joey wasn't the only one getting leaned on from above. No doubt he'd had to explain his decision to release one of his senior detectives to assist in what was a Glasgow Police investigation.

Fraser didn't invite them to sit as he folded his arms. 'OK, DS Rougvie. Let's hear it.' He glanced from one to the other. 'I want a progress report on what you two have been up to.'

Rougvie shifted his weight uneasily from one foot to the other. 'I'm sorry, boss. I should have let you know I was back in Inverness.'

'That's my fault, sir,' Drummond cut in quickly. 'It was me who asked DS Rougvie to help me out this morning. I understand DCI Buchan has informed you there's a strong possibility of an Inverness connection in the strangler case. We might have a suspect. I needed DS Rougvie's local knowledge when I interviewed a witness this morning.' He pulled an apologetic expression. 'I know should have run it past you first, but there really wasn't time.'

DCI Gavin Fraser's eyebrow arched. 'DCI Buchan only mentioned enquiries. She didn't say you had a suspect.'

Drummond nodded. 'It's still early days, sir, but yes, could be.'

Fraser eyed him. 'I take it your enquiries aren't confidential?'

Drummond smiled. 'There's nothing I can't share with you, sir.'

'Then what are we waiting for? Spill.'

The DCI shifted in his chair as he listened intently to Drummond relating the information Joanna Flugg had given them and how this led him back to Inverness – and the Free Church and Angus McLeod. His eyebrow lifted again. 'And you think this could be your man?'

Drummond frowned. 'Not for sure, no, but we're certainly not ruling him out.'

Fraser shook his head. 'It all sounds very unlikely. Why would a serial killer drive from Inverness to Glasgow to commit these murders? If this McLeod really is your man, why doesn't he seek out victims right here?'

'You're right, sir. It doesn't make any sense, but we're not dealing with a normal, rational person.' Drummond held Fraser's stare. 'This is why I need your help. I'm only here for another day or so.' He glanced at Rougvie who returned an expressionless stare. 'And I really need Nick's help and maybe the use of a computer or two?' He gave a hopeful smile.

DCI Fraser pursed his lips and nodded. 'I'm not sure I go along with this, DI Drummond. I'll have to speak to your governor in Glasgow, but for the time being I'll give you the benefit of the doubt.'

'Does that mean I can carry on working with the DI?' Rougvie was clearly pleased.

Gavin Fraser nodded. 'Just don't go disappearing without keeping me in the picture. Understand?'

Both detectives gave him a broad smile. 'Thanks, guv,' Drummond said. 'I appreciate this.'

Drummond grabbed the empty desk next to Rougvie's and settled himself in front of the computer. 'So, what's first?' Rougvie asked, tapping at his keyboard.

'Everything. I want to know everything about this man. Where he was born, what school he went to, what girl-friends he had. If he breaks wind, I want to know about it.'

'We can't access his phone data unless we arrest or detain him,' Rougvie said.

'Not yet.' Drummond was frowning at his screen. 'It doesn't stop us seeing what he gets up to on social media.'

'Have you found him on Facebook?' Rougvie asked.

Drummond shook his head. 'But I've got his church here and there's pictures and biographies on the three church elders.'

'Including McLeod?'

'Yup. Not much, but according to this he's the son of a Free Church minister on Stornoway.'

'I have a good friend up there. I'll give him a ring.'

'Let's do it,' Drummond said, hitting the print tab. Some-where across the room a printer clattered into action and two copies of Angus McLeod's bio slid out. He studied the longer biography on the minister, the Reverend Andrew Guthrie, his eyes sliding to the picture of him and his wife, Elizabeth, who according to Rachel McLeod, Angus had managed to capture in his thrall. She was a plain, severe-looking woman. She didn't look like someone who would be easily led, but photographs didn't always reflect the true nature of the subject. There was an address for the manse and Drummond scribbled it into his dog-eared notebook. They would speak to her later.

Rougvie was finishing the call to his contact on Stornoway as Drummond returned from collecting what he'd printed. 'Well?' he said. 'What've you got?'

'Loads,' Rougvie said, flicking through the pages of his notebook. 'The McLeods were practically infamous on the island for their fierce, Bible-thumping Free Church philosophies. Angus moved to the mainland years ago, but Mac says he vaguely remembers some scandal involving his mother.'

'Scandal?' Drummond's ears perked up.

Rougvie nodded. 'Apparently she had affair with a local man. Angus's father, the Reverend Murdo McLeod disowned her and she was forced to leave the island in shame. I'll see if I can dig out some newspaper cuttings and photos.'

'Where is McLeod's mother now?'

'Mac wasn't sure, but he's going to do a bit more scratching around.'

Drummond nodded, flicking his hand at the notebook for him to continue. Rougvie went back to his notes.

'When the mother left, Angus's father brought a local woman into the manse as housekeeper. She took the boy under her wing, but according to the gossip she wasn't above bad-mouthing his mother. It's rumoured she coached Angus into hating his mother.' He looked at Drummond. 'Word has it that this woman took over more than her house-keeping duties. She took on the mantle of the boy's mother. The pair of them would be in the front pew every Sunday hanging on every word the minister ranted at the congregation.'

'It sounds like this man was a big influence on his son.'

'Absolutely,' Rougvie said, consulting his notes again. 'He was a crusading force in the Free Church community and a leader in the campaign to stop the ferries sailing on the Sabbath.'

Drummond's brow wrinkled into a frown. 'If this minister was such a crusader and Angus looked up to him, why did he opt for banking over the church?'

Rougvie took a deep breath. 'You're going to love this, Jack. Apparently, the scandal wasn't restricted to Angus's mother. His father was said to have "borrowed" money from church funds. The local bank manager bailed him out with a loan and said nothing so long as he agreed to let Angus come under his wing. An agreement was made, and young Angus was duly put to banking.'

Drummond caught the excited glint in Rougvie's eyes. 'There's more?'

Rougvie nodded. 'I've kept the best till last.' He blinked. 'According to my contact, the bank manager tried to abuse the boy, but Angus was sixteen years old and having none of it. He threatened to expose him, and the man was later found hanged at his home.'

'Christ,' Drummond said. 'Do we know if Angus's father still alive?'

'Yes, he's in his eighties now and retired. The house-keeper still lives with him and looks after him.'

Drummond chewed his lip. 'I think we need to go over there. Can you check ferry sailings, Nick?'

## TWENTY-NINE

'You're what?' The voice exploded at the other end of the phone.

'On the ferry to Stornoway,' Drummond repeated. 'Now don't get excited, Joey. We'll be right back after we've spoken to McLeod's father.'

'You're having a laugh, aren't you? You were told to get yourself back to Glasgow by tomorrow. And less of the Joey. It's DCI Buchan to you.'

'Sorry, Ma'am.' Drummond grinned into the phone. 'I thought you would have wanted me to tie up all the loose ends here before we arrest McLeod.'

'Arrest him? You didn't tell me you had evidence to arrest him.'

'Emm, well I don't. At least not yet, but if I'm right his father will hopefully supply that.'

Joey Buchan gave a loud sigh. 'You'd better hope the strangler doesn't get himself another victim down here while you're messing about on ferries.'

The words gave him a jolt. He'd arranged for Inverness CID to keep an eye on Angus McLeod while he and

Rougvie were away, but the man was a devious character and more than capable of giving his Highland colleagues the slip. 'I'm having him watched,' he said.

'Oh, that's all right then.' Joey Buchan did nothing to disguise her sarcasm. Drummond tried not to let it unnerve him, but they did need hard evidence. He was pinning his hopes on getting that from McLeod senior.

Rougvie watched him end the call. 'Everything all right?'

'Just my boss getting her knickers in a twist again. I think she's missing me.'

'I booked us back on tomorrow afternoon's ferry, so you could drive back to Glasgow and be there by tomorrow night if it would make your DCI any happier,' Rougvie suggested.

'Let's not jump the gun. We could have arrested a killer by this time tomorrow, in which case I'll be staying for as long as it takes.'

'You really think McLeod is our man?'

Drummond narrowed his eyes against the wind as the ferry approached the quay on Stornoway. 'He's guilty all right. I can taste it. Let's just see what his old man has to say.'

Rougvie slung his rucksack over his shoulder as they disembarked from the ferry. 'I've booked a couple of rooms at the B&B across from the harbour. I've also arranged for us to meet my contact in the pub once we've signed in and dumped our bags.'

Drummond cocked his head and gave him a look. 'Is there anything you can't organize, DS Rougvie?'

'I thought that's what you wanted.'

'It is. This is me being impressed.'

.   .   .

The rooms Rougvie booked were small and basic, but they were cosy. Drummond wasn't interested in the comfort. It was a bed for the night. He was anxious to get on with things.

The contact they were meeting was standing at the bar nursing a pint. He looked up as they came in and shot his hand out to Rougvie. 'How're you doing, you old devil?'

'Yeah, I'm good, Mac. How about you?'

'Can't complain. How's the family?'

'Elaine and the bairns are fine. What about your lot?'

The man laughed. 'Mad as ever.'

Rougvie turned to Drummond. 'This is the DI I told you about, Mac.' The man offered his hand. 'Michael Mackenzie, police sergeant and general dogsbody around here. Call me Mac.'

'Jack Drummond,' Drummond said, shaking the man's hand. He nodded to his glass. 'Same again?'

They waited for their pints to be filled and then took them to a table on the far side of the pub. 'Thanks for agreeing to meet us,' Drummond said.

'Nick mentioned you were interested in the Rev Murdo McLeod. What's the old devil done now?'

'You make him sound like a troublemaker.'

'He was...in his day. He was the Free Church minister here in Stornoway before he retired. And if you haven't already heard, he was ferociously against the ferries operating on the Sabbath. He and some of his cronies also campaigned against shops trading on the island on Sundays.'

'Campaigning isn't against the law,' Drummond pointed out.

'No, but intimidation is. The Rev McLeod and his

followers intimidated people, threatened to boycott local shops and incited their followers to do the same.'

'I take it they didn't succeed?'

'What do you think?' Michael Mackenzie said.

Drummond lifted his beer. 'So, not a popular man?'

'Oh, don't get me wrong. His congregation loved him. In their eyes he could do no wrong. But he ruled his flock with an iron fist. He could make life very difficult for anyone who defied him.'

'Like his wife,' Nick Rougvie cut in.

Mac nodded. 'So the story goes. It was before my time, but nobody was surprised when Mary Ann left him. What did surprise people was her taking off with James Shaw.' He gestured around the pub. 'He used to run this place.'

Rougvie pulled a face as he put his glass back down. 'Disloyalty, fornication, and the demon drink. In McLeod's eyes she had committed all the sins in the book.'

'And this was Angus McLeod's mother?' Drummond asked.

Mac nodded.

The pieces were beginning to fall into place. 'Tell me, how old would Angus have been when all this was going on?'

Mac screwed up his face and studied the ceiling as he worked that out. 'About ten I'd say. Certainly old enough to know what was going on.'

Rougvie frowned. 'Can't have been easy being abandoned by his mother.'

'The story goes she wanted to take the boy with her when she left, but old McLeod wasn't having any of that. I'm told he threatened to kill her if she came near Angus again.'

'So where did Mary Ann and James go?' Drummond wanted to know.

'James had a croft up on the hill so they moved in there and kept a low profile until the bairn was born.'

'Bairn?' Drummond's head snapped up. 'They had a child?'

'They did, a wee lassie they called Morag.' Mac shook his head. 'But she was a sickly bairn and didn't survive beyond a few weeks. The couple reportedly moved away after that.'

'Some folks said losing the bairn was their punishment. It would have been more ammunition for Angus's father and the old crone he took on as housekeeper to brainwash him.

Drummond was remembering Nick saying the woman took the boy to church every Sunday to sit in the front pew to hear his father addressing his flock.

'What about this woman? Was there any talk that she was more than a housekeeper?'

Michael Mackenzie laughed. 'Tongues never stopped wagging about that. Sarah Duff wasn't, and still isn't, popular in the town. She has a vicious tongue in her head and you felt the lash of it if you had the audacity to mention the Sunday word.'

Drummond frowned. 'What's wrong with Sunday?'

'The Free Church doesn't recognize it. According to them it has heathen origins. It has to be the Sabbath or the Lord's Day.'

Drummond was thinking back to his conversation with Rachel McLeod. She had talked about the Sabbath.

'Most people reckon Murdo and Sarah were having it off even before the wife left,' Mac said. 'Not that either of them would ever admit it.'

Rougvie pulled a face. 'Do as I say, not as I do.'

'That's about the size of it,' Mac said.

'I've been telling Jack what you said about Angus McLeod and the banker.'

Mac's brow wrinkled. 'I've been thinking more about that since you called, so I looked out the old police files. Alan Rogers, the bank manager, wasn't liked around here. People didn't trust him. Rogers enjoyed bragging about how much he did for the local youth club, but there was talk he was over friendly with some of the boys. Nothing concrete but talk sticks.'

Drummond's eyebrow lifted. 'So the bank manager was a paedophile?'

Mac spread his hands and shrugged. 'It was only talk. Apparently he was very strict...looked after his job.'

Drummond nodded.

'One loan he did approve, however, was £500 to no other than the Rev Murdo McLeod, but it seems the minister missed more than a few repayments. Soon after this, young Angus is taken on by Rogers as an apprentice.' Mac looked up, his glance travelling from one to the other. 'And Murdo's loan was mysteriously paid in full.'

Drummond stared at him. 'Are you saying Murdo sold his son to this man?'

'That was the word at the time and very soon after this Angus left the bank. Alan Rogers was found days later. He'd hanged himself in his shed. My colleagues at the time found a diary. Apparently, he had made advances to Angus that weren't well received. Angus threatened to report him.' Mac broke off and reached for his glass. 'It was all in the diary,' he said.

'Could we have a look at those files, and the diary?' Drummond asked.

'No problem. I'll get them ready for you in the morning.'

'I meant tonight,' Drummond said. 'We could go back to your nick with you.'

Mac blew out his cheeks. 'OK, but that just might cost you another pint tomorrow.'

Drummond flashed a grin to Rougvie. 'It's a deal,' he said.

# THIRTY

THEY WERE BACK in the B&B and Drummond had spread the police files Mac supplied across the bed.

'What are we looking for?' Rougvie asked.

'Anything that suggests Alan Rogers' demise was not self-inflicted.'

Rougvie frowned. 'You don't think it was suicide? But everything at the time pointed to that.'

'Exactly,' Drummond said. 'So, nobody would have been looking for anything else.' He was flicking through the pages of the post-mortem report. 'Listen to this.' He read from the report. *"Slight bruising to the neck from the rope used by the deceased to hang himself."* He looked up. 'Surely there would have been massive bruising?'

'I suppose that would depend on how efficiently the deed was done,' Rougvie said. 'I've known suicides where the bruising wasn't that bad.'

But Drummond's lips were pressed hard together. 'Something's not right here. Come and have a look.'

Rougvie came to stand beside him. He tilted his head, frowning at the images. 'What am I supposed to be seeing?'

'How high is that beam?' Urgency had crept into Drummond's voice. 'Look man!' He jabbed a finger at one of the pictures.

'I'm sorry.' Rougvie blinked. 'I don't know what you want me to see. I...' He frowned, staring at the image. 'The chair? Something about the chair?'

The wooden kitchen chair lay on its side under the hanging man. 'Look at that beam Rogers is hanging from,' Drummond said. 'Can you see how high it is?'

'Well, yes, but...' Rougvie was still uncertain.

'And how far off the floor the body is? If he had put that noose around his neck and jumped off that chair, as we're meant to assume, the body would have been suspended much closer to the floor, not five feet in the air.' He swallowed. 'So how the hell did he get up there to hang himself?'

'Jesus,' Rougvie said. 'How did they miss this?'

'They weren't looking for it,' Drummond said.

'Or they deliberately ignored it,' Rougvie suggested. 'We need to know who the investigating officers were.' He was already on his phone. 'Mac? Look I'm sorry about this, but we could really do with your help. We need a list of everyone involved with the investigation into Alan Rogers' death.'

Drummond gestured for Rougvie to put his phone on hands free so he could hear Michael Mackenzie's responses. He was reeling off names of the officers involved and Rougvie was frantically scribbling them down.

'Ask him if he knows if any were members of the Free Church,' Drummond cut in.

'I heard that,' Mac said. 'I can tell you right now. Douglas Mathieson – Sergeant Mathieson – was a cousin of Angus McLeod's. What's this all about?'

Rougvie held out the phone for Drummond to take over

the call. 'Is this Sergeant Mathieson still living?' Drummond asked.

'He died about five years ago. You still haven't told me what's going on.'

'We need to make a few more enquiries, Mac, but we'll put you in the picture as soon as we can. Thanks for your help.' He ended the call and looked up at Rougvie. 'How do you think Mac will feel about reopening the case? This time as a murder enquiry.'

Rougvie blew out his cheeks and stared down at the photographs of the death scene. 'I don't think we're going to be popular if we stir all this up again.'

Drummond gave him a hard stare. 'You're not suggesting we let a murderer go free? Think about it, Nick. Alan Rogers makes an attempt to sexually abuse Angus McLeod, the kid he's supposed to be taking under his wing. But young Angus is having none of it. He's the Free Church's minister's son after all and Alan Rogers has just proved he is a paedophile. He has to be punished. Angus is only sixteen, but he's big for his age, bigger and stronger than Rogers. He makes the man write that entry in his diary saying how ashamed he is. The scene is now set for suicide, except it's not suicide. It's murder.'

'You're saying Angus McLeod murdered the banker?'

'Yes,' Drummond said grimly. 'I'm saying that's exactly what happened. Angus McLeod's murderous career started long before he moved to Inverness.'

Rougvie sighed. 'It's all circumstantial. How do we prove it?'

'That's up to your mate, Sergeant Mackenzie, but Angus has to be his number one suspect.'

. . .

The Rev Murdo McLeod and his housekeeper, Sarah Duff, lived in a cottage high on the hill above the town. It was a traditional West Highland croft, but in a state of serious disrepair. Drummond glanced at the unkempt garden as he and Rougvie approached the shabby black-painted front door.

'I'm not sure we should be here under the circumstances,' Rougvie muttered under his breath.

Drummond gave an innocent shrug. 'Emily Ross was his son's stepdaughter. Maybe she confided in him.'

Rougvie rolled his eyes. 'Yeah and watch out for the flying piglets.'

Drummond grinned at him. 'You worry too much, Nick,' he said, raising his hand to knock on the door. Grubby net curtains twitched as they waited. It took a second knock before the door slowly opened and a cross-looking face poked out at them.

'We don't make purchases from uninvited callers,' the old woman snapped. 'Go away.'

'We're police officers. It's about Emily Ross, Angus McLeod's stepdaughter.'

The woman's suspicious grey eyes moved from one to the other. 'What's this got to do with us?'

'We would like to have a word with the Reverend McLeod.' Drummond smiled. 'If he could spare us a moment.'

'Let them in, Sarah,' a rasping voice from inside the cottage ordered.

The woman narrowed her eyes, still not sure she was doing the right thing, but she stepped aside and let the two officers pass. The place was a tip. If Sarah Duff's role here was as housekeeper, she wasn't very good at her job.

The kitchen was big and untidy, but dishes had been

washed and were stacked, however untidily, on the drainer. A wizened old man, in a stained grey woollen cardigan, sat in a high-backed chair by the fire. 'What about my son?' he growled at them.

Drummond cleared his throat. 'We're investigating the murder of your son, Angus's, stepdaughter, Emily Ross.'

'Never heard of her,' the old man snapped.

Drummond blinked. 'You've never heard of Emily? Is your son not in touch with you, sir?'

Sarah Duff stepped in front of him and twitched her black shawl around her thin shoulders. 'Angus never comes here,' she said. 'He doesn't bother with us these days.'

'And that's fine by us.' Murdo McLeod spat out the words. 'If the boy chooses to live his life as he does, we want no more to do with him.'

'Ungrateful brat,' Sarah hissed out of the side of her mouth. 'And after all you did for him, Murdo.'

'Hold your tongue, woman,' the old man snapped. 'You have too much to say for yourself.'

'I says it as I find it and nobody can tell me different.'

Drummond looked away and caught Rougvie's look of amusement.

'Well, if that's all you came to find out we won't be keeping you,' Murdo McLeod's rasping voice said.

But Drummond wasn't going to be dismissed that easily. 'Does that mean you have no contact with your grand-children?'

'Grandchildren? What grandchildren? I've met no grandchildren.'

'You have three grandchildren, Mr McLeod, and another on the way. Angus never told you?' Drummond was incredulous.

'He didn't say that.' Sarah Duff thrust her face in front

of Drummond's. 'We know about the bairns, but their father has never seen fit to bring them here.'

'And Angus has never mentioned his stepdaughter, Emily?' Rougvie asked.

'You've been told everything you need to know,' the old man hissed. 'I'll ask you to be on your way now.'

'When was the last time you saw your son, Mr McLeod?' Drummond persisted.

The minister's old eyes were staring into the glowing embers of the fire. Neither he nor Sarah appeared to notice the amount of ash that had spread untended over the black-tiled hearth. It was like he was seeing into the past. 'He brought his woman here years ago...wanted me to marry them.' He shook his head. 'Think on that. He dared to think I would welcome such a woman into our church.'

Drummond frowned. 'What kind of woman was that, Mr McLeod?'

It was Sarah who answered. 'A sinful unmarried woman with a child.' Her lip curled in a distasteful sneer. 'That's what kind of woman Angus was bringing into the family.'

Out of the corner of his eye Drummond was aware that Rougvie was staring at the woman in disbelief. He opened his mouth to remonstrate but Drummond made a gesture to silence him. What was the point in even engaging with such bigotry when the people involved had such closed minds?

Drummond turned, signalling to Rougvie that they were leaving. 'Thank you for your time, sir,' he said curtly. It was a struggle to keep the anger from his voice. The old man didn't take his eyes from the fire as Sarah followed them out. She opened the front door and stood back as they left. Drummond saw her glance back into the cottage as she lowered her voice. 'Angus's mother, Mary Ann, you might try looking for her and her fancy man. Funny how nobody's heard of them since they were found out.'

Drummond spun round. 'Mary Ann and James Shaw?' He fixed her with a hard stare. 'What about them? What do you know?'

Sarah pulled the old shawl tight around her and made another furtive glance back into the cottage. 'Ask Angus,' she said before closing the door in their faces.

'Well,' Rougvie said. 'What d'you make of that? Is she suggesting Angus McLeod did something to his mother and her boyfriend?'

But Drummond was silent. He didn't like the feeling that was growing inside him.

## THIRTY-ONE

DRUMMOND's mobile phone rang as they got back to the car. It was Joey Buchan. He tapped the screen. 'Yes, boss?'

'We've got him, Jack! We've got the strangler.'

Drummond flinched as Joey's excited words hit him. 'You've got him?' He could hear his voice rising. This wasn't the way it should have happened. If they really had caught Angus McLeod, he should have been happy about it. Surely the important thing was to get him off the streets before he could harm another woman. But something was sticking in his craw. McLeod was *his* man. It should have been *him* who made that collar.

He swallowed. 'How did you catch him?' He tried to hide that he was struggling for words.

'We're waiting for DNA results, but it's him, Jack. I can feel it in my water.' He could hear the eagerness in her voice. 'I know, I can hardly believe it too. But we have him in custody. I'm going down to interview him now.'

'So, you're in Inverness?' Drummond was surprised. The magnitude of what he was hearing still hadn't sunk in.

'Inverness? What? No. He's here in Glasgow.' She

paused. 'Ah, I see. You think it's your suspect up there, well it's not. You were wrong, Jack. Your Wee Free Church man had nothing to do with this.' He heard her laugh. 'You'll never believe this, but he walked into the station. Joanna Flugg was here being interviewed and she recognized him.' There was second of charged silence. 'He's a solicitor, Jack,' she said. 'He was here to interview a client. He almost dropped dead when Joanna stepped out of the interview room in front of him. She went crazy, jabbing a finger in his face and screaming he was the one...he was the man who'd attacked her.'

Drummond was stunned into silence.

'You know what this means, don't you?' she said.

'What?' Drummond felt his skin tingle.

She laughed, hardly able to contain her delight. 'It means you can get yourself back down here...like pronto!'

Rougvie was staring at him.

'It's not him,' Drummond said. 'They think they've got the strangler and it's not Angus McLeod.'

Rougvie frowned. 'Not McLeod?'

Drummond's hands went to his head, the tips of his fingers working his temples. 'They've got somebody else in the frame.'

'Are they sure?'

'They're waiting for a DNA match. Apparently Joanna Flugg, has identified him.'

'So, what about McLeod?'

Drummond threw his head back and blew out his cheeks. 'McLeod is a wrong 'un Nick. He killed Alan Rogers, I'm sure of it - and that father of his helped him. What was it the old witch of a housekeeper said – "after all you did for him"? What was it he did for him?'

'We can't get involved in this, Jack. There's no proof to

back up what you're suggesting, quite apart from the fact that it's way out of our remit to get involved. We need to leave this to Michael.'

But Drummond was thinking of Sarah Duff's caustic remarks as they left Murdo McLeod's cottage. Was she attempting to thrust Angus into the frame for something they didn't even know had happened? Or was it just a bitter old woman trying to cause trouble?

'Let's see what your pal, Sergeant Mac, has to say about this.'

Michael Macintosh greeted them with a cheery grin as they walked into the police station. Drummond wondered if Nick's pal would still have such a broad smile when he shared what he'd come to say. 'Kettle's on,' Mac said, leading the two detectives to a back room.

Drummond watched the man pour boiling water onto the instant coffee in three white mugs. He would have preferred a stiff whisky but guessed there was no chance of that.

'We've been up to see Murdo McLeod and his house-keeper,' Drummond said.

Mac passed him a mug and smiled. 'No doubt they rolled out the red carpet.'

Drummond wrinkled his forehead. 'How did you guess?'

'They're a queer old couple. Do you have much to do with them?' Rougvie asked.

'No, they keep themselves to themselves. They don't even attend church these days.'

'Don't you think that's odd?' Drummond asked.

'They're an odd couple. The old woman comes out first thing in the morning to buy what provisions they need.

Most people know to steer clear of her. She's not exactly sociable.'

'We've been having a look at that Alan Rogers file and there's a few things that struck us as unusual,' Drummond said. There was no point beating about the bush.

'Like what?' Mac frowned at them.

Drummond put the file on the table and opened it, spreading out the photographs. 'Notice anything odd about the scene?'

Mac studied the pictures, picking one up for a closer look.

His brow creased. 'I'm sorry. What is it I'm supposed to be seeing? This case is more than twenty years old and way before my time. Alan Rogers committed suicide. It's here in black and white.'

'But is it? Think outside the box, Mac,' Rougvie said, moving closer to look over his friend's shoulder.

Drummond waited, avoiding the urge to point out the anomaly. Mac's head suddenly jerked up, looking from one to the other. 'The beam's too high. Even if Rogers stood on that chair, he couldn't have done it.'

'Give the man a prize,' Drummond said. 'Rogers didn't end his own life. Somebody did it for him.'

Mac was still staring at the photo. 'You're not suggesting this was deliberately overlooked by the investigating officer at the time?'

'I've no idea,' Drummond said. 'I only know the case has to be reopened in view of this new evidence.'

'I can run it past my superiors, but I'm making no promises.'

'Just remember the Free Church minister's son, Angus McLeod, was staying with Rogers at the time and according to his own admission in his diary, he had tried to sexually abuse the boy.'

Mac narrowed his eyes at him. 'Are you saying Angus McLeod murdered Alan Rogers?'

Drummond shrugged. 'If he did, he had help. Whoever did murder the man would have needed a ladder to get up there to that beam.' He pulled a face, staring at the image. 'How did a young boy, as Angus would have been at that time, manage to carry a body up a ladder without help?'

Mac rubbed a hand over his mouth, considering this.

'The old minister is pretty bitter about how his son treats him. Apparently he has nothing to do with his father,' Rougvie said. 'His housekeeper, Sarah Duff, is very vocal about it. She's furious with Angus for treating his father like this, especially, as she says, *after what Murdo did for him.*'

Mac swung round and stared at Rougvie. 'What did he do for Angus?'

'That's what you have to find out,' Drummond chipped in. 'But if a teenage boy was going to kill his abuser, who do you think he would go to for help?'

'His father,' Mac said slowly.

'That would be our thinking,' Drummond said. 'But there's more. The housekeeper went out of her way to stir things up even more for Angus. She suggested we should investigate what happened to his mother. Apparently, Mary Ann and the innkeeper, James Shaw, have never been heard of since they left the town.'

Mac held up a hand. 'Don't tell me. Sarah Duff is saying something sinister happened to them.'

'More than that,' Rougvie said. 'She was hinting that Angus had something to do with the disappearance of his mother and her lover.'

'Do you know if that was ever followed up?' Drummond asked.

Mac raised his shoulders in a shrug. 'Again, all this was well before my time. I suppose I could have a look, but remember, Sarah Duff is a nasty, vindictive old wife. She's also completely nuts. We should take what she says with a very big pinch of salt.'

Drummond nodded. 'It's still strange that nobody has heard from the couple after all this time. Shaw walked out on his pub, remember.'

'He didn't own the business though,' Mac pointed out. 'It belonged to a brewery. James only managed the pub, but I will make enquiries.'

'Can you keep in touch with us?' Drummond asked. 'I have to get back to Glasgow but Rougvie here will always be around.'

Rougvie slanted a look at him and then turned back to Mac Mackenzie. He grinned. 'And if there are any problems, we'll get Jack to sort them out.'

'I'll remember that.' Mac laughed, reaching out to shake their hands as they left to make their way to the ferry terminal.

## THIRTY-TWO

Rougvie had dropped Drummond off at his car outside the River Inn. 'Let me know what happens with your suspect,' he said.

'I'll ring as soon as he's charged,' Drummond promised, shaking the hand Rougvie offered. He stood for a minute watching the man drive off. Over the past few weeks they had become friends, an unexpected pairing, but Drummond knew he was going to miss Rougvie. He was itching to contact Joey Buchan for an update on that interview, but she beat him to it.

'Tell me you're on your way back,' she said. The elation of the earlier call had gone. She sounded tired.

'I'm driving as we speak,' he lied. 'How did the interview go?'

Joey sighed. 'Frustrating. I was hoping for a nice easy confession after Joanna Flugg identified him, but he's saying nothing.'

'What about the DNA match?'

'I've requested a fast track on the results. We should have them later today.'

'Who is this solicitor guy? Would I know him?'

'James Mortimer Dalrymple, and you probably don't know him. He's newly qualified and just been taken on by that big firm in West Nile Street.'

'He'll be sorted for representation then,' Drummond said, getting into his car.

'No, he asked for the duty solicitor. Look, Jack, I need you here. What's your ETA?'

Drummond cleared his throat. He should have told his DCI that he was only just setting off. His stupid lie had the potential to come back and smack him between the eyes.

He'd also planned to pay Rachel McLeod a quick visit, even if only to assure himself that she was all right. It was ridiculous that he was being pressurized to get back to Glasgow, especially as he suspected the real reason Joey wanted him there was to boost her confidence when interviewing James Mortimer Dalrymple. 'I'm caught up in traffic. I think there might be an accident up ahead,' he said, cringing at yet another lie.

'For Christ's sake, Jack. Just put the boot down and get yourself here.'

'I'll do my best,' he said, but she had already cut off the call.

There was an ambulance outside the McLeod's house. Drummond cursed and rammed on his brakes. He was out of his car in seconds and charging across the road. Two paramedics were carrying Rachel out on a stretcher. Even from here he could see the blood on her face. Her eyes were closed. She wasn't moving.

'What's happened?' Drummond flashed his ID at them.

One of the medics nodded to a distraught-looking Mandy Stranger standing by the gate. 'Ask her. She's the one who made the call.' But the woman had already seen him and was hurrying forward. 'He did this...Angus. He tried to kill her. You have to arrest him!'

'Where are the kiddies?' Drummond asked, his face tight with anger.

Mandy nodded back to her house. 'My assistant, Shona's looking after the three of them. They'll be fine with her.' She switched her attention back to the ambulance. 'I should go with her.'

Drummond nodded to the paramedics to allow her into the ambulance as he put his phone to his ear. 'Nick? It's Rachel McLeod. Angus has attacked her. It looks serious. She's on her way to hospital now. We need to find McLeod.'

'OK, we're on it.' The authority in Rougvie's voice helped calm Drummond's rage.

Mandy had turned back as she stepped into the ambulance, 'If you're looking for Angus, try his girlfriend.'

'Girlfriend?' Drummond stared at her.

'That's where he'll have gone,' she said. 'You'll find an address in a red box in my bureau. Rachel did a bit of detective work and tracked her down. She couldn't risk Angus knowing she'd found out about his other woman, so she gave me the address for safekeeping. Tell Shona I said you could take it.'

Drummond could see the paramedic inside the ambulance working on Rachel as Mandy climbed in beside them and the doors closed. The vehicle took off at speed as he headed for Mandy's house. He recognized the young woman supervising the children's play from his previous visit. She looked up, surprised as Drummond walked in.

'Remember me, Shona?' he said. 'I'm a police officer. I need to find something Mandy says is in her bureau. Can you help me find it? She said it's in a red box.'

Shona narrowed her eyes at him, clearly not at all sure

he should be in the house. 'The bureau is in the next room,' she said. 'But I can't leave the children.'

Drummond smiled at the curiosity on the little faces as they turned to look at him. 'No problem. I'm sure I'll be able to find it.'

The room next-door appeared to be a study. He crossed to the bureau, opening it as he scanned the bundle of papers. He couldn't see a red box. 'Try the top drawer,' Shona called to him from the other room. He did and found the box nestling beside a pile of neatly stacked folders. It contained a few receipts and a folded note in neat handwriting. Judy Meadows, 3, New Pasture Lane, Shawlands, Glasgow. He put the note in his pocket and replaced the box, sliding the drawer closed. He ducked his head into the playroom as he left. 'Thanks for your help, Shona.' The girl gave him an unsmiling nod.

Drummond called Rougvie as he hurried to his car. 'Any news from the hospital?'

'Not yet. I'm in McLeod's office at the bank. The staff say he hasn't been in today. We've had a sniff around his office but haven't found anything that throws any light on where he might be.'

'I have an address in Glasgow. I'm going there now. You need to have a word with the minister of McLeod's church. Make sure you speak to his wife as well. Angus has been filling her head with stories about Rachel.'

'Will do,' Rougvie said. 'I'll also keep in touch with the hospital. I'll let you know when I have any more news.'

'Thanks, Nick,' Drummond said as he raced through the Inverness traffic.

He waited until he'd reached Aviemore before checking in again with DCI Buchan. 'How's it going with our man?' he asked when she picked up his call.

'Still no DNA results,' she said over a heavy sigh. 'I'm letting him cool off for a while.'

'Is he definitely our strangler? You're not sounding so confident, Joey.'

'He's our man all right. I know it and I can't wait to wipe the smug leer from his face when I charge him with the murders.' She paused. 'Where the hell are you, Drummond? You should be here by now.'

'I'm driving past Aviemore. It's slow going. I think the world and his wife are out on the A9 today.'

'I don't know what you're up to, Drummond. Is this another tale you're spinning me? You could be sunning yourself on a beach in Cornwall now for all I know.'

Drummond laughed. 'I promise you I'm not in Cornwall, unless I've missed a turning somewhere.'

'You better not have.'

'I do have a bit of a detour to make when I get to Glasgow. There's an address I have to check out.'

He could almost see Buchan's eyebrows shoot up. 'Does it have anything to do with the case you're *supposed* to be on?'

'It's Angus McLeod. He's attacked his wife and left her for almost dead. I've had a tip-off that he's at an address in Glasgow.'

'Sounds like you might need some backup.'

'Thanks, Joey. I'll contact you when I get closer.' He wasn't passing on any address, not yet. The last thing he wanted was for some flat-footed uniforms to go charging in and chasing him off. McLeod was *his* collar and he wasn't planning on letting him slip the net.

Drummond's mobile buzzed and his heart gave a little jolt when he saw the caller was Rougvie. Was he about to be told that Rachel had died? He was still fired up by how brutally she'd been beaten. His hands tightened on the wheel. 'Nick. Hi.' He didn't get a chance to say more when Rougvie cut in. 'Rachel's out of theatre. She's going to be fine,' he said. 'She'll need a spell of rest and recuperation before she's back to normal but the medic I spoke to said she was a strong woman.'

An involuntary smile spread across Drummond's face. He'd been picturing those curious little faces at Mandy Stranger's nursery and wondering how Rachel's young family would cope if their mother was suddenly wrenched away from them. 'What about the baby?' He was bracing himself for Rougvie to inform him that she'd lost the child.

'Oh, didn't I say? It's a little girl.'

Drummond's smile widened. He was glad Rougvie couldn't see him getting so soft about a family who had nothing to do with him...except he did have a connection. He felt responsible for Rachel and her children. He had already let Emily down and she had died. He needed to look out for the family she left behind. He swallowed the lump in his throat. And that meant bringing Angus McLeod to justice.

Rougvie ended the call and Drummond glanced at his satnav. It showed he was thirty minutes from the Shawlands address he had punched in for McLeod, the place where, by all accounts, he had set up his little love nest with this Judy woman.

He needed to do this by the book. Every muscle in his body itched to hurl the man against a wall and beat the living daylights out of him for what he'd done to his wife.

But there were other punishments awaiting McLeod. He could be patient.

New Pasture Lane, in Shawlands, was lined with grey terraced houses. It was the kind of respectable place where net curtains twitched when neighbours had visitors. The curtains would soon be on overdrive.

Drummond parked a few doors down from number 3 and stared at the car parked in the drive. It was McLeod's car. He could of course have ditched it here and taken off elsewhere, but why would he? The man had no idea anyone had this address. He would feel safe at this house. Drummond was imagining him toasting his toes in front of a roaring fire with the child he'd bought that pink rabbit for playing at his feet. He was here all right. He reached for his phone and tapped in Joey Buchan's number. 'Send in the troops, Joey. Angus McLeod is at home.'

'What's the address?' she came back quickly.

Drummond told her.

'OK, sit tight. We're on our way.'

Every muscle in Drummond's body tensed as his eyes travelled over the end of terrace house. He was weighing up the man's possible escape routes if he tried to get away. The houses backed onto similar properties in the next road. They would have to get people round there.

His face split into a grim smile. But that wouldn't happen. Angus McLeod was going nowhere, except back to the station – in handcuffs.

## THIRTY-THREE

DRUMMOND'S EYES were glued to the driving mirror as the two police cars came silently into the road and pulled up behind him far enough away to be out of sight of the house. Joey Buchan was getting out of the first vehicle and Drummond walked quickly to meet her. This was the dangerous time. If Angus McLeod saw them now, he would run. 'We need to get a couple of bodies round the back,' he ordered.

Joey made some hand gestures to the officers with her as two others got out of the second vehicle. They waited for Joey and Drummond to approach the front door before following them up the path and round to the back of the property.

The blonde woman who opened the door was heavily pregnant and they could hear a child crying from somewhere inside the house. The commotion started before she had even raised a surprised eyebrow at them. Behind her McLeod was racing across the hall and through the back of the house.

'The back door!' Drummond shouted, flying past the DCI. 'Grab him!' he yelled. 'Don't lose him.'

'But he needn't have worried. One of the two burly officers who had stationed themselves at the rear of the property had pinned Angus to the ground while the other grabbed his arms behind his back and was slapping handcuffs on him. They yanked him back up to his feet.

'Is this what you're after, guv?' The stout PC grinned, giving McLeod a little push.

Drummond stopped, catching his breath. He gave McLeod an icy smile. 'Yes,' he said. 'He's the one.'

Angus McLeod's face was contorted with rage, but he'd stopped struggling. 'You'll pay for this, Drummond,' he hissed, his eyes narrowed to slits.

'Put him in the car,' Drummond said, turning his back on the man and walking back to the house.

The pregnant woman was standing on the path and beginning to whimper. 'What's happening? I don't understand.' She sounded dazed as she wrapped protective arms around her bulge.

Drummond took her arm and gently led her back into the house. The neighbours behind the twitching curtains had had enough entertainment for one day.

She shook off his hold. 'Why are you arresting my husband?'

'Angus McLeod is your husband?' Drummond stared at her.

'No!' she screeched back at him. 'You've got the wrong man. My husband is Alan Rogers. You've got the wrong man!'

Drummond screwed up his face. Alan Rogers! McLeod was calling himself Alan Rogers? Why would he want to connect himself to the Stornoway banker who had tried to abuse him all those years ago? The criminal psychologists would have a whale of a time with this. Drummond could still visualize that picture of the banker's body dangling from the end of a rope. He shook his head slowly. Angus McLeod was a piece of work.

The woman made another attempt to push past him to get to McLeod, but Drummond blocked her way. He could still hear a child was crying. 'Shouldn't we check on that bairn?' he said.

Judy Meadows turned back and he followed her into a front room where a screaming toddler had hauled itself up the bars of a playpen. She ignored the child, turning furious blue eyes on Drummond. 'You'll have a lot of apologizing to do when you see you've arrested the wrong man.' She was pulling a phone from her apron pocket and was tapping at it. 'Mum? It's Judy. Look, something's happened. Can you come over?'

Drummond could see she was trying to stay calm. 'Yes, the police. They've arrested Alan and they won't tell me why.' She nodded at the phone. 'Thanks, Mum,' she said, ending the call before turning her fury back on Drummond. 'You've got the wrong man. You do know that, don't you?'

'That's a chance we'll have to take but if you want to help your husband, I should contact your solicitor.'

Judy's eyes filled with tears again as she shook her head. 'I don't understand any of this. It's all a mistake. Why won't you believe me.'

'How long have you been married?' Drummond asked.

'What? What does that matter?'

Drummond held her stare as he waited for a response. 'Almost a year,' she said, going to the crying child. She bent over the wooden rail and picked her up, holding her close, murmuring soothing words as she patted the child's back. Gradually the crying stopped, and the woman carried the baby back to her chair.

'What kind of business is your husband in?'

The woman looked up sharply. 'Stop trying to quiz me. I'm sure you know quite well that he's an insurance executive.'

'Does that mean he travels a lot?'

She nodded and drew the child closer. 'We don't see much of him during the week. He has to drive all over the country staying overnight in Travelodges, but he phones regularly.'

'That must be difficult,' Drummond said, forcing himself to control his rising temper. Angus McLeod had totally deceived this poor woman. While she lived here looking after his child and preparing for the arrival of another, he was strutting around Inverness acting out the farce of being the respectable bank manager and God-fearing churchman. He wondered what the man's staff, never mind Rachel, would say if they knew about the little set up he had here. He was living a second life as husband and father to a totally different family. Could this have been why Emily left home? Had she discovered her stepfather's little secret? Had she told Rachel? He turned away; his expression grim. They still weren't sure if Emily had been another victim of the strangler. If that was true and the man Joey was currently holding in a cell really was the killer then it let McLeod off the hook, for that at least.

They still didn't know for sure that the solicitor, Dalrymple was their man. Drummond was keeping an open mind.

His eye was taken to a picture of Angus McLeod in a frame on a bookcase on the far wall. Drummond stared at it. They knew the man was responsible for beating up Rachel. Could he also have killed Emily?

His train of thought was interrupted by a knock on the

front door. The caller hadn't waited for it to be opened. The woman rushed in and flew across the room, throwing her arms around Judy and the baby. Her appearance sent Judy into more floods of tears.

'Everything is fine, darling. We'll sort this,' the woman soothed, stroking Judy's hair and glaring at Drummond. 'You'd better have a good excuse for this. What are you doing here?'

'It's no good, Mum,' Judy said. 'He won't tell you. They've taken Alan away and they won't explain why.'

Judy's mother kept up her hostile stance. 'Is that right?' she demanded. 'Have you arrested Alan?'

'He's helping us with enquiries.'

'I'll take that as a yes, then. What's he done?'

Drummond kept his voice even. 'Like I said, he's helping us with enquiries.'

'And you're not going to tell us what they are?'

'I've told you as much as I can.'

'In that case, if you have nothing more to tell us why are you still here? I want to talk to my daughter in private.' She began to shoo him to the door.

Drummond took a card from his pocket and put it on a nearby table. 'This is where you can reach me if you need to get in touch.'

'Don't hold your breath,' Judy called after him as he left the room.

Back in his car Drummond tried to collect his thoughts. He felt bad that this poor young woman had been caught up in the mess made by Angus. None of it was her fault.

He frowned, going over his conversation with her. Why had McLeod used the name Alan Rogers? Could he have taken on Rogers' identity as well as his name? Was this some kind of twisted obsession to keep the deceased banker alive?

It crossed Drummond's mind that Angus McLeod could be on some kind of guilt trip. Had he murdered Rogers? He still believed his father, the dubiously respectable Free Church minister of Stornoway, the Rev Murdo McLeod, had also been involved. He was convinced this had been what Sarah Duff was referring to when she said how much Murdo had done for his son.

He rubbed his hands over his face trying to clear his mind. He had to focus. If all this had really happened and Angus had killed before, he might not think twice about silencing Emily, especially if she had been threatening to expose him.

Drummond felt the nausea heave in the pit of his stomach. Why did this stuff still affect him so much? He was a highly trained Glasgow cop. He was supposed to be a hard man. The villains who rubbed him up the wrong way certainly thought so. It was the women that got to him...the vulnerable women. He couldn't deal with men who treated women badly.

He was already thinking about Angus's mother, Mary Ann, and her lover, James Shaw. Where were they now? Were they even alive? Had McLeod killed them and buried their bodies somewhere? He shuddered. He hardly dared think about that.

Angus could only have been about ten years old when his mother left, but who knew what kind of twisted evil the old minister had filled the boy's head with. Drummond swallowed.

He was trying to imagine the minister's shame and fury when his wife's infidelity was so publicly revealed. Could the man have persuaded the young Angus to help him murder his mother? A shudder went through him. He'd been convinced that Angus was their serial killer, the one who had strangled all those sex workers. But then James Mortimer Dalrymple had crawled out of the woodwork.

It looked pretty conclusive given the strangler's latest victim, Joanna Flugg, had identified him. All they were waiting for was the DNA confirmation.

Angus McLeod may not be the strangler, but he could still be a serial killer. Drummond narrowed his eyes at the road ahead as he fired up the car engine.

Joey Buchan was waiting for Drummond outside the interview room. He had briefed her on the phone about Angus McLeod's background and his suspicions about the man, but he had to keep reminding himself that they were only suspicions. At the very least, McLeod would be charged with the assault on Rachel, possibly attempted murder. And then, if he really had gone through a marriage ceremony with Judy Meadows, there was the possible bigamy. But Drummond wanted more than that. He wished it was Nick Rougvie he had with him, he could do with the DS's insight, but Joey was pretty savvy too. He knew he could depend on her.

Angus McLeod sat bolt upright as they entered the interview room. He fixed his attention on Drummond, totally ignoring Joey.

The officers settled themselves in front of the man as he was informed the interview was being recorded.

'What's your name?' Drummond asked.

The man's eyes slid away, but Drummond persisted. 'Your name please.'

'You know my name.'

'For the recording,' Joey Buchan said.

Drummond saw the muscles in the man's jaw twitch. 'Angus McLeod,' he said.

Drummond waited a beat, his eyes still on McLeod's face. 'You haven't asked how your wife, Rachel, is. Why would that be?'

McLeod looked up, frowning. 'Rachel? What's wrong with Rachel? Has something happened?'

Drummond could hardly believe the man's gall. 'She was badly beaten and left for dead,' he said coldly. 'You left her for dead, Angus.'

'I don't know what you're talking about. How is my wife? I need to go to her.' He attempted to stand up, but the uniformed officer behind him pushed him back into his chair.

Drummond sighed. 'I hope you're not planning to deny this, Angus. We have a witness who saw you running from the house.'

'Did this witness say they saw me attack my wife?'

'No, but...'

'Then you have no witness,' McLeod cut in, sitting back, arms folded, as Drummond and Joey exchanged a glance.

'Do you want to know how your wife is?'

'How is she?' Angus frowned.

'Not great, but she is alive.' Drummond gave the man a slow smile. 'Rachel is in hospital and I'm told she can't wait to tell us what you did to her.'

'I don't know what you're talking about. Rachel isn't well, ask anyone. She makes things up. You can't trust her.'

Drummond could feel his fists clenching. He so wanted to smash one of them into the man's smug face. What kind of sick bastard brutally attacks the pregnant mother of his children leaving her bloody and semi-conscious on the kitchen floor? How could any man do that and feel no remorse? The blood was pumping through his veins. He knew Joey was giving him a concerned look. She was right. He must not allow his feelings about this man to cloud his judgement.

Drummond forced himself to breathe. 'Can you tell us who Alan Rogers is?'

'Angus rolled his eyes to the ceiling as though he was trying to recall the name. 'Rogers?' he said, shaking his head. 'I don't think I know any Rogers.'

Drummond blinked. What was the man playing at? He was in total denial. 'The lady in the house where we arrested you said you were Alan Rogers. She also said she was your wife.'

'I've no idea what you're talking about. My wife is in Inverness.'

DCI Buchan leaned forward. 'So, what were you doing in that house?'

McLeod's gaze never wavered. He stared wide-eyed at Joey. 'I had a call on my mobile to go there. The woman said I wouldn't know her, but it was urgent, so I went. That's why I was in that house.'

'Where is your mobile now, Mr McLeod?' Drummond asked quietly.

The man shrugged. 'I don't know. I must have dropped it, perhaps when your officers so brutally attacked me.'

'Convenient,' Drummond muttered under his breath. 'We knew exactly where to find you. How do you think we managed that?'

McLeod pursed his lips and examined his fingers. 'Surely it must be clear to you that I am being persecuted. Someone is trying to make trouble for me. That woman in the house in Shawlands...I never set eyes on her before.'

'So why is she saying you're her husband?' Drummond asked, trying to keep his expression bland.

'You'll have to ask her that.' The man was actually smiling. So, this was it, McLeod was going to deny everything. Drummond thought he must be deluded if he imagined he could get away with that. Both Rachel and Judy would give evidence against him and then there would be the testimonies of the women's neighbours. He didn't have a leg to stand on.

He cleared his throat. 'I'll ask again. Can you tell us who Alan Rogers is?'

McLeod gave a vacant look. Drummond had no intention of giving up. 'Isn't that the name of the banker in Stornoway that your father, the Rev Murdo McLeod, asked to take you under his wing and introduce you to banking?'

'Is it? I don't remember.'

'Can you remember Alan Rogers was found hanged in his garage?' He paused and tilted his head at McLeod. 'Surely you remember that, Angus?'

The man gave another shrug. 'Are we finished now? I need to go to the toilet.'

One more question and then we'll take a break. 'Where is your mother?'

For a split second Angus McLeod's carefully ordered composure slipped. Drummond's eyes were glued to the man's face. 'Are you sure you don't want a solicitor?' he asked, allowing a cold smile to spread over his face.

'All I want is a toilet,' McLeod said. 'Right now!'

## THIRTY-FOUR

DRUMMOND FOLLOWED DCI Buchan back to the incident room where the dead faces of the killer's victims took up much of the Murder Wall. 'What's keeping those DNA results?' he said, his eyes scanning the pictures and taking in the familiar scenes where the bodies had been found.

'Good question,' Joey said, stabbing at her phone. 'OK, Maurice! Where are those results? You're supposed to be fast-tracking them.' Drummond watched her brow crease. 'We're all busy,' she hissed back. 'We have a serial killer making himself comfortable in one of our cells and I can't charge him until I have those results.'

Drummond was only listening to the call with half an ear. He'd been so immersed in these murders, but nailing the killer no longer felt as important as exposing Angus McLeod.

'Why didn't you say that in the first place? I'll send somebody down to collect them.' Joey ended the call with a grin. 'The results are in.' She punched the air. 'We've got him!'

'What if it's not him?' Drummond swung round to look at her.

'It's him,' she said, signalling to one of the young detectives to come over. 'The DNA results for Dalrymple are ready,' she said. 'Can you get down there and grab them?'

DC Murray Anderson nodded. He looked excited. 'Right away, Ma'am.'

Drummond watched him stride from the room, the jauntiness in his step showing he was clearly motivated having been charged with such a potentially important task. He was obviously confident the Glasgow Strangler was about to get his comeuppance and he was the one who would bring the proof of his guilt. Drummond hoped he and Joey were right.

It was ten minutes before Anderson came back and handed the file to DCI Buchan. Every pair of eyes in the room watched as she scanned the words. A slow smile crossed her face and she punched the air. 'It's him!' she shouted. 'We've got him!'

A cheer went around the room and Drummond caught the excitement. How could he not be delighted when they were about to take a killer off the streets?

'Come on, DI Drummond, you've earned the right to be there. Let's go tell James Mortimer Dalrymple the good news.'


Two uniformed officers brought the man to the interview room next door to where they had questioned McLeod. He avoided their gaze. Behind the dark-rimmed spectacles his eyes darted nervously about the room as they entered. The solicitor by his side gave a cursory nod. Joey put her folder on the table and waited as Drummond set up the recorder.

Each of the four identified themselves for the tape.

'You can't keep me here.' Dalrymple's voice was shaking. 'I've done nothing wrong.' He still wasn't looking at them. 'I can have you for wrongful arrest, you know.'

The lawyer put a warning hand on his arm. 'If you have evidence against my client tell him now, otherwise we will be leaving.'

Joey looked down at her file. She was in no hurry. She opened it and glanced over the contents. 'We have the results of your DNA test, Mr Dalrymple.'

The man moved uneasily in his chair.

Joey smiled at him. 'And guess what?' She waited, enjoying the moment. 'We have a match.'

Dalrymple shot a wild look to his solicitor.

'The forensic evidence we collected at the scenes of where four murder victims were found places you at each one. Your DNA was also found on Joanna Flugg. What do you have to say about that, Mr Dalrymple?'

Drummond watched the man's hands trembling. His shoulders slumped and his dark, curly hair shone greasily under the light. The solicitor put a hand on the man's back and bent to whisper something in his ear. Dalrymple leapt from his chair and backed away, his eyes on fire. 'Let me out of here. I've done nothing wrong.'

Joey's nostrils flared. 'Tell your client to sit down, please.' She was in no mood for compromise.

'Do as the officer says, Mr Dalrymple,' the solicitor said quietly. 'Come back and sit down.' He nodded to the chair.

Dalrymple wrapped his arms around himself and backed further into the corner. 'It was them, not me. They wanted to die.'

The solicitor jumped to his feet and put a hand out to

the man. 'Don't say any more,' he said sharply. He drew his client back to the table. 'Sit down, Jimmy.'

Joey Buchan waited until the man sat and gave him time to compose himself. He was still trembling uncontrollably. 'You said they wanted to die, Jimmy. Can you tell us why you said that?'

'It wasn't my fault. I've done nothing wrong,' the man bleated.

'You can help yourself by just telling us what happened. You said it was their fault. Why was it their fault? Why did you kill those women?'

Drummond gave the man a hard stare, ignoring the wave of anger that swept over him. He forced sympathy into his voice. 'The court will take your co-operation into consideration, Jimmy. What is it you'd like to tell us?' He could feel Joey's eyes on him. She wouldn't like him jumping in like this, but they needed answers – and quickly.

Dalrymple kept his eyes fixed on the table. They could hear the involuntary rapping of his feet on the floor as his legs trembled violently. They waited. The man raised his head and looked directly at Joey. There was a sneer on his face.

'I did it,' he said. 'I killed the four whores and I almost got the other one.' He raised his voice. 'They were tarts. They wanted it!'

Drummond held his breath. He desperately wanted to smash his fist into this man's insolent face. How could he have no conscience about what he'd done? There wasn't an ounce of remorse in him. He had taken the lives of women he probably didn't even know and had the audacity to suggest they deserved it. He fixed the man with a disgusted stare.

'Which other one?' he asked coldly.

'The one that got away,' Dalrymple said, shaking his head. 'That shouldn't have happened. I slipped up there.'

Drummond shot Joey a glance and she gestured for him to continue. 'Haven't you left somebody out?'

'I don't think so.'

Drummond tried to steady the way his heart was thudding in his chest. He hardly dared ask what he had to say next. He took a deep breath, aware that the others were watching him. 'Emily Ross,' he said, keeping expression from his voice. 'The young woman you killed in the alley behind the pub in the city centre. Have you forgotten about her?'

Dalrymple frowned. 'She wasn't one of mine. I don't know anything about her.'

Drummond's heart gave a mighty lurch. Emily wasn't killed by the strangler! He had to stop his fist coming down on the table. The piece of scum who killed Emily, the girl he'd taken pity on and had tried to help, wasn't the Glasgow Strangler. It was Angus McLeod. It *had* to be him. He just needed to prove it. The pieces of the puzzle were coming together and the net would soon tighten.

A cocktail of emotions swirled around Drummond's insides. He had interviewed hundreds of offenders in this small, claustrophobic room but he had never before felt the walls closing in on him.

The Glasgow Strangler had held such power over all of them for so long. Detectives had been pulled in from all over Scotland to join the hunt. Their prey had seemed almost invincible, killing one woman after another and every time escaping unchallenged into the night.

And now here he was...the serial killer every cop in Joey's team had been looking for. Through narrowed eyes

Drummond stared at the twitching, pathetic creature in front of him. It felt like an anticlimax. Maybe he hadn't been so committed to catching this killer as he'd thought. Could it be the chase that excited him and not the conclusion? He hoped not, but he didn't know.

DCI Buchan got to her feet. 'Stand up, Mr Dalrymple,' she said. Drummond watched the man's face as the murder charges were put. He looked confused. Buchan signalled for the PC behind her to take Dalrymple away.

The man's face twisted into a grin. 'Is that it? Can I go now?'

Joey Buchan frowned. 'The only place you are going, Mr Dalrymple, is back to a cell. And if there's any justice in the world you will stay locked up for a very long time.' She and Drummond stood back while the man was led away. They followed him out and watched as he was escorted along the corridor.

'I won, didn't I?' he called back at them. 'I won the cat and mouse game. I had you all fooled. You didn't know it was me.' He was still calling out as he rounded the corner back to the cells. 'I'd like to go home now.'

Drummond shook his head. 'He's a total nutcase.'

A grim smile crept over Joey's face. 'It's down to the procurator fiscal now, but I don't think there will be any problems.' She hugged the file she was carrying to her chest. 'We've caught the bastard. I'm beginning to like this day.'

There was a spring in her step as she and Drummond walked back to the incident room to give the troops the good news that Dalrymple had confessed.

'What about Emily Ross?' Drummond asked.

'Four out of five isn't bad.'

'Is that it?' Drummond stopped and swung her round, his eyes blazing. 'Is that how much you care about Emily

Ross? For God's sake, Joey. She was seventeen years old and some evil bastard squeezed the life out of her and left her body amongst the filth in that alley.'

Joey glared at him. 'You know I didn't mean that. What's wrong with you, Drummond? If Emily Ross wasn't one of Dalrymple's victims, we'll find out who did kill her.' She gave him a sideways look. 'You still think it was the stepfather, don't you?'

Drummond cast his eyes to the floor and nodded. 'I know it was. Angus McLeod murdered Emily.'

There was a buzz of exhilaration around the incident room as the news of the strangler's confession spread. Several bottles of whisky had unsurprisingly appeared from desk drawers and most people were sipping amber liquid from plastic cups.

Drummond's heart wasn't in the celebrations. He was thinking about the other man they still held in custody – Angus McLeod. He had to get his head together. Detectives from Inverness were already on their way to Glasgow to pick him up and take him back north to be interviewed about the attack on his wife, Rachel. But in Drummond's eyes murder took precedence and he had no intention of handing him over until he'd got some answers about Emily's death.

He glanced around the room and caught sight of Joey. She beckoned him into her office. 'What's happening about your man McLeod?

Drummond knew Rougvie's pal, Sergeant Michael Mackintosh from Stornoway, or somebody very like him, could also be turning up soon to snatch him away for interviewing about Alan Rogers' death and maybe even the disappearance of McLeod's mother and her lover all those years ago. Whatever the future held for the man, his life from now on wasn't going to be easy, and neither should it be.

Drummond heaved a weary sigh. 'I haven't finished with him yet. Can I take those files?' He nodded to the pile of fat folders on her desk. They contained the printed interviews with witnesses in the strangler case.

Joey shrugged. 'Be my guest, although I doubt if you'll find anything new there.'

He hoped she was wrong. She had to be. Now that a different killer was in the frame for Emily's murder everything had to be scrutinized differently. He needed a break, a tiny scrap of evidence that placed McLeod in that alley with Emily.

Joey had taken two glasses from her drawer and extricated a half bottle of whisky from the file cabinet. She poured two generous measures and handed one to Drummond. 'Ease up, Jack. You deserve this as much as any of us.' She was smiling at him in a way he might have responded to at a different time. He lifted the whisky and threw it back in one go. 'I can't let it go, Joey, not yet. McLeod killed Emily; I know he did.'

'Let the Inverness boys take him. He'll go down for what he did to his wife. There's plenty of time to investigate his involvement or otherwise in his stepdaughter's murder.'

Drummond met her eyes. 'What about the woman in Shawlands who's pregnant with McLeod's child...his second child to her? She also believes she's his wife and she's right here on our doorstep.'

'You don't let go, do you, Jack?'

'I'm just doing my job,' he threw back at her, but he knew it was more than that. Angus McLeod had got to him. The man was a sanctimonious, bigoted bully – and he'd killed Emily. He wasn't getting away with that, not if Drummond could help it.

'OK, go, if that's what you want,' Joey said. She sounded annoyed as she turned and poured herself another whisky. 'But you don't know what you're missing.'

Drummond scooped up the folders, looking away as he left the room. He did know what he was missing.

He felt Joey's eyes on his back as he walked away. He still felt guilty about how their relationship had ended. It had been a fling, a little dalliance, nothing more. It wasn't his fault if she'd read more into it – or was it? Drummond's reputation with women wasn't great, but violence never had, and never would play a part in it.

The number of people in the incident room had thinned out. His colleagues were beginning to drift away to further celebrations in the pub. He wouldn't be following them, not tonight. He dropped the folders onto his desk and they landed with a thud. He pushed his fingers through his hair as he sat down. There was a lot of reading to do.

'Call me if you come up with anything, I'll be in the pub,' Joey called across to him as she left incident room. He raised a hand in acknowledgement without looking up. Pulling Emily Ross's file in front of him he flicked it open and began to scan the pages.

In his mind's eye he was back in that dark alley staring down at the girl's body and seething with anger at the bastard who had done that to her.

He pressed his lips together, thinking. Emily had been dressed for business – a short, tight black skirt and low-cut red blouse. The clothes being very different from the jeans and sloppy T-shirts she wore around his flat.

He forced himself to remember how her body had been sprawled amongst the rubbish that had escaped from the bins at the back of the pub. It had been established that Emily had died in that lane. She hadn't been taken there after death, like the strangler's victims. Once again Drummond cursed the useless, broken CCTV system. If it had been operational that night they might have seen the girl's killer.

Drummond sat back in his chair and ran his hands over his hair. There was nothing to connect McLeod to that alley, but the man didn't know that.

They had established that McLeod hadn't been in Inverness that night, so where had he been? Would pregnant Judy give him an alibi? That's where he had to start. He closed the file and grabbed the jacket he'd carelessly thrown over the back of his chair and headed for the back stairs to the car park.

Judy's mother opened the door him. 'It's that detective, Judy, the one that took Alan away. He wants to speak to you.'

Judy came hurrying to the door, her hands steadying her bulge. 'Have you brought Alan back?' She strained to look behind Drummond. 'Where is he? I don't see him.'

'He's back at the police station,' Drummond said quietly. He cleared his throat. 'We need to ask him more questions.'

The woman's shoulders slumped, and she turned away.

'You'd better come in,' the older woman said.

Judy went into the front room and they followed her in. The big TV in the corner was on, but he got the impression nobody had been watching it. Judy lowered herself carefully into an armchair and stared into the fire.

'We went to the police station, but nobody would tell us why my husband has been arrested.' She turned huge confused eyes on Drummond. 'That can't be right. Why won't they tell me what Alan's supposed to have done?'

Drummond spread his hands. 'He's helping us with an investigation. I'm sorry but that's all we can say at the moment.'

He was aware the older woman was watching him with narrowed eyes. 'It would help if you could remember what you and–' he paused '–Alan, had been doing on certain dates.' He reeled off a few dates, burying the important one – the night Emily was murdered – in the middle of them.

Judy looked up at her mother. 'Can you bring that calendar in from the kitchen, Mum?' The woman disappeared into the next room and returned with a calendar, which she handed to her daughter.

'What were those dates again?' Judy had begun to flick through the pages. Drummond listed the dates again. Judy shrugged. 'Nothing here, except for...' She smiled. 'We were at the hospital that day for a scan.'

'So, Alan was with you?'

Judy nodded. 'Of course, he was, it was a very important day for us. It was the day we learned we were having a boy. Alan was overjoyed.' She gave a wistful smile. 'Alan was so excited he couldn't sleep that night. He had to get up and go for a walk.'

Drummond felt his insides flip over. 'You're sure of this date?'

Judy held out the calendar for him to see where she had jotted down the hospital appointment for the scan. 'No mistake. That's the date. Is it important?'

'And Alan went out for a walk that night? What time would that have been?'

Judy's brow wrinkled. 'I don't know, about ten I suppose. It wasn't long after I'd gone to bed. Alan said he was too excited about the baby to sleep.' She looked up at him. 'He'd always wanted a son you see and now it was actually happening.'

'So, Alan went out around ten? Do you know when he got back?' Drummond could feel his blood pumping.

'I don't know, but now that you mention it, he was out for ages. He certainly hadn't come back by three. I remember looking at the clock, but I fell asleep again.'

He could see the woman's mother was surprised. 'You never mentioned Alan was out all night.'

'It wasn't something to mention. It's just how Alan is. He has trouble sleeping and the only thing that helps is to get out and walk. Time isn't important to him.'

Drummond had a smile on his face as he drove back to the station. He was making progress. If Angus McLeod was relying on Judy to give him an alibi, she had just smashed a hole in it.

## THIRTY-FIVE

'We meet again,' Drummond said, coming into the interview room and dropping the folder with Emily's name on the table. He set the recorder going, instructing McLeod to identify himself. Drummond gave no sign that he'd noticed the man's eyes flick over the file and then quickly look away.

'Your wife sends her love,' he said, smiling.

It took McLeod only a split second to react. 'Dear Rachel,' he said. 'Is she feeling better now?'

'Rachel? No, she's still in hospital recovering from the injuries you inflicted on her.' He paused. 'I was referring to Judy.'

McLeod shrugged. 'I have no idea who you're talking about.'

'I'm talking about Judy, or Mrs Rogers, as she believes herself to be.'

'I don't know any Mrs Rogers.'

'But you do know who Mr Rogers is...Alan Rogers?'

McLeod looked blank.

'Let me refresh your memory. Alan Rogers is the man who took you in, at your father's request, to train you for a career in banking. He's the man who described in his diary how he tried to sexually abuse you.' His eyes were glued to McLeod's face. 'That was before he was found hanged in his garage in Stornoway.' Drummond smiled. 'Remember him now?'

Angus McLeod swallowed.

Drummond kept up the pressure. 'We've reopened that case, you know. The police up in Stornoway are not happy about that original suicide verdict.'

Panic flashed across the watchful eyes and was gone in an instant, but Drummond hadn't missed it. His feeling of optimism was growing. Time to rev up the pressure. He opened the folder and looked up. 'Where were you on May 5th, Mr McLeod?'

'What? Without checking my diary, I have no idea.'

But the stiffening of the man's jaw gave him away. The date was definitely significant to him.

'Let me help you. May 5th is when your stepdaughter, Emily Ross, was murdered,' Drummond said. He slid a picture of the murder scene from the file and stared down at it. Surely you remember that?'

The man was fidgeting now. 'I didn't realize that's what you were referring to. I was home, of course.'

Drummond pursed his lips, still fingering the photograph. 'Which home would that be? Are you talking about the one in Inverness, or the one in Glasgow?'

'Inverness of course. I have no home in Glasgow. You're trying to provoke me,' he snapped. His eyes were on the photograph of Emily's body.

Drummond sighed. 'Well, the thing is, Mr McLeod, I've already asked Rachel about this and she told me you were not at home that evening. In fact, you didn't return until the next day.' His brow creased as he stared at the man. 'Is that why you attacked Rachel? Was it a warning to her to keep quiet?' He shook his head. 'But the thing is, I'm better at this than you, Angus, because I had already talked to Rachel and she confirmed your absence that night.'

'So, I'll ask again. Where were you on that date?'

McLeod swallowed. 'Rachel was mistaken. She fantasizes about things, says things happened when they hadn't.' He blinked. 'It's not something I like to talk about, but Rachel is not stable. Ask Mrs Guthrie, the minister's wife, she knows.'

'Knows what, Mr McLeod?'

'Elizabeth knows Rachel has mental health problems. She's experienced in dealing with these things. She's been trying to help Rachel.'

Drummond had had enough. This man didn't deserve to be treated with consideration. He slid the shocking photograph of Emily's body further across the table. 'Do you recognize this place, Mr McLeod? This is where Emily died. Someone put his hands around her throat and squeezed it until she was dead. Then he scurried away, like the rat he was, leaving her body amongst the filth and rubbish in this miserable alley.' He couldn't keep the disgust from his voice.

Angus McLeod was staring wide-eyed at the photograph. He looked transfixed. Tiny beads of sweat glistened on his forehead.

To Drummond's surprise, tears began to slide down the man's cheeks and his shoulders heaved as his body was convulsed with sobs. Was it grief or remorse? Drummond didn't know. He left the photograph on the table.

'Did you kill Emily, Angus?'

McLeod turned wild eyes on him. 'Me?' He sounded genuinely shocked. 'No. I didn't kill her. It wasn't me.' His breath was coming in gasps. 'You have to find who did this to my lovely girl. You have to find him. It wasn't me.'

The uniformed officer behind McLeod was looking anxious. He stepped forward, but Drummond waved him back, leaning across the table. 'The thing is, Angus...we have CCTV.'

'What? You're lying!' McLeod suddenly sprang from his chair and lunged at Drummond.

The young PC bounded forward and got him in an arm lock, forcing him back into his chair.

'Why does CCTV upset you so much, Angus, if you weren't there?'

'There was no CCTV. I was told. The camera wasn't working that night.'

'That's what we all thought originally, but it actually was. I've watched the video, Angus. It's very interesting.'

Drummond tilted his head, watching the man. He was coming apart. All the bravado, the carefully constructed wall of granite was fast disappearing. Angus McLeod was guilty as hell. All he had to do now was to keep pushing and he'd get his confession. And if he had to throw in a few lies along the way then so be it.

The man jerked up and squared his shoulders, fixing Drummond with a defiant glare. 'I want a solicitor,' he said.

Drummond felt exhilarated as he watched McLeod being led back to his cell before heading off to the custody desk. Sergeant Ronnie Ryan, the custody sergeant, lifted his head from his newspaper. 'Everything all right?' he asked.

'He wants a lawyer. Can we contact the duty solicitor?'

The sergeant nodded.

'Like I said before, you better keep an eye on him,' Drummond said. 'I don't think he likes our five-star accommodation.'

He was in the corridor on his way back to the incident room when he met Nick Rougvie and the junior officer sent to escort Angus McLeod back to Inverness. 'I'd love to say I'm pleased to see you, but I've got McLeod on the verge of confessing to his stepdaughter's murder. Any chance you could leave him with us for another hour?'

Rougvie's eyes lit up. 'He's ready to confess? But that's brilliant.' He slapped a hand on Drummond's shoulder. 'Congratulations.'

'We're not there yet, but I'm hopeful.'

The constable who'd been in on the interview was coming along the corridor. 'The duty solicitor was in the building. I'm off to take him to see McLeod now.'

'Thanks,' Drummond said. 'I'll give them half an hour.'

Rougvie introduced the officer he'd brought with him. 'This is DC Faraday.' The man shot out his hand. 'It's Colin, sir,' he said, his plump pink face crinkling into a smile.

Drummond nodded. 'Look, Colin. The canteen's on the floor below. Fancy grabbing a coffee for yourself while I have a word with DS Rougvie here?'

The DC looked at Rougvie who nodded his agreement. He put his hand in his pocket and pulled out a banknote. 'Get yourself a sandwich as well.'

Colin Faraday's grin widened as he accepted the money and hurried off.

Rougvie turned to Drummond. 'I really can only give you an hour. We're under orders to get the prisoner straight back to Inverness.'

'Prisoner?' Drummond queried.

'That's right. Rachel McLeod has come round. She's confirmed it was her husband who attacked her. We're charging him with attempted murder.'

Drummond smacked his first into his hand. 'Yes!' he said. 'Let McLeod try to squirm out of this.'

Rougvie checked his watch. 'Fancy joining young Colin in the canteen while you wait for McLeod's solicitor to do his thing?'

Drummond felt he should stick around, but ten minutes wouldn't do any harm. They were on their way back from the canteen when the alarm bell started to clang along the corridor. Drummond's first thought was Angus McLeod. 'It's him!' he yelled, breaking into a spontaneous charge towards the cells with Rougvie fast behind. The sound of running feet was coming up behind them.

They came to an abrupt halt as they reached the open cell door. The young PC who'd hit the alarm button was staring in horror at Angus McLeod's body, blood still seeping from gashes in both his wrists. Beside him was a cheap plastic pen that was also covered in blood.

'Jesus!' Drummond flew across the room, grabbing a hankie from his pocket and trying to staunch the flow of blood while he yelled to Rougvie to do the same. Outside more feet pounded towards them. Three uniformed officers piled into the cell, pushing the shocked-looking solicitor out of the way.

'Call an ambulance,' Drummond shouted at them. But even as he spoke, he knew it was too late. Angus McLeod was dead.

Rougvie put a hand on Drummond's shoulder. 'I'm sorry, Jack,' he said quietly. 'He's gone.'

Drummond's hands went to his head as he let out an ear-splitting wail. 'Nooooo. He can't die!' He rocked his head. 'He can't die, not yet.'

'Come away, Jack,' Rougvie said gently, leading Drummond away from the body.

'I had him, Nick. He was on the point of confessing to Emily's murder. Now he gets away with it.'

'I'd hardly call taking his own life getting away with it,' Rougvie said. 'Wasn't he on suicide watch?'

'What? No!' Drummond screwed up his face. 'Why the hell should he have been? Angus McLeod wasn't suicidal. He was arrogant. He was chancing it out.'

Rougvie gave a deep sigh. The custody sergeant had arrived now and was staring at the body.

'I told you to keep an eye on him,' Drummond yelled. 'Why didn't you watch him?'

The man backed away, shaking. 'Don't you blame this on me. Nobody asked me to put this man on suicide watch.'

Rougvie stepped between them. 'This can wait. You need to get the duty doctor down here, DI Drummond. Like now!' He moved closer to Drummond. 'Get a grip, Jack.' Rougvie's whisper in his ear was urgent. 'This has to be done by the book from here on in.'

Rougvie began to walk from the cell with Drummond. 'We have to get DCI Buchan down here,' he said. 'D'you have her number?'

Drummond fumbled for his phone but Rougvie took it from him. 'I'll do it,' he said.

The two detectives were pacing the floor in Joey's office when she arrived. 'I want to see the body,' she ordered. 'You stay here, Jack.' She turned to Rougvie. 'You'd better come with me and put me in the picture.'

She marched ahead of him to the cells, passing the custody sergeant's desk on the way. 'You come too, Sergeant Ryan. Tell me what the hell's been going on here.'

'I wasn't here when Inspector Drummond and this officer found McLeod's body,' the sergeant bleated, puffing after her.

'Were you aware that he was a suicide risk?' Buchan demanded.

'Not that I was told. We would have been checking him regularly if that had been the case,' Sergeant Ryan said breathlessly.

Joey Buchan put her hands on her head at the sight of the body on the cell floor. 'Christ,' she said. 'How the hell did he manage to cut his wrists?' She turned her fury on Ryan. 'Was nobody watching him?'

The sergeant shifted his weight uneasily from one foot to the other. 'You'll have to ask DI Drummond about that. Apart from the duty solicitor, he the last person who saw the man alive.'

Joey Buchan put her fingers to her temple. 'How in shit's name did he manage to do this?'

Rougvie swallowed and nodded to the pen that was still lying beside the body.

'Christ,' Joey Buchan said, narrowing her eyes at the sergeant. 'Why was this not taken from him?'

Sergeant Ryan caught his breath. 'He was searched same as all prisoners in the cells. He had no pen on him then. Somebody's given this to him.'

Joey released a long sigh. 'Don't anybody touch anything in here. Is that clear?' It was the sergeant she was looking at. He gave a glum nod as she turned sharply, marching out of the cell with Rougvie at her heels.

'DI Drummond won't be blamed for this, will he?' Rougvie said, striding fast to keep up with her.

'Well what would you think, DS Rougvie? Everybody knew Jack had it in for McLeod. He made no secret of it. He hassled the man, no doubt accused him of murdering his stepdaughter when there was no evidence. And he taunted him about the death of that banker in Stornoway, not to mention the disappearance of McLeod's mother and her boyfriend way back when.'

'And a possible bigamy,' Rougvie muttered under his breath.

But Joey was still in full spate. 'He certainly gave the man grounds for being suicidal,' she hissed. 'I just hope he didn't give him that pen. So yes, I'd say Jack Drummond is a prime candidate for blame, wouldn't you?'

Drummond was still in Joey's office and keeping an anxious eye on the door into the incident room as he waited for her return. The look on her face when she appeared with Nick Rougvie gave him no solace.

'I'll have to call this in, Jack. There will be an investigation. You'll have to prepare yourself.'

'It's an unexplained death in the cells.' Drummond frowned.

'And that's what you're going to tell the investigating team, is it?' Her voice was rising. 'You're going to suggest this is an unexplained death?' She gave an exasperated sigh. 'But it's not, is it, DI Drummond? Angus McLeod took his own life because somebody gave him a pen.' She couldn't keep the anger from her voice. 'And oh yes, there's also the little matter of how you goaded, taunted and bullied the man!'

'But I didn't...'

'The tapes will show you being nice to him, will they?'

Drummond hung his head.

'I think you should make yourself scarce. You'll be contacted when they want you.' She glanced to Rougvie. 'Get him out of here.'

They had reached the door when Drummond looked back. 'I didn't give him that pen, you know,' he said.

# THIRTY-SIX

ROUGVIE WATCHED Drummond staring morosely into his whisky glass having waved aside any suggestion that he should go home. He needed to get his friend out of here before Drummond's aggressive, drunken behaviour got them both thrown out. He had already informed DCI Gavin Fraser, in Inverness, of their prisoner's unexpected demise. Fraser agreed that he and Faraday should stay overnight in Glasgow and Faraday had gone off to find them a B&B.

Rougvie leaned in closer to Drummond, lowering his voice down. 'You have to keep everything together until all this gets sorted, Jack.'

'Sorted? You think this is going to get sorted?' Drummond gave a drunken grin. 'This won't get sorted. The top brass want me out and now they have the perfect excuse.' He was waving his hands with a flourish. 'They'll say I caused a man to kill himself in the cells. This is my fault.'

'You can stop that talk right now. Stand up for yourself, man.' Rougvie was losing patience. 'And while you're at it you can stop this drinking.'

Drummond pulled a face and drained his glass. 'Like that's going to happen.'

'So, what then? You're just going to sit here and drink yourself to death? Brilliant idea!'

Drummond shrugged. 'What the hell. I'm finished in the Force. They don't like insubordinate buggers like me. It suits them better when we're obedient muppets jumping to attention and playing everything by the book.' He looked up and met Rougvie's frown. 'Don't you get it, Nick? They want rid, and this is their chance.'

'You don't know that.'

Drummond picked up his empty glass and headed for the bar. Rougvie watched him stagger across the floor and made no attempt to stop him. What would have been the point? Anyway, why should he care about this bolshie, stubborn man when he clearly cared nothing for himself? He'd thought they were friends, but Drummond was throwing it all back in his face. The man was on a collision course for disaster and taking his foot off the brake. Rougvie shook his head, watching him downing a fresh whisky and asking for another.

What the hell! He and Faraday would be on their way back to Inverness in the morning. Drummond would have to look out for himself.

The barmaid had caught Rougvie's eye as she leaned in to speak quietly to Drummond. He waved her away. But the woman still looked concerned as he took his glass and weaved his way back to the table before announcing he was going for a slash.

Rougvie waited until he had disappeared into the gents before making his way to the bar. 'I couldn't help noticing you seem to know my friend.' He gave the barmaid a smile.

She sighed. 'Jack Drummond? Yeah, I know him. Why is he getting so smashed? I couldn't get a thing out of him.'

'Probably better not to even try,' Rougvie said, wondering if Drummond and the barmaid had been an item. 'I don't suppose you know any of Jack's mates?'

She gave him a suspicious look. 'Why?'

'The thing is,' Rougvie started. 'I have to get off soon and I don't like leaving him like this.'

The barmaid wrinkled her nose. 'I might do.'

'Could you give them a ring?'

She nodded thoughtfully, her eyes on the door of the gents as Drummond re-appeared.

'I wouldn't let him have any more booze,' Rougvie said. 'Strong coffee might be an idea.'

His mobile pinged a text coming in. It was Colin Faraday telling him he'd found a B&B up near the university. He passed on the address saying he would go straight there and see him in the morning.

The barmaid arrived at their table with two mugs of coffee, which Drummond immediately pushed away. She gave Rougvie a nod, which he took to mean she had contacted somebody to fetch Drummond home. He mouthed a 'thank you', pushing the coffee back in Drummond's direction. He shoved it away again, but Rougvie persisted and eventually Drummond began to sip at it.

The pub was busy but Rougvie's eyes kept flicking to the door, watching for any sign of this friend. And then the big man walked in and he saw the barmaid catch his eye and nod to their table. Rougvie got to his feet as the man approached.

Drummond's head came up. 'Pete! Come away in. What are you having?' He started to get unsteadily to his feet, but Pete put a hand on his shoulder and pushed him back down. He gave Rougvie a wry smile. 'Pete Mullen,' he said. 'This young reprobate and I go way back.'

'Nick Rougvie,' he said, extending his hand. 'I'm a newer mate. Can I get you a drink?'

'Coffee would be great,' Pete said.

Rougvie went to fetch it. He had to wait while the barmaid served other customers, but she was smiling as the coffee machine hissed away behind her. 'Pete will sort him out. He's the only one Jack will listen to when he's in this frame of mind.'

'Who exactly is Pete?' Rougvie asked, glancing back to the table. He could see the two men had their heads together, deep in conversation.

'One of the good blokes. He's the community copper around here. Everybody knows him.'

Rougvie's eyebrow arched. 'He's a copper?'

'He's Jack's mentor.' She nodded, watching them. 'Jack will be fine now.'

'What's your name?' Rougvie asked, as the barmaid turned to leave.

'Just call me Lucy.'

'Thanks, Lucy,' he winked. 'I can see Jack has more than one good friend around here.'

She blushed and he saw how pretty she was. 'It's no more than Jack would have done for me.'

Drummond didn't look quite so drunk when Rougvie returned with Pete's coffee. The man looked up and smiled. 'Jack tells me you're down from Inverness.'

'That's right. I'm a DS up there.'

'So, I've been hearing.'

'Nick and I have been working together on the strangler case,' Drummond interrupted, making an effort not to slur his words.

Pete nodded. 'Do you have a car, Nick?'

'Well, yes.'

'Could you give us a lift to Jack's place?'

'Of course.' Rougvie got to his feet. 'I'm parked just outside.'

Pete attempted to take Drummond's arm to support him out of the pub, but he shook him off, holding his head high and giving Lucy a backward wave as they left.

Rougvie wasn't sure what he'd expected as he and Pete followed Drummond into his flat, but it wasn't the pleasant, orderly place he'd stepped into. He wouldn't have described it as cosy though, not the way his and Elaine's house in Inverness was cosy, but then he doubted if Drummond actually spent much time here.

'I don't suppose either of you have eaten much today,' Pete said, heading for the kitchen. He clearly knew his way around the flat.

'What have I told you about keeping your fridge stocked, Jack?' he shouted through.

Drummond shook his head. 'He's such a bully.'

'I might just manage a couple of bacon rolls,' Pete called again after inspecting the contents of the fridge. 'Will that do?'

'Sounds great,' Rougvie called back, grabbing the whisky bottle before Drummond got his hands on it.

It wasn't until the smell of grilled bacon permeated the flat and Pete arrived with the bacon rolls that Rougvie realized how hungry he was. Even Drummond devoured the food with apparent relish.

'Now then,' Pete said. 'Is somebody going to tell me what this is all about?'

'I think I've lost my job,' Drummond said.

Pete threw Rougvie a questioning glance. 'Is that right?'

'You tell him, Nick. I don't think I can trust myself. I might have killed the bugger myself if he hadn't got to it first.'

Pete raised an eyebrow.

'Don't listen to him,' Rougvie said. 'He's his own worst enemy, but then I'm sure you already know that.'

Pete waited.

'A man called Angus McLeod topped himself in one of the cells today, a man Jack had been interviewing. He cut his wrists with a broken plastic pen.' He put up a hand. 'And before you ask, the answer's no. We don't know how he got hold of a pen in the cells.'

'I was going to ask what this has to do with Inverness?'

'The man who died was from Inverness. He hightailed it down here after beating the daylights out of his wife. Jack was up in the Highlands at the time investigating this man's activities. He was there when the poor woman was found. She almost died.' He blew out his cheeks. 'A colleague and I got here this afternoon to take the man back to Inverness to face a charge of attempted murder.'

'The guy was a monster, Pete,' Drummond chipped in. 'I had him in the frame for the strangler until the last victim identified Dalrymple.'

'So, what are you saying, Jack – that you had it in for this character?' Pete frowned.

Drummond shrugged. 'OK so he wasn't the strangler, but he murdered his stepdaughter, Emily. I know he did, and he knew that I knew. He was on the point of confessing when I left him to mull over his options.'

Pete leaned forward. 'Did you browbeat him, Jack?'

'I did what I had to. You didn't see what he did to his

wife. He was a total maniac. I wasn't going to treat him with kid gloves. He killed Evie. I needed him to admit it.'

'Evie?' Pete was staring at him. 'Is that what this is all about? You've been beating yourself up because you couldn't save Evie?' Pete threw up his arms in frustration. 'This girl was never your responsibility, Jack. You have to let it go.'

Rougvie put out a hand. 'Wait a minute. Am I missing something? Who's Evie?'

Drummond hung his head.

'Tell him, Jack. If you trust him, tell him.'

'Tell me what?' Rougvie wasn't sure he wanted to hear what was coming.

Drummond stared across the room. He was imagining Evie curled up on his sofa like a vulnerable kitten. 'Evie was what she called herself when she was here. You know her as Emily Ross.'

Rougvie screwed up his eyes, not sure what he was hearing. 'Emily Ross was here? D'you mean here in your flat?'

Drummond gave a slow nod. 'We were in the throes of the hunt for the strangler and I'd taken to going out at night warning the street girls to be on their guard, not that they paid any attention.' He swallowed. 'I found Evie soliciting with the others on a street corner. She looked about twelve. At least the older hookers were a bit savvy, but this girl, despite the front she put up, didn't look like she would have had a clue how to protect herself if a punter turned nasty.

'I took her aside, told her to go home. She refused of course. I said I would arrest her if she didn't get off the streets. She wasn't happy. I insisted. She said she had family in Edinburgh so I gave her a few quid and bundled her on a train.

'It felt good seeing that train pull out of the station. It was like I'd saved the girl from a life of misery.'

He sighed. 'I didn't think I would see Evie again, but I was wrong. It was weeks later she came to see me at the station. Her clothes were filthy, and she had a black eye. She was trembling, pleading with me. She had nobody else to turn to, she said. She begged me to put her up for a few nights until she got herself straightened out.'

Rougvie threw up his hands. 'Don't tell me. You let her stay here in your flat.'

'What else could I do? She was hardly more than a kid and she was in a terrible state. It was no skin off my back if she stayed here for a couple of nights.'

'But you must have known she was trouble,' Rougvie persisted.

Drummond sighed. 'It's easy to see sense after the event but at the time I really felt I could help her.'

'And did you?' It was the first time Pete had commented since Drummond started talking.

'No, it got worse. I knew Evie was taking drugs, but she seemed to be doing her best to kick her habit. At least that's what I thought. I wanted to help her.' He heaved another sigh. 'The last time I saw her she was curled up here on this sofa. When I got back from the station late one night the flat looked like it had been turned over. Drawers had been emptied, cupboards ransacked...and Evie had gone! It was later that I discovered she'd taken the emergency £500 I kept hidden in my wardrobe.'

'Oh, Jack.' Rougvie sighed.

Pete shook his head.

'That was the night Evie's body was found in that filthy alley,' Drummond said flatly. 'It was assumed she was another victim of the strangler, but it didn't look right.'

'Tell Nick about the phone,' Pete said quietly.

Drummond raised his head, swallowing. 'I found Evie's phone down the side of the sofa, the phone she used to contact her mother.

'Reading those messages between her and Rachel was heartbreaking. This was the real Evie, or Emily as you later told me she was. It was easy to learn from the text messages that she had lived in Inverness. I needed to know more about her.'

'And that's where I came in,' Rougvie said.

Drummond nodded. 'Pretty much.' He spread his fingers and stared at his hands. 'When I became suspicious of McLeod, I couldn't let it go. If he had been involved in his stepdaughter's death I had to know.'

'And now he's dead,' Rougvie said.

'I think it's more serious than that,' Pete commented. 'McLeod has taken his own life in a police cell and the PIRC will be wanting answers.'

Drummond looked up, his eyes going from one to the other. 'Oh great. An enquiry by the Police Investigation and Review Commissioner is all I need. I don't imagine whoever investigates this will trouble to look very far for a fall guy. I made no secret of how convinced I was that McLeod had killed Emily Ross.'

'But it wasn't your fault the man did what he did,' Rougvie said. 'Whoever gave him that pen is the one who needs to be worried. Anyway, surely if there had been any worries about his mental state, he should have been put on suicide watch.'

Drummond pulled a face. 'I did get a bit heavy with him during that last interview. It will all be on the tape, but I did tell the custody sergeant to keep an eye on him.'

'Will he back you up on that?' Pete asked.

'It was Ronnie Ryan. What do you think? He's not going to put himself in the firing line for me.'

'You think he'll lie?' Rougvie said.

'Of course, he will. If he'd kept an eye on McLeod as I asked him to then the man might still be alive.' He bit his lip. 'And he'd have to face up to what he did. That's what I can't forgive. Angus McLeod took the easy way out – and we let him!'

## THIRTY-SEVEN

'Am I confined to barracks?' Drummond asked next morning, poking his head around DCI Buchan's door.

'Come in, Jack.' She looked up from the computer screen. Her expression was not amused. She indicated he should sit. He wasn't in a mood for arguing.

She sat back, watching him. 'You need to talk to me. What the hell happened here last night?'

'A worthless piece of trash topped himself in one of our cells. I thought you knew.'

'Cut the comedy. You're in no position to joke about this.'

'Joke?' Drummond felt his blood rising. 'You think I would joke about this? Angus McLeod killed his stepdaughter. I *know* he did. He beat his wife so viciously that she's still in intensive care in Raigmore Hospital.' He got up and began pacing the small room. 'He was supposed to be this respected banker, this holier than thou elder in the Wee Free Church in Inverness.' He wheeled round and glared at Joey. 'Was he repentant for what he'd done? Was he hell!

He took the coward's way out and gouged out his veins. It was all about him again.'

'Sit down, Jack! Getting steamed up like this helps nobody, least of all you.'

Drummond ignored her.

'Did you hear me?' She said, her voice rising. 'Sit down!'

He took a deep breath and let it out in a long sigh before pulling out a chair and trying not to throw himself into it.

'Now listen here, you.' Joey tapped her desk. 'You could have been suspended...you would have been if I hadn't persuaded the top brass upstairs to let you go on working.'

Drummond was tempted to leap in again with what he thought about the top brass, but his good sense told him to hold his tongue. Making an enemy of Joey Buchan would help neither of them.

'You have to control that anger, Jack.' She fixed him with an earnest stare. 'It won't look good if you kick off like that when they interview you. Just think about it. A man is dead and apart from his solicitor you were the last one to speak to him. I believe you when you say it wasn't you who gave him the pen, but that doesn't let you off the hook.' She was studying his face for any sign that he was taking her seriously. 'I've watched the playback of that interview, Jack, and you didn't exactly go easy on McLeod.'

'I was doing my job,' Drummond muttered.

'Some might think you were overdoing it. Did it not cross your mind that he might do something like this?'

Drummond shook his head. 'I know he was rattled. I saw that as progress. But I did tell the custody sergeant to keep an eye on him.'

The DCI blinked, frowning. 'Sergeant Ryan didn't mention that.'

'Well he wouldn't, would he? The lovely Ronnie will be more than happy to drop me in it.'

'We'll see about that. I'll make sure the investigators know about this.' She got to her feet. 'In the meantime, I'm trusting you to keep your head down. No more angry outbursts. The man's dead now and we can't bring him back.'

Drummond gave a resigned nod.

'You'll find a stack of paperwork on your desk, DI Drummond. I suggest you concentrate on that.'

The incident room had officially been stood down now that James Dalrymple had admitted the murders, so the frantic activity he'd got used to surrounding him during the strangler investigation had been replaced by the occasional tap of a keyboard and a ringing phone. The stack of papers Joey had mentioned was bigger than he'd hoped. He pulled a face as he sat down and reached for the top of the pile.

'What will happen to DI Drummond now?' Colin Faraday asked Rougvie as they crept past the eternal roadworks on the A9 on their way back to Inverness. Once the work to extend the dual carriageway was completed, driving north from Glasgow and Edinburgh would be a treat. But for now, it was a matter of road users gritting their teeth and exercising patience.

'I don't know, Colin. A suicide in the cells is a serious business. There will be an investigation and DI Drummond will get interviewed.' He stared at the queuing traffic ahead. Faraday's question had been foremost on his mind too since he'd left Drummond's flat the previous night. If what he'd learned about his friend's relationship with the murdered girl, Emily Ross, got to the ears of certain others, the man's career in Police Scotland would be finished. Then there was the issue of Drummond finding the girl's mobile phone. Rougvie knew only too well why handing it over to the authorities could never have been an option, but that was nothing to the trouble he'd be in if it was discovered that he'd 'planted' it at the scene for another colleague to find. God it was a mess. No wonder Drummond had been in a bad way the previous night. At least he had the support of Pete Mullen behind him now. He was in good hands. Rougvie had got the impression that if anybody could help him it would be this man. A highly respected officer like Mullen would have serious standing in and out of the Force. He would also understand the internal working of police investigations such as the one Drummond now found himself in the middle of.

'Do you think he'll get a fair hearing?' Faraday's question interrupted his thoughts.

'Let's hope so,' Rougvie muttered.

The traffic hold-ups were behind them now. Inverness was only an hour away and despite what DCI Fraser was expecting, Rougvie had decided he was calling in at home before setting foot in the nick. He needed the comfort of Elaine's arms around him and that injection of normality back in his life.

DC Gail Swann had been assigned to organizing the paper-work and preparing the documents in the strangler case for the procurator fiscal's office. She'd tucked herself away in a dusty corner of the basement, but Drummond found her. She looked up as he came into the room.

'Thought you could probably do with this,' he said, putting a cardboard cup of coffee from the machine down beside her. He glanced over the litter of documents. 'You drew the disclosure straw. Sorry...'

She pushed a strand of hair out of her eyes and reached for the coffee he'd brought. 'I don't mind. It's better than you doing it.'

'What? You think I might kick off on one if I read all these witness statements again?'

Gail raised an eyebrow that clearly said that was exactly what she'd meant.

Drummond nodded. 'I've been warned to stay a million miles away from the case. The DCI doesn't want me digging up any new evidence.'

'So, what are you doing here?'

'I don't really know, other than I'm drowning in the mind-blowing banality of paperwork upstairs.' He'd caught sight of one of the statements and was reading the name of the witness upside down. Olivia. He'd forgotten about Olivia. He'd still have her number in his phone.

Gail noticed his interest and quickly bundled up the papers. 'Was there anything else, DI Drummond?' She looked up at him.

Drummond pulled an expression of hurt. 'If you're telling me my company is not wanted then I'll leave you in peace.'

'Thanks for the coffee,' she called after him.

There was a smile on his face as he walked away.

Back at his desk Drummond got his phone out and scrolled through his contact list, pausing when it came to Olivia's name.

Joey came out of her office and glanced across at him as she left the room. He wondered what she would say if he rang Olivia now. She wouldn't be happy, but he guessed that would be more on a personal level than a professional one.

He hit the name and listened as Olivia's number registered the engaged tone. He cursed. That wasn't what he'd wanted. It put the ball in Olivia's court. He knew she would ring him back as soon as she saw the missed call. They had only gone out a couple of times and he liked her, but Olivia had wanted more. She had turned up unannounced at his flat one night and narrowly missed meeting his house guest, Emily, but she saw enough to realize Drummond had a woman staying with him. She'd jumped to a wrong conclusion that he was in another relationship and fled. That was the last time he'd seen Olivia. He stared at his phone. Maybe he was kidding himself imagining she would ring back.

It was two hours before her call came. 'What do you want, Jack?' She sounded supremely bored.

'Just a catch-up. It's been a while. I wondered if you fancied meeting up for a drink?'

'A drink? Why would I want to have a drink with you?'

'I can't think of a single reason,' he said. 'What about the Blue Lobster at six?'

'That won't be happening,' she said. 'I never met a man with such colossal cheek.'

'You're right,' he said. 'It was presumptuous. Would seven thirty be better for you?'

He heard her heave a sigh at the other end. 'OK, the Blue Lobster, but I'm only staying for one drink.'

Drummond glanced around his flat after Olivia left next morning. No arrangement had been made for them to meet up again, but he knew they probably would. He liked Olivia and now they had straightened out previous misunderstandings they could be good together without the complication of strings. He had no doubt Olivia would put him in his place when necessary. He kind of liked that. She was one of the few women he knew who got him.

But now that he was here on his own again all the old insecurities returned. He hadn't discussed his current situation with Olivia. He didn't want her sympathy. Allowing himself to be swept along by the moment in the company of a warm and loving woman had been more than enough. For a few wonderful hours he had forgotten his problems and felt like a member of the human race again.

Everything had changed so much in the last forty-eight hours. Two days ago, he was in the depths of despair, still full of anger that Angus McLeod had taken the knowledge that he had murdered Emily to his grave with him. Drummond's career in the police force was undoubtedly over, and all he'd wanted was to sit morosely in a corner of the pub getting drunker than drunk.

He gave a grim smile as Nick Rougvie's serious face swam before him. Nick and Pete...friends who cared. They had taken him home that night, stopped him drinking, but more importantly they had let him talk until all the anger had been talked away.

And yesterday he'd gone into the nick expecting to hear he'd been suspended. But Joey...lovely Joey, had spoken up for him.

And now he had Olivia back in his life.

So many good people around him. He could feel himself becoming emotional. Two days ago, all he'd wanted to do was to give up. But fighters didn't give up. If he did that then Angus McLeod would have won. And he had no intention of allowing that to happen!

## THIRTY-EIGHT

The Reverend Andrew Guthrie ran a finger around the inside of his dog collar as he and his wife, Elizabeth, waited nervously for the senior police officer to arrive. 'I suppose we're doing the right thing by coming here,' she said uneasily.

Andrew wasn't entirely sure either, but they were here now. He glanced at the letter he'd placed on the table and wondered what Angus McLeod would have thought about his letter being passed to the police. When the contents became public, as they surely must, the implications of what he had written would be far reaching. They would also cause much grief for the man's family, especially his widow, Rachel. And what about the church? Would the things Angus had done reflect on that? The repercussions it could cause were unthinkable and yet here he was ready to hand over the damaging letter.

It was only minutes before Detective Chief Inspector Gavin Fraser came into the room. Andrew got to his feet and offered his hand. 'The Rev Andrew Guthrie,' he said solemnly, his eye going to the seated woman. 'And my wife,

Elizabeth.' The officer introduced himself and they all shook hands.

'It's about this letter,' he said hesitantly. 'We think you should take a look at it.'

Fraser glanced at the letter and sat down, pulling it towards him. The couple watched uncomfortably as he began to read. They saw his eyebrows rise as he took in the contents. Andrew had experienced the same shock when he'd read the stark words. He hadn't been prepared for what the church elder had written. When he'd been handed the letter, he hadn't questioned it. Members of the congregation occasionally left such things with the minister to be held in trust and opened after their death. It usually meant there was to be a bequest to the church. He had no reason to believe Angus McLeod's letter was any different.

Andrew had opened it on the day news of the man's untimely death reached him. His heart lurched even now as he remembered the words.

"I have entrusted this letter into the care of the Rev Andrew Guthrie in the understanding that it will be read after my demise.

There are things I have done in my life for which I will be criticized, but they had to be done and I will set out here the reasons why.

I was ten when my mother, Mary Ann McLeod, left us and ran off with James Shaw. I cried and cried and was broken-hearted that she didn't love me. Father said she was evil. He preached from the pulpit that those who turned their back on family and God must be driven out and never be permitted to return.

I was fourteen when I killed them both. No need for me

to go into the details except to say their bodies are buried by a rowan tree on the hill behind the croft where they lived in Letters overlooking Loch Broom.

My next transgression – although I have always seen this as a good deed on my part – involves Alan Rogers, a local banker in Stornoway and a despicably evil man who sought his pleasures with young boys. The creature offered to take me under his wing and teach me banking. Father was enraged when I told him what Rogers wanted from me in return. Together we decided he must pay. We forced him to confess his evil ways in his diary and then we took him to his garage and strung him from a high beam until he was dead. I took great satisfaction at the sight of his body dangling there. I would have taken the credit for it, but the court decided Alan Rogers had taken his own life in a fit of remorse over those boys he abused.

Emily – my beautiful stepdaughter, Emily, was different. Every day I feel sad knowing I will never see her again, never touch her soft cheek or stroke her shining hair. She knew I loved her and yet she rejected me. I only wanted to care for her, to take her to that place where life is exalted, but she cast me aside.

Emily broke my heart. I know I shouldn't have taken my despair out on her mother, Rachel, but what was I to do? I wanted Emily and all I had was Rachel. It was so unfair!

Emily knew how much her leaving would enrage me, but still she went.

My association with Judy Meadows was purely for convenience. It provided me with respite and somewhere to stay latterly on those trips I made to Glasgow to look for Emily. Our marriage took place in a register office. In my eyes that didn't count.

It was weeks before I found Emily. It was by chance in a

*place I would never have thought to look. She was on a street corner in the red-light district of Glasgow mingling with the prostitutes. Emily was offering complete strangers the thing she denied me...and she was doing it for money. She had betrayed me. She had betrayed God. I knew I had to show Emily the error of her ways.*

*It was hurtful the way she hurried off when she saw me approaching. I only wanted to speak with her, to persuade her to return home.*

*The night I followed her into the alley she had been taking drugs, lots of drugs. Her speech was slurred, and she was swaying, pointing a finger and yelling abuse at me. Even in that state I itched to touch her, stroke her face, hold her body close to me, but she struggled.*

*I don't remember putting my hands around her neck, only the silky softness of her skin and how it yielded to my touch. I felt more and more aroused as my thumbs pressed deeper into her throat. Suddenly she stopped struggling. I thought she was surrendering herself to the passion of the moment. But that wasn't it.*

*When I released my hold, Emily slid to the ground, her body lifeless. I stared at her and almost vomited. The woman at my feet was no longer my beautiful girl. She was a prostitute in revolting prostitute clothes who had destroyed her body with drugs. She was a vile creature and a complete stranger to me. I felt totally crushed as I walked away.*

*I don't regard any of the aforementioned things as true transgressions. Each one was justified and understandable, but I know there will be those who will not agree with this.*

*I do not want to go to my maker without laying out the things I have done. I am a Godfearing man. Only He can judge me. So be it.*

*This is an accurate and true testimony of the things I have done.*

*Angus McLeod."*


Andrew swallowed as he watched the officer re-read the letter and frown. 'You see why we felt it was important to bring this on to you.'

'When did Mr McLeod give this letter to you?'

'It was some weeks ago. It was after he and his wife came to the manse for dinner.' He gave a little smile. 'I've only recently been appointed as minister for this church. Angus McLeod was one of our elders and we wanted to meet him and his wife in an informal setting.'

Elizabeth Guthrie nodded. There was a catch in her voice. 'We had such a lovely evening. Who could know it would end like this? Such a tragedy.'

'Did he explain why he was giving you the letter?' DCI Fraser asked.

'No. He gave no indication of the contents, if that's what you mean. He simply asked me to put it away safely and treat it with confidence until the day it was opened, or he had asked to have it back.'

'Were you not curious?'

'Not really. I assumed it had something to do with his estate...something he didn't, for whatever reason, want to put in his will.'

'So, you had no idea of the contents until you read it?'

Andrew shook his head.

'It's two weeks since Mr McLeod's demise. Why are you only bringing this letter to us now, sir?'

'I...err...I wasn't sure what to do. What Angus put in his

letter affects so many people, especially his widow. It was a difficult decision to make.'

'Have you shown the letter to anyone else, Reverend Guthrie?'

'No, of course not.'

'Not anyone in the church?'

'No.'

Fraser stood up. 'You should have brought this letter to us sooner, but now that you have you can leave it with us.' He made no move to offer his hand, but the interview was clearly over.

Andrew shot his wife a glance. 'Is that it?'

'Yes. We will deal with this now.'

Fraser saw the couple out and watched from the window of his office as they got into their car and drove out of the car park. The letter they left behind had the potential to be a bombshell. He sat at his desk and spread the pages before him, staring at them.

He would have to hand the letter over to the investigation into Angus McLeod's death in the Glasgow cells. And the investigations that had been reopened into banker Alan Rogers' death in Stornoway and the disappearance of Angus McLeod's mother and her lover would have to be halted.

He frowned, glancing out to where Nick Rougvie was on the phone at his desk. He had a right to know about this, but could he be trusted not to get right on the phone to his pal, Drummond?

## THIRTY-NINE

DCI Buchan was heading up the briefing session into a spate of burglaries in the Drumchapel area that had recently turned violent. She was aware of Drummond's repeated glance to the clock. His attention was clearly elsewhere, and she didn't blame him.

At nine forty-five she nodded to him. 'You should get off now, Inspector. A chorus of 'good luck' followed Drummond from the room.

Drummond's heart pounded as he took the stairs to the top floor. He could have taken the lift, but he felt his legs might buckle under him unless he kept them moving. In just a few minutes he would know his future. His career in the Force could be about to end and there wasn't a thing he could do about it. His hand shook as he entered the interview room. A man and woman he didn't recognize sat serious faced at the table. Neither of them looked friendly. He gave them a courteous nod.

'Take a seat, Detective Inspector Drummond,' the woman said, lowering her spectacles to examine him. 'I am

Chief Superintendent Monica Salt, and this is Chief Inspector Graham Wright.'

Drummond sat, hoping he wasn't looking as nervous as he felt. Nerves could be seen as guilt. And he wasn't guilty, no matter how high the odds were stacked against him.

He was wearing a new shirt and the collar felt uncomfortably stiff around his neck, but he resisted the urge to loosen it.

Both officers were giving him a cold stare. Drummond suspected it was a stance designed to intimidate. He had employed it himself numerous times when questioning a suspect. But this time it wouldn't work. He needed to focus, to get the measure of these two. His future career could be in their hands and right now he suspected they wanted to hang him out to dry.

Little stabs of anger were beginning to rise from somewhere inside him. He'd have to watch that. He would force himself to stay calm and look them in the eye when he answered their questions, no matter how probing they were. These people were no better than him. If they were going to shaft him then let them do their worst.

The woman glanced down at the papers in front of her. Drummond waited. She looked up. 'Can you take us through that last interview you conducted with Angus McLeod?'

'It's all on tape, isn't it?' Drummond flashed a frown from one to the other and immediately regretted the comment. Bad move. He shouldn't be snapping at them.

'We want your version of events, DI Drummond,' the woman said.

Drummond tried not to sigh. 'The reason Angus McLeod was arrested and in the cells was because he viciously attacked his wife in Inverness and then took off down here to Glasgow hoping his *other* wife would give him an alibi.

'I also had reason to believe he had murdered his step-daughter, Emily Ross. This is what I questioned him about.'

The woman straightened her papers. 'How would you describe your attitude during that interview?'

'Professional.'

'Not forceful?'

'It was a robust interview,' Drummond conceded. 'I am a trained and highly experienced officer. The interview was conducted correctly.'

'Was it now?' Inspector Wright tilted his head to look at him. 'It sounded to us like you were browbeating the man. Wasn't it the case that you had decided this man was guilty and you had no intention of letting him wriggle off the hook, no matter what it took?'

'He *was* guilty. I knew he was.' Drummond was aware that his voice was rising. If he lost his temper now this pair would win.

He was aware of Chief Superintendent Salt's eyes assessing him. 'We've been having a look at your records, DI Drummond,' she said. 'Taking an overall view of what we read we've concluded you are insolent, insubordinate and frequently ignore instructions from senior officers.'

Drummond pressed his lips together. It was coming now. This is where they would tell him he was getting the bullet. He braced himself.

'On the other hand,' Salt continued. 'You appear to get results, and apart from rubbing some of your colleagues up the wrong way most of them speak highly of you.'

'Really?' Drummond blinked. 'Was she complimenting him?'

'And there's this,' she added, sliding what looked like a

handwritten letter across the table to him. 'Would you read this, please.'

Drummond reached for the letter and pulled it towards him and began to read. The words McLeod wrote were jumping from the page. He murdered Emily, he murdered all of them. He was admitting it. Drummond felt the blood drain from his face. Everything he had suspected about McLeod was true. His hands shook as he looked up, eyes wide. 'McLeod wrote this?' He made no effort to disguise the shock in his voice.

Chief Superintendent Salt nodded. 'What are your thoughts?'

Drummond's head was all over the place. The image of Emily Ross's poor body discarded like a piece of rubbish in that lane was racing before his eyes on a loop. McLeod had admitted in the letter that he'd murdered Emily, but there wasn't an ounce of remorse in his words. He'd accepted no responsibility for the evil he'd done.

Drummond leapt to his feet with a force that sent his chair flying across the room. He ignored it as he began pacing the room. He'd killed Emily! The words seared across his mind. McLeod had killed all of them and he couldn't have cared less about his victims. The blood was coursing through Drummond's veins. The man was a monster!

'Please sit down, Inspector.' The woman's tone was firm. 'We understand how you feel but you must try to remain calm.'

Drummond's rage was so fierce he could feel the prick of tears. He turned away, forcing himself to control his breathing, aware that Salt was waiting for him to regain his composure. He made a colossal effort. 'I apologize for my behaviour,' he said quietly, recovering the chair and sitting back down, still not looking at them.

Chief Superintendent Salt was watching him. She sat back. 'We were expecting a reaction from you, Inspector, but just not that one. You have a wild temper. It will be your undoing unless you get it under control.'

He swallowed. She was right, but his anger was as much against himself as McLeod. Emily had been so desperate to get away from the man that she subjected herself to the degradation of being a prostitute. He could feel the bile rise in his throat. She had called herself Evie and she'd come to him for help. And he had let her down! He should have been more patient, encouraged her to talk more. He should have coaxed all this background story out of her. But he hadn't. He'd thought giving the girl a roof over her head for a few days was enough. It hadn't been enough – and Emily had died. How could he not feel responsible?

Drummond took a deep breath to steady himself and nodded. 'I'm fine,' he mumbled.

The woman managed a stiff smile. 'Look, we can see how much this written confession has shocked and distressed you, but you must not let yourself become so involved. We expect you to do your job efficiently and now you must stand back and take stock of your actions.' She paused, still watching him.

'We are not happy about how you conducted this inter-view with Angus McLeod and yes, maybe you do have to take some responsibility that he took his life. Perhaps he could see you would never stop pursuing him until the truth was out.' She shrugged. 'Perhaps the man felt taking his life was his only option. Who knows? It's still a fact that if he hadn't died in that cell we wouldn't now be in possession of this letter of confession.'

She sat back in her chair with a sigh. 'A prisoner taking his life in a police cell is a serious business, DI Drummond. We have considered this letter written by Angus McLeod. It's important and the contents will be investigated further.' She ran the tip of her tongue over her lips. 'However, it does not absolve you of any blame for his death.'

Drummond blinked, confused. He was still having trouble taking all this in. 'You're saying it's my fault that Angus McLeod killed himself?'

The woman nodded. 'You have to take some of the responsibility for what's happened.' She paused, meeting his eyes. 'We can't allow you to resume your duties here as though nothing had happened. Angus McLeod took his own life in that cell. Granted you were not the one who gave him the pen he used on his wrists. We will deal with that officer separately and there are others who must share responsibility for what's happened.'

Drummond's heart was in his shoes. So, this was it, they really were going to drum him out of the Force. He was aware she was watching him, but he couldn't meet her gaze.

'Is my dismissal immediate?' he said.

Monica Salt took her time. 'There will be no dismissal, DI Drummond, but my report will recommend you be transferred to another station outside Glasgow. I will suggest that should be Inverness as you have already done some work up there.'

'What!' Drummond shot bolt upright. 'You want to banish me to the Highlands?' Why didn't she just order his dismissal and be done with it? Dozying around Inverness dealing with low-level crime might suit Nick Rougvie, but it wouldn't do for him.

Her words had hit Drummond like a cannonball between the eyes. His whole purpose of being a copper was to do his part in cleaning up the streets of Glasgow. Nothing else mattered. They might as well drum him out of the Force altogether.

Monica Salt was meeting his hard stare. 'I can see that doesn't meet with your approval, but it's where we're at.' She put down the pen she'd been twiddling in her fingers. 'We have no reason to believe that if you found yourself in a similar situation with another suspect you wouldn't behave in exactly the same way.'

'Angus McLeod murdered his stepdaughter. I was right. And now we know he killed the others,' Drummond said.

'That's true,' Monica Salt agreed. 'But at the time you didn't know any of that. You bullied that man, Drummond, and he took his own life in a police cell.' She picked up her pen and began twiddling it again.

'But Inverness, Ma'am? What good could I do up there?'

She gave him a slow smile. 'It's not a crime-free zone, Inspector. You've already had some experience of that, but I accept it will be different.' She sighed. 'Look, I think your career will benefit from you being taken off the streets of Glasgow. Of course, you don't have to accept this, the choice is yours.'

'You mean I could resign?'

She put her hands up. 'That's up to you, but I hope it won't come to that. You're a good officer, DI Drummond. You just need to calm down a bit.'

Drummond's legs shook as he stood up and left the room. So, he was to be thrown to the dogs after all!

# FORTY

He was still shaking when he passed DCI Buchan's office. She waved him in. 'Shut the door,' she ordered. 'I want to know everything.'

The muscles in Drummond's jaw tensed. 'Not a lot to say.' He paused. 'I've been shafted and now they want rid of me.'

Joey looked genuinely shocked. 'They fired you? Why the hell did they do that?'

'They haven't exactly fired me, just encouraged me to jump.'

'You're talking in riddles, Jack,' she said. 'Just tell me what happened.'

Drummond pulled out a chair and slumped onto it. 'There was a letter, a nice long letter from our friend Angus, in which he confessed to murdering Emily, his mother and her boyfriend, and an old banker in Stornoway who liked to fiddle with wee boys.'

'McLeod was a serial killer?' Joey stared at him. 'And he murdered Emily?' Her voice was rising.

Drummond nodded.

'So, you were right all along.'

He nodded again. 'Can you believe that bastard murdered all those people and didn't show one speck of remorse? He wrote as though he thought he was doing God's work, eliminating people who didn't live by his weird standards.'

Joey went on staring at him. 'So, have you been dismissed or what?'

'Transferred,' he said flatly.

'Transferred?' She frowned. 'To where?'

'It really doesn't matter because I won't be going. I've had enough, Joey. Police Scotland and I will be having a parting of the ways.'

'You're resigning?' She stared at him. 'Don't be a bloody fool, Drummond. Why would you want to do that?'

'I'm clearly not wanted around here, that's why.' He shook his head. 'Even though I was right about McLeod they still want rid of me.'

'But that letter should have cleared you. Why are they suggesting a transfer?'

'Apparently I'm insubordinate and don't obey orders.'

'Well, they're right about that. You never could take orders and you're an awkward bugger when it suits you, but that doesn't explain why they want to transfer you.'

'Might have had something to do with the way I kicked off and sent a chair flying across the room when I read that letter.'

Joey winced.

'I tried to stay calm, but the sanctimonious way McLeod described how he'd killed all those people, how he'd tried to manipulate Emily before he murdered her.' He shook his head. 'Something inside me just snapped and I lashed out.'

'You need to forget him. The man was a pervert, but it's all water under the bridge now. He's admitted what he did.'

'Maybe so,' Drummond said. 'But that won't bring any of his victims back. It's the ones still living that I'm worried about.'

'You're thinking about his wife.'

'Rachel...yes. I can't imagine how she'll deal with hearing the man she was married to murdered her daughter. It's been one nightmare after another for her.' He heard the glasses clink as Joey took them from her filing cabinet together with a new half bottle of whisky.

'It'll be worse for her hearing news like that from a stranger,' she said, pouring two stiff drams and handing one to Drummond. 'Maybe you should be the one to tell her, Jack?'

It was a decision he had already made. 'I'll leave for Inverness later today,' he said. 'But it will be a flying visit. It's not my kind of place.' He threw back the whisky in one go and held his glass out for a refill. He'd expected the back of her tongue for his audacity to demand another shot of whisky, but he had nothing to lose now. To his surprise she said nothing and poured him another drink.

'Leave Inverness until the morning,' she said. 'I'll get onto the plods up there and warn them to leave Rachel to you. We'll also give McLeod's other woman, Judy, the bad news that she's not his wife.'

'Some might see that as good news,' Drummond said. The second whisky had also gone down quickly. He was in a mood to find a pub.


Rougvie rang as he left the building half an hour later. 'I wasn't sure you'd be out of the interview yet. How did it go?'

'You don't want to know,' he said sharply. 'Never mind about me, tell me about Rachel McLeod.'

'She's fine, Jack. She's been asking for you. She says you saved her life when you arrested Angus.'

Drummond felt a ridiculous stab of pride. It wasn't true, but it felt good to hear. 'How did she take McLeod's death?'

'I think she was relieved. She wouldn't have stayed with him anyway after what he did to her.' He paused. 'I know about McLeod's confession, Jack...the letter he left with the Free Church minister.'

'I guessed you would,' Drummond said. 'How do you think she'll take it when she hears it was Angus who murdered Emily?'

'To be honest, I think she already suspects as much. Rachel is pretty savvy. She will have picked up clues from the way McLeod behaved. She knew he had another woman somewhere. She's not stupid and Angus was certainly not as smart as he thought he was.'

'That's for sure,' Drummond said. 'I've volunteered to be the one to tell her about his confession. It has to be me she hears it from.'

'When are you coming up?'

'In the morning. I'll go straight to see Rachel and then maybe we can meet up. I have something to tell you.'

When he cut the call, he tapped in Pete Mullen's number. He should know before Rougvie that he was leaving the Force. It was answered immediately. Drummond got the impression his old friend had been waiting for his call.

'Well?' Pete asked. 'How did it go?'

'Angus McLeod confessed to everything in a letter he left with the minister of the Free Church in Inverness.'

'Glory be!' Pete said. Drummond could almost see the

grin on his face. 'So, it was him who killed the girl, Emily, all along? You were right, Jack. Well done. Look, my shift ends at five. I'll buy you a drink.'

'Sounds like a plan, Pete. What about the Five Stars?'

Pete had arrived at the pub before Drummond and grabbed a quiet table. 'A pint and a half is it, Jack?' he said, rising and heading for the bar.

'Just the pint, thanks.' Drummond ignored Pete's raised eyebrow.

'So, tell me,' he said when he returned with their beer. 'I want to know all the gory details of the interview. Are they giving you a commendation?'

'I'm resigning,' Drummond said.

Pete's mouth fell open. 'Why would you want to do that?'

Drummond pulled the pint across to him. 'It wasn't nearly as bad as I'd expected. I thought they were going to throw the book at me and then they produced this letter and told me to read it.'

'You must have been elated when you saw that.'

'I wasn't actually. Just the opposite. You should have read it. McLeod put down all the murders he'd committed but–'

'Wait a minute,' Pete cut in. 'What d'you mean ALL the murders? I thought it was just your lassie, Emily.'

'She was never my lassie, Pete.'

'No, I know. I just meant you'd been looking out for her. So, who were all these others?'

Drummond picked up his beer. 'He mentioned the banker in Stornoway who apparently liked wee boys more than he should have. McLeod also implicated his old father, the local Free Church minister, the Rev Murdo McLeod, in that one. He also suggested he'd murdered his mother and the man she ran away with and buried their bodies on a hill opposite Ullapool.'

Pete sat back, frowning. 'I call clearing up all these murders as a reason to celebrate. Why would that not please you?'

'Like I said. You should have read the letter. Angus McLeod took no responsibility at all for what he'd done. It was like he was writing about somebody else.'

'And that upset you?'

Drummond allowed his gaze to wander over the pub. It was filling up as customers came in for a drink before heading home. He didn't look at Pete. 'I wanted him punished. It shouldn't have been up to him to decide he could duck out of life without facing up to what he'd done in court.' He pulled a face. 'I kicked off a bit. They didn't like that.'

'What did you do?'

'Got angry, kicked a chair away, paced about a bit...Oh, I don't know. I just kicked off.'

'Don't you think it's time you stopped being a fist with a warrant card?'

Drummond laughed. 'That's more or less what this chief super who interviewed me said. She said I needed anger management.'

'I've been telling you that for years.'

'I know.' Drummond sighed. 'And now it doesn't matter because I'm going.'

Pete was watching him. 'So, you'll be going on a bender tonight?'

'No. It's been too long since I last saw my dad. I'm going over there tonight.'

'Good idea,' Pete said. 'And then what?'

'Tomorrow I'm driving to Inverness to tell Rachel McLeod that it was her husband who killed her daughter. I'm not looking forward to it, but it has to be me who passes on this news. I feel responsible.'

'You have a good heart, Jack Drummond. And give me heart over fist any day.'

Drummond swallowed a sudden lump in his throat and looked away.

'What happens after Inverness?' Pete asked.

'I'm not sure,' Drummond said. He felt on the verge of something he couldn't explain, but he knew his life was about to change. He just didn't know how he would cope with it.

After he left Pete at the pub, Drummond walked to his flat and let himself in. He looked around him. The room was as neat and tidy as always, but there was a greyness about the place he'd never noticed before. A kind of emptiness that made him shiver.

All he wanted was to crash out and make an early start for Inverness. Rachel shouldn't have to wait any longer to know the truth about the man she married, even if that knowledge would devastate her.

Drummond's mobile rang as he stepped out of the shower. 'Nick! I thought we were catching up in the morning,' he said, pulling on his bathrobe.

'Pete tells me you're leaving the Force,' Nick said bluntly.

'Well, that was the plan,' Drummond said, his eye on the sofa he hadn't sat on since the last time he saw Emily there.

'You do know you're making a huge mistake.'

'Am I,' Drummond said. 'I hear they're crying out for street cleaners here, or I could run a pub, or join the church.'

He could hear Rougvie sighing at the other end of the phone. He took a breath. 'Or maybe you could rustle up a few bad guys for me to nick up there in Inverness.'

There was a moment's silence and then Rougvie's confused voice. 'Are you saying what I think you're saying?'

Drummond swallowed. It was the visit to his dad that had made up his mind. 'There's always a job for you here in the shop, son,' his dad had said. A sudden vision of himself selling sweeties and newspapers from behind a counter, with a spreading waistline and a hopeless kind of defeat in his eyes, had flashed before him. Was that to be his future? He didn't think so. He was a cop. He would always be a cop

He grinned into the phone. 'I'm saying I'm not ready to quit being a copper – not yet.' He paused. 'I'm going to be your new neighbour, Nick.'


End

## AUTHOR'S NOTE

Can you spare a few minutes to leave a review? Reviews are important to everyone as they help readers to find the books they love. They are the lifeblood for authors and the best way for readers to express their thoughts about a book. Reviews can be long or short, so long as they are fair. This author would be very grateful if you could take a few moments to leave a review on Amazon. Thank you.

∼

Cover design by Craig Duncan
www.craigduncan.com/creative

Printed in Great Britain
by Amazon

64804564R00184